# I, Strahd

BOOKS

# I, Strahd

## P. N. Elrod

# I, STRAHD

First Printing: October 1993
Printed in the United States of America.
Library of Congress Catalog Card Number: 93-60256

9  8  7  6  5  4  3  2  1

ISBN: 1-56076-670-0

TSR, Inc.
P.O. Box 756
Lake Geneva, WI 53147
United States of America

TSR Ltd.
120 Church End, Cherry Hinton
Cambridge CB1 3LB
United Kingdom

For the three "M's" in my life,
Mark, Mac, and the Mite.

## Acknowledgments

With sincere thanks to
Tracy and Laura Hickman,
Christie Golden, and
the many other explorers who
came to Ravenloft first.

And a special thanks to
Forrest J Ackerman,
who had a hand
(or was that a claw?)
in influencing my work.

# Prologue

Though it was a bright, hot dawn outside, there were no windows in this part of the castle. Van Richten had to provide his own light in the form of a small lantern, which he gripped with a white-knuckled fist. He paused on the last, rough-hewn step at the top of the spiral staircase, caught his breath, and held the lantern as high as his slight stature allowed. Its feeble glow only managed

# P. N. Elrod

to push back the darkness for a scant few yards, just enough for him to see that the room was apparently empty of threatening occupants. That fact, of course, meant nothing in this place.

He glanced back the way he'd come. Cold stone walls curved sharply down into utter blackness, utter silence. The fingertips of his left hand, which had brushed against the walls as he'd gone up, were still numb from the chill, as if the rock itself had sucked the warmth right out of them. With a thin but rueful smile that tugged at only one corner of his mouth, he flexed his stiff hand. *Like master, like castle*, he thought, then his smile vanished as he turned into the room.

If not the true heart of the place, the chamber was certainly a vital organ. Each high wall was covered with books—hundreds, thousands of them, more than Van Richten had seen in one place in his fifty-odd years of scholarly life. The yellow glow of his lantern picked up the sheen from well-oiled leather covers and gilt titles, the occasional flash of a gem, and the dull face of a tome so ancient that no amount of care or restoration could revitalize it. But the outer shell hardly mattered; it was what lay inside that was important.

Van Richten breathed in the books' scent and felt his heart begin to race a little. If the monster had a weakness, and they all did in one form or another, perhaps it would be found here. As a man might be judged by the books he reads, so might a clue be revealed in the neat ranks of titles that marched up the walls. Van Richten suppressed another smile. Not by *any* stretch of fancy could Count Strahd Von Zarovich be considered a mere man anymore, though the local people seemed unaware of his true nature. He'd lost his allotted portion of humanity . . . how many centuries ago? And at what cost in lives and misery and agony of spirit for those hapless souls he'd touched in that time?

*But I can't think about that now. Time is too short.* Life *is too short.*

He had all the day ahead of him, midsummer day to be sure, the longest of the year, but brief enough now that he saw how much work lay before him. And where to start?

He moved quickly, lighting candles in their sconces as he found them. The black shadows grudgingly retreated. Though the room was cold like the rest of the castle, Van Richten decided to leave the great fireplace dormant. He was comfortable enough in the coat he'd thought to bring and two layers of sweaters. Besides, the telltale smoke would only let all and sundry know the place was occupied, and Van Richten had excellent reasons for keeping this visit as discreet as possible.

The gypsies knew about him, of course; one couldn't enter or leave the place without their help. He had paid them dearly for a guide to take him to the ring of poisonous fog that surrounded Castle Ravenloft. The potion they'd sold him to neutralize the poison had cost extra, but they'd only charged him half as much for the second dosage—macabre indication that they did not expect him to return. In the course of centuries, many bold explorers, well armed and highly magicked, had gone in to deal with 'the devil Strahd,' as he was known locally. None had ever come out—at least not in the same condition as they'd gone in. What hope did a lone, middle-aged herbalist have?

*None*, he answered truthfully.

However, he did have knowledge, and upon *that* he was willing to gamble his life. Indeed, more than his life. If he was wrong . . . well, there were much worse things than dying, but he had a kind of escape prepared should it become an eventuality. Not pleasant, but better than the alternative.

So the gypsies had been more than willing to take his money and leave him to his fate. Van Richten had no doubt Strahd knew of his presence in the castle, but he was certain Strahd would do nothing against him. Correction, Strahd *could* do nothing against him.

It had taken Van Richten nearly a decade to guess the truth, and yet another five years of waiting to be sure, and this day, this one midsummer day, he'd proved it by simply walking unchallenged into Castle Ravenloft.

In those fifteen years the place had shown no sign of life. The merchants in the village that lay in its shadow had not received any orders for goods in all that time. The youngest of them even complained about the lack of custom. His father had known something of prosperity, but *these* days? The man had thrown up his hands in well-rehearsed despair for those lost profits. The others were silent or grimly amused by him.

In fifteen years, Lord Strahd had not collected the taxes, though the taxes had been dutifully compiled, the burgomaster proudly stated. There were many old wives' tales about burgomasters who had failed in this task and had come to very bad ends, indeed. Just wives' tales, to be sure, but sometimes there was truth to be found in such fancies. Anyway, none of the villagers, let alone the burgomaster, would risk complaint from their lord. The money, quite a lot of it by now, was stored in a special stone house in the center of town. Thieves? No. They had no fear of thieves. Even the gypsies would not dare to touch it.

Also in that time there had been few unexplained or unusual deaths, as had once been common. Young girls in the prime of their looks no longer disappeared without trace—unless they decided to elope with their lovers. Fifteen years of relative peace, fifteen years of nights that were not so dark as before, fifteen years that Strahd had . . . left them alone.

Some cautiously whispered that perhaps Death had caught up with him at last and taken him away. But if so, then why was the poisoned wall of mist still thick about the castle base? No one had a reply to that one, nor were any too curious to find out. One could ask the gypsies: they knew everything. Aye, and *told* everything. To Strahd. Best not to ask; you might not like the answer.

But Van Richten was sure he had the answer.

Strahd the Ancient, Strahd who was the Land, Strahd the great and awful Lord of Barovia—genius, necromancer, ruthless killer—was now at his most vulnerable.

Strahd Von Zarovich, the vampire, was in hibernation.

Van Richten, who knew as much about the undead as any living man, was reasonably certain that for a few more years the master of the castle would be unable to stir from the sleep that was not sleep. The odd fact that he stood where he stood—that he hadn't encountered

Strahd's undead minions and necromantic guardians—seemed confirmation enough. Perhaps Strahd's dark magics could not last through his years of quiescence.

But Van Richten was only reasonably certain, which was why he'd allowed himself only one day to investigate. Though he could have spent months poring through the rare books in this room alone, he did not believe in taking unnecessary risks. A single, isolated intrusion that would brush against the dimmed consciousness of the monster was as far as he planned to take it for now. Perhaps later—a year, maybe two, as the vampire settled back into his sluggish dreams—he would return . . . and then he would not be alone.

But for that future expedition Van Richten needed more knowledge. He needed facts, not rumors or folklore or tall tales.

Candles lighted, he looked around the room for a hint on where to start. Even without the implied wealth of the books, the place was a study in opulence. The richly stained wood trims, grass-thick carpet, and inviting couches and chairs all indicated that though Strahd was a monster, he valued his comfort.

Van Richten's brows lifted as he noticed one *objet d'art* in particular. Well. Von Zarovich certainly had excellent taste. Over the exquisitely carved mantelpiece hung an enormous portrait of a young woman. She was breathtakingly lovely, painted by an artist with the skill to capture not only her outer beauty, but the lively purity of her inner soul. There was no date on it, no signature to be seen, but the antique costume the woman wore indicated several centuries had passed since the paint had been wet.

She was mesmerizing, bewitching . . . and long dead. Possibly even one of the Count's early victims. If so, her fate had been a grim one, and Van Richten had no wish or time to speculate on it. His purpose now was to see that other young girls were spared from such horrors.

In the center of the room was a low and massive table, so highly polished that the multiple flames of the candles reflected from its surface as if it were a mirror. Smooth and bright, no speck of dust anywhere. . . .

Van Richten went very still as he regarded the implications of the missing dust. After a moment's thought, he swallowed and hoped his heart would return to its proper place in his chest. Though impossible to detect, it was logical to assume Strahd had placed some sort of magical spell on the room to preserve its contents while he slept. Who knows what damage could be done to the fragile volumes by the gentle onslaught of dust, worms, and nibbling rats? Strahd obviously did—and had allowed for it.

A great book and some sheaves of paper covered with writing lay on the table. Within easy reach was a pot of ink and some quill pens, all expertly cut to a proper point and ready for use. A chair was pulled away from this spot, as though the last occupant had only just walked out and not bothered to push it back into place.

As though at any moment he might return.

Van Richten firmly shrugged off *that* idea. If Strahd had been active, he would have done something by now. The master was asleep, and his castle, like one in some half-remembered child's tale, was in much the same condition. That was how the little herbalist from Mordentshire had been able to pass through the great gates, aware of the dangers, of the torpid guards living and . . . not living. It had been grim going to walk past the dragons that glared down at him from their stone perches and the gargoyles and all the other things that he'd sensed or imagined were lurking in the shadows around him, but he had done it. The traps still worked, but those could be avoided if one had the right skills. He'd gotten in, and, most importantly, he expected to get out again.

He moved toward the table and gently set his lantern down, using a stack of yellowing paper to keep its metal base from scratching the pristine wood.

*You're a foolish old humbug, Rudolph*, he chided himself. But he had an ingrained respect for workmanship, and the table was a beautiful piece of art, however terrible its owner.

Carefully and not a little nervously, he ran his fingers over the fine leather cover of the book. It had an odd texture to it, odd and repulsive, as if it were made from . . .

He yanked his hands away as he realized the source of the unusual leather.

*Damn the creature. Damn the* thing *that was capable of such an obscenity.*

After a moment's pause to offer a prayer for the soul of the book's victim, he inhaled a great breath, and reached out again, swiftly opening it.

It wasn't precisely a book, so much as a collection of various folios loosely bound together in such a way that more could be added or removed as needed. Some of the parchment pages were the color of cream, thick and substantial, made to last many, many lifetimes. Other pages were thin and desiccated, positively yellow from age, and crackled alarmingly as he turned them over. There were no ornate illuminations, no fussy borders, only lines of plain text in hard black ink. The flowing handwriting was a bit difficult to follow at first; the writer's style of calligraphy had not been in common use for three hundred years. No table of contents, but from the dates it looked to be some kind of history.

He turned to the first page and read:

I, Strahd, Lord of Barovia, well aware certain events of my reign have been desperately misunderstood by those who are better at garbling history than recording it, hereby set down an exact record of those events, that the *truth may at last be known. . . .*

He caught his breath. By all the good gods, *a personal journal?*

# Part I

# Chapter One

## *Twelfth Moon, 347*

"There is a traitor in the camp, you know," Alek Gwilym said, not looking at me, but at the bottle of wine standing tall on the table between us. He studied the graceful shape of the dark green glass as an artist might admire an especially beautiful model. After a long moment during which he satisfied his aesthetic sense, he finally reached for it, blandly intent on satisfying some other senses as well. Touch, in the way his hands closed around the bottle's dusty surface, and smell, once the cork was off and the contents were breathing. Taste would come later. I had little understanding of such ritual for myself, but Alek's obvious enjoyment of the process had taught me to respect it.

I raised one eyebrow when his eyes briefly shifted my way.

"I think he will try to kill you," he added, in the same lazy tone.

"There are always traitors in every camp. They have to kill somebody."

"You should worry about this one, Strahd. You really should."

Having been my fighting comrade for fifteen years, he was more than entitled to use my given name in private. This time, however, it irritated me, perhaps because he managed to work in a slight, patronizing tone as he spoke. I was expected to ask him why I should worry more about this one than any others, but remained silent. Sooner or later, he would tell me. Alek always seemed to know all the gossip worth knowing in the ranks and, despite his coolly amused manner, found it physically impossible to keep anything really interesting to himself.

He reached for the wine and carefully poured some into a gold chalice he'd acquired on a long-ago campaign. The heavy red fumes drifted over to tantalize my own senses. The flavor, I knew, would be ambrosial, but unless I drank it with food I'd have a headache before finishing my second cup.

With eyes closed, Alek sipped slowly, holding a few drops on his tongue to take in all the subtleties of flavor. When the last of it was gone, he opened his eyes again and shot me a chagrined smile. "Anyone else would be demanding explanations from me at sword point, but there you sit like a cat before a mouse hole, waiting for the inevitable to happen."

I said nothing.

The need to share his news finally overcame him. He put his cup on the table and leaned forward, though there was no one within earshot who could have heard him. "The traitor is a Ba'al Verzi assassin, Strahd," he whispered.

The time for games ended with the utterance of that name. I straightened in my chair, fighting down the burst of rage that wanted to rush out. "Who? Who would *dare?*"

He shook his head. "If I knew, he would be dead by now."

"How did you learn of this?"

"From one of our wounded. He thought he could buy special treatment with the information. Unfortunately, he waited too long and died."

"Lady Ilona can still find a way to speak with him."

"I've already seen to that. She found out no more than what I've been able to tell you now."

"Have him raised."

"That's been tried as well. Once she was aware of the threat to you, she made the preparations and performed the spell." He lifted one hand, palm up. "Nothing."

"Why not?"

15

# P. N. Elrod

"The very question I put to her. She said he was simply not strong enough to survive the attempt."

Other alternatives came to me, each to be dismissed. Between them, Ilona and Alek would have done everything possible to learn all that they could. "Who else knows of this?"

"No one. Others are being questioned. So far none of them knows anything about an assassin."

"Unless you're the assassin."

"An excellent point, my lord," he said evenly. "And the first one I thought you would consider. But I decided to take the chance and warn you anyway."

A wise thing to do, especially since Ilona would have also told me.

"If you should wish to put me out of the way, though, then please do not relax your vigilance, for I can promise that the Ba'al Verzi will still be out there, waiting for his moment."

Indeed, yes, for deception was the greatest weapon of that particular guild of killers. Once they had operated openly, brazenly, until strict laws and liberal executions forced them into society's shadows. Your oldest friend, your most faithful servant, by the gods, even the mother that bore you could be a Ba'al Verzi. Their ways were a secret among secrets, and should one be hired to kill you . . . why then, you would die.

Unless you got him first. The Ba'al Verzi were uncannily sportsmanlike about their victims. Should one of their number be caught out and stopped, then the assassination was called off, never to be completed. The target had earned the right to live, and an unworthy assassin

16

had been handily culled from their ranks.

"Why?" I repeated. "The war is over. What enemy could benefit from my death now?"

"The man's exact words were 'beware the Ba'al Verzi, the great traitor who will take all for himself.' I would rather expect the beneficiary would be among your friends . . . such as you have."

True. A man in my position could not afford to have friends. The art of forming friendships had not been one I'd ever sought to cultivate, anyway. Of all the people I worked with or commanded, Alek Gwilym came the closest to fulfilling that position. By right of battle skills and quick wit he'd earned his own place in the ranks as my second-in-command, no small feat for a man who'd initially joined our forces as a hired mercenary—and a foreigner, to boot. He said his homeland was so far away that the name would have no meaning, so he never bothered to name it. I couldn't honestly say that we really liked one another, but we worked well together, and there was no little respect between us.

"Until he or she is discovered, you can trust no one. I expect that common sense will guide you to include me in that number. I shan't be offended." His thin lips quirked into a smile, and he sat back in his chair again.

"I'm so relieved to hear it," I informed him.

"There's no need for me to remind you what precautions must be taken."

"No," I agreed, and called to the guards standing just outside my tent. Both hustled in with a minimum of noise, waiting for orders. If their instructions puzzled them, they did not show it, being well trained and used to

17

my ways. While one remained inside, the other went off to roust out two more for duty. From now on, or until I found the traitor, I would not be alone, waking or sleeping. The Ba'al Verzi were known to strike only when their victim was isolated, their chosen weapon being a special dagger. At least I would not have to worry about being poisoned, smothered, or shot by an arrow or crossbow bolt. Cold comfort, I thought darkly.

The guard watched over us with a stoic face as our supper was brought in and consumed. He was insurance for us all. If either of them was the assassin, neither could take action for the other's presence. It was a tidy little standoff, but not one I planned to maintain forever.

I was not inclined to think that Alek was the man, not unless he wanted to make things difficult for himself in order to enhance his reputation within the killers' guild. Then again, I was not inclined to take chances, period. On the field of battle it was different: you had a clearly defined enemy to fight, and the blood rage was upon you. But when the battle was over and the political gaming began, caution was the best watchword for survival.

A half-dozen names churned through my mind as we ate and discussed tomorrow's activities as though nothing were wrong. I could assume that, since the Ba'al Verzi would directly benefit from my death, he would be among my inner circle of officers and retainers. Anyone of lesser rank would not have as much to gain from the risk. There was the Dilisnya clan, the Wachters, the Buchvolds, even Gunther Cosco. For each one that came up, I could think of many reasons they should not kill me, balanced by an equal number of reasons they should. Beyond that core were others, and still others beyond them. After a long life of soldiering, I'd made many, many enemies, a bitter return for all my service.

The candles burned low around us, flickering whenever a servant came in with another course of food. Alek's look followed one young woman in particular, and he got a shy answering wink for his trouble. Despite his hard gray eyes and a sharp blade of a nose, which did not flatter his long face, women seemed to find Alek handsome enough. He enjoyed his ladies as thoroughly as he did his wine. In the fifteen years I'd known him, he'd never suffered through a lonely night unless he was too drunk or too battle-tired for such amusements. This night looked to be no different from any other.

When he took his leave to pursue this new conquest, two more guards came in to take his place. I did not inform any of them about my situation. There was no need for the entire camp to know that a Ba'al Verzi was after me. Alek's desire to share his news had been fulfilled; it would go no farther now. Lady Ilona, too, could be trusted to remain discreetly silent.

Could she be the assassin? Very unlikely . . . but not impossible.

Another problem to consider was that by keeping the guards around me, I was informing the assassin I knew of him. A moot point if he turned out to be Alek or Ilona, a warning to be more cautious if not. I pinched the bridge of my nose wearily. With this kind of worrying I could think myself into circles within circles, ultimately meeting myself along the way. Perhaps that was another Ba'al Verzi strategy: let the victim exhaust himself with suspicion and speculation before striking. The task would be all the easier.

I smiled sourly. The only way to overcome the assassin was to strike first. Unless he chose to flout the guild's traditions and do something tonight, it was safe enough to indulge in some restorative sleep. The day had been hard, and a more difficult one lay ahead. Just because the battle had been won and a generations-long war was ended did not mean the work was over. There were bodies to bury or burn, spoils to divide, honors to bestow, and a thousand other details awaiting us in the morning.

And so the morn provided. I dragged my aching body from my cot and began the day with a fresh loaf of cheese bread and a hot cup of beef juice drained from yesterday's joint. Gradually, the pains in my limbs began to recede as the rich liquid performed its usual miracle of waking me up. I was in better shape than most men half my age, but that knowledge did not gainsay the fact that I was forty-two years old and growing older. Every day it took longer for the night's stiffness to wear off, longer still on a cold and damp morning like this one. The charcoal braziers in my tent could do little against the chill and nothing at all against the approach of age.

My barber was sent for, and he silently scraped at my chin and cheeks as the guards watched his every move. Though they'd been given no specifics, they knew something was up. After all, a man getting a shave is in a singularly vulnerable position: head thrown back, neck exposed to a sharp razor. But a razor was a razor, and a knife was a knife. I could trust the Ba'al Verzi would cleave to tradition and so relaxed as usual for this daily necessity.

# I, Strahd

The bristles that were wiped off on the barber's towel had a gray cast to them. At least the hair on my head was not yet affected, being thick and black as ever. When the time came for it to go gray, would I resort to some sort of dye to hide it, or simply cease to look into mirrors?

With some disgust, I shrugged off the bout of self-pity even as I shrugged into my fur-lined cloak. Men grow old, I was no different, and there was little point in wasting any thought on the fact.

Flanked by the guards, I emerged from my tent just as the sun broke free of the horizon. Its light flooded the valley and bounced off the high peak beneath which we'd made camp. It shone, too, on the more formidable crags to the north and west. A thousand feet up, perched on a natural and most convenient outcrop of rock, stood the castle. Its high walls of cream-colored stone caught the new sun's rays, reflecting them back like a beacon. For miles around, it was the most visible of landmarks and something of a lodestone for every army that had ever passed through this country.

Its warlord had allied himself on the wrong side during the conflict, and now his head was on a pike near the place where the dead were buried or burned. I'd killed him myself, and though not an easy task, he hadn't been an especially skilled fighter. His talents had lain in bluster and bullying, which were of no use against the strong downswing of a sharp broadsword.

And now his lands and the ruined castle overlooking them were mine, by right of combat and conquest. Today I would enter its walls for the first time and take

# P. N. Elrod

formal possession.

The camp was already well astir as the cooks and their innumerable helpers worked to get the morning meal ready. Other servants attached to various officers were busy with their chores. I saw them and ignored them, this invisible army that kept my own army afoot. They were part of the normal background of the camp, always there, like one's own heartbeat.

*And any one of them could be the Ba'al Verzi in disguise,* I thought with a new and entirely unpleasant alertness.

I managed to throw off the feeling. I was as safe as I could be until the assassin was caught. Beneath my outer tunic, I had on a finely worked shirt of chain mail. Heavy, but I'd worn it so much over the years that the weight was noticeable now only when absent. It could be penetrated only by the thinnest blade, and I knew the Ba'al Verzi's traditional weapon would be something more substantial than a slender stabbing dirk. Few had ever seen the assassins' knives and survived, but many knew that the blades were small, with hilts decorated in red, black, and gold. Red stood for the blood the assassins took, black for the darkness of death they brought to their victims, and gold for the payment they accepted for their grim work.

Ah, well, every guild was entitled to its symbolism.

The knives were also said to be magical, which meant that even someone with a less than strong arm could cut deeply into some vital spot and make a kill. I'd studied enough of the Art to take such hearsay very seriously.

High Priestess Lady Ilona Darovnya came striding

"Trying to bring me around, Lady?"

"That will happen when it happens," she answered. "I'm only offering you an alternative to looking over your shoulder for the rest of your life."

"A choice that might not be what it seems, should you be the one."

"I expected to hear that from you, my lord," she said, taking it without insult. "Decide as you will. There are others besides me who can help you if help is needed."

"The Most High Priest Kir? He's a bit far away to be of much use."

"There are many right here in the camp."

"And all subordinate to you, Lady," I pointed out.

She smiled again, gently giving up with a shake of her head. "Very well." She sighed and fell in beside me, walking back the way she'd come, toward the tents of the wounded. "If I could hate anything, it would be the Ba'al Verzi guild. They destroy trust, and how can one live without trust?"

I almost argued the point with her, until I thought of my barber again. It was true. I trusted him not to nick me, much less cut my throat. Every moment of the day I trusted all those around me to one degree or another. The Ba'al Verzi could be any of them, and unless I flushed him I would spend all my time waiting, waiting, waiting for him to strike. What pleasure was to be found in that kind of skulking existence? None.

There was work waiting for Ilona when we reached the tents, and she went straight into it, as though the stench of the dying and dead was nothing to her. Perhaps it was so. She was a dedicated woman with an unshakable faith. Had she worn it like a proud banner as did some others, she'd have been insufferable, but she had no time for such posturing and no patience for those who did.

I left her to it and set a good pace over to where the horses were kept. The grooms stood a little straighter and worked a little harder when they caught sight of me. It was only to be expected, so long as the discipline continued without my inspiring presence. Judging from the condition of the animals in their care, it did.

One of the older men bowed as I approached. "All is ready as you ordered, my lord."

He indicated a number of horses, saddled and waiting. Close by stood their riders; Alek Gwilym stood with them. His eyes flickered as he looked me over, no doubt assuring himself that I hadn't picked up any stray blade points during the night. He was refreshed and ready to go, having a natural resilience for surviving a good victory celebration. Few of the others possessed his gift. Next to him, barely standing, was Ivan Buchvold, who was a better soldier than drinker. Propping him up were his younger brother, Illya, and his brother-in-law, Leo Dilisnya, who also looked worse for wear. All three had proved themselves a dozen times over in battle, so I wasn't going to chide them for their excesses. The morning's ride would sweat the wine from their blood soon enough.

Behind Leo stood his oldest sibling, Reinhold Dilisnya. He was only a few years younger than I, but managed to look much older. His grim face seemed daunting until one learned that it was the result of chronically poor digestion. On his left was his sister's husband, Victor

Wachter, on his right, their old family friend, handsome Gunther Cosco. Though the oldest in the group by some ten years, he still cut a dashing figure, but his famous looks were a trifle blurred this morning from too much wine and too little rest.

"Good morning, Lord Strahd," he rumbled, bending slightly forward. The others imitated him.

*Could he be the one?*

Of course he could, I impatiently answered myself. Alek glanced at me as though he'd somehow heard my thoughts. I ignored him and mounted my horse. The others followed my example, along with their retainers and the rest of our entourage. We made quite a parade, walking the length of the camp, and even collected a few cheers on our way to the Svalich Road.

Once there, we took the southwest branch, seemingly the wrong direction to get to the castle. The northwest turning looked like a shortcut, but the local guides agreed with our sketchy maps that though it cut off many miles from the journey to the Tser Falls, it also led to a dead end at their base, rather than to the bridge over them.

The road curved and climbed, making a lengthy switchback into this edge of Mount Ghakis. The air grew colder, not warmer, as the morning progressed, and patches of snow became more frequent until they were unbroken. I'd already sent a sizable party ahead of us to secure the castle, and evidence of their previous passage lay clear on the road in the form of churned and frozen mud. Our horses struggled through it, up and up to more rocky ground. This firmer footing had its own slippery hazard from hidden ice, and Gunther's mount nearly threw him off when its hind feet encountered some. He kept hold of his reins and head and even laughed about it later, though a careless fall in these mountains was tantamount to a death sentence.

The morning was almost gone by the time we reached the bridge. A dozen guards had been posted there and made their report of having spent a relatively quiet night. The falls made a very noisy rush, after all, in their nearly six-hundred-foot drop to this end of the valley. I peered over the high parapet of the bridge, taking my first real look at the land, at *my* land, at Barovia.

Almost directly below was the dead-end trail winding through dense thickets of trees. Except for the pines, the trees were bare and gray from the winter, making this the only time of year one might spot the Gypsy camp by the Tser Pool. Their wagons were gone now, driven far to the east, away from the war. Locals said that they would doubtless return in the spring. Beyond the campground to the right, I could just glimpse the crossroads where my army quartered. Hundreds of fires sent up thin lines of smoke into the still sky. In the center of the valley sprawled the village of Barovia, neatly cut in two by the Svalich Road. The trees were considerably thinner there, or missing altogether from marked off stretches of cultivated fields and pasture. Though hard to judge now, the land looked to be rich enough to make living here worthwhile.

Days earlier, when the army had marched through the village, the inhabitants had not impressed me much. Dark and stocky, either surly or too anxious to please, but one could hardly find fault with their ill-behavior in wearily trading one ruler for another. My predecessor had been a hard man, but better the devil you know than the one you don't—as Alek had said later, repeating their sentiments to me. I didn't care what they thought, as long as the taxes were collected and promptly turned in.

On my left stood the castle on its high spire of rock, but I couldn't see it from the bridge as an even higher outcrop bulked in between.

Alek Gwilym appeared suddenly at my side. I hadn't heard him because of the falls. I did not quite jump.

"The food is ready, my lord," he announced, shouting over the water's constant roar.

I ate with the men, but silently, watching their faces in vain hope that I might discover a clue. Leo Dilisnya and Illya Buchvold had recovered enough to joke about the previous night's revels. Reinhold listened to his younger brother's bragging with amused tolerance, but Ivan Buchvold barely heard them at all, appearing to be pre-occupied with something.

"Your thoughts are very much elsewhere, Ivan," I said.

He jerked and blinked, offering a thin smile. "Yes, my lord."

"Perhaps if you shared them with us they would not distract you so."

"'Tis nothing of any great interest to you, Lord Strahd."

"I will make my own judgment on what I find of interest."

Reinhold looked ready to jump in at that point, but my eye was on his brother-in-law, not him.

"Well, Ivan?"

31

He offered a sheepish smile. "I was only worried about my poor wife, Gertrude. She's nearing her time, and I've heard no news of how she is doing."

"Her time?" Perhaps she had some fatal disease, I thought.

Now Reinhold did speak. "He's hoping the brat he got with my sister on his last leave will be a boy, my lord, as if the two fine daughters he has were not enough of a handful to raise."

Family matters. Ivan was right: I had no interest in such things, and they all knew it. But there was another level to discuss, and I went straight to it. "If you have a son, then will you not get an additional share from your father-in-law's estate?"

"Yes, my lord. But that hardly matters to me now. My wife . . ."

He went on to speak of his dear Gertrude's many virtues and his concern for her continued good health. I quickly lost the thread of his talk. After all the honors and booty he'd picked up on this last campaign, Ivan's disinterest in the Dilisnya estate seemed genuine. Not so for Reinhold, the eldest and the head of the clan for the last two years. He hadn't done as well as he'd hoped during the war. The Dilisnyas were not a small family, what with a brother and two sisters and nearly a dozen offspring to support along with various in-laws, poor relations, servants, and serfs. Among them only Leo had not yet married, probably a wise choice. He was the youngest and thus had the least share in the family fortune.

Reinhold drifted across my thoughts again. Were I to die, control of Barovia would naturally pass to him as the senior officer. A rich prize indeed for a man with the boldness to strike for it. Except for Gunther and Alek, all the others were related by blood or by marriage. The Dilisnyas had served the Von Zarovich family for generations, but betrayals had happened before and for less cause.

As I watched, Reinhold's face twisted from some inner torment. He passed his half-finished plate of food back to his servant and got up, clutching his stomach. Indigestion, then, not guilt, though I could hardly expect a Ba'al Verzi to possess a mundane vulnerability like guilt.

*There is a traitor in the camp, you know.*

Alek's words turned my own meal to ashes. I gave my plate back even as had Reinhold and signed for the others to remain seated as I rose.

Reinhold had walked along the road for a little distance. I followed him. I'd left my guards behind. On purpose.

He noticed my approach and nodded companionably, one hand rubbing his abused stomach. "My lord."

"Seeking solitude, Reinhold?"

"I was thinking a walk might ease the pains."

"You should see Lady Ilona for such trouble."

"She has enough to keep her busy. Besides, what are the cramps in an old soldier's belly compared to the sorely wounded men who really need her help?" His hand went inside his coat, but he drew out only a small flask. He removed the cork and treated himself to a good swallow. "Medicine," he grimaced. "Catnip and fennel. It cools the fire."

We put some distance between us and the bridge; he

paused and pointed. "There, you can see the edge of it, past that mountain."

I looked. One of the outer walls of the castle was just visible, a flash of white against the harsh winter sky.

"Will you live there?"

"That depends on what condition it's in. Old Dorian had the reputation of a pig. It may be a wreck not worth the salvage."

"True, but he was still a fool to leave it and meet us in the valley. He should have waited for us to come and lay siege to him. One good snowstorm before the season's end this high up and half of us would have frozen to death, with the other half coming down with winter fever."

"Whose side are you on, Reinhold?"

"Yours, my lord, but I can't abide sloppy tactics no matter who's using them. Why, at this bridge alone he could have held us off for weeks. He might have placed some archers up on those cliffs on the other side and picked us off as we crossed, or rolled boulders down and blocked the road. I wonder what could have possessed him to be such a fool as to discard all his advantages."

"Just be glad that he did."

"Eh? Oh, yes, of course."

Not that Reinhold didn't have an excellent point. My one guess was that Dorian had wanted to go out as a fighter instead of wasting away in his castle like a rat in a hole. A siege can best be survived when you expect relief to come and take the attackers from behind. Dorian was alone and knew it. No help of any kind would come to him, and after his many depredations elsewhere, he could not expect quarter. No one would care to ransom him. He was dead and knew it. Yes, better to die fighting than to swim in your own sweat while waiting for gaunt hunger to take you.

Alek appeared, striding toward us on long legs, one hand on his sword hilt to keep the blade from swinging too much. He didn't look happy, probably thinking that I was taking too much risk, but he said nothing and only told us that everyone was ready to leave.

We resumed our ride at a slightly faster pace. The worst of the climb was behind us, though the land still gradually rose. We made it to a three-way crossroads within an hour. The left-hand branch was the Svalich Road, the right led to the castle. Two more switchbacks, a narrow pass, and *it* loomed into sight.

Twin towers had been built right at the edge of the mountain, and either would have made a fine keep for any conquering lord. But they were nothing compared to what lay behind them.

It was enormous. Overwhelming. Overpowering. The eye could not take it all in at first.

The curtain wall was nearly fifty feet high, interrupted by squared-off turrets that rose even higher. As massive as these were, they were made small by the round towers of the keep, the tallest soaring three times the height of the curtain wall. I was astonished not only for the sheer size of the structure, but by the unspoken fact that men— mere men—had designed and built such a wonder.

We crossed the drawbridge, which was in reasonably good repair, and marveled at the depth of the chasm it spanned. Ivan Buchvold got only laughter for his trouble when he upbraided young Illya for spitting over the edge.

The front gate was so huge that a giant might have easily passed through it. The man-sized doors beyond the portcullis seemed like something the builder had grafted on as a jest, like making a special entrance in a house for the mice to use. The guards standing at attention before them only added to the illusion, looking like a child's toy soldiers in their puny self-importance.

Passing through a short tunnel and under the portcullis, which was rotted through and useless for defense, we stopped just inside the courtyard for a long look at the keep itself.

"Magnificent," breathed Gunther.

"It's a wreck," Alek muttered.

"You're both right," added Victor Wachter. "It's a magnificent wreck."

Reinhold, who must have noticed I was not amused, told them to be quiet.

Without doubt, the place had seen better days. Trash and offal had collected in the corners of the yard, and where the wild grass could not find root, mud held sway. There was evidence of abuse and neglect, but they were but superficial details. The true lines of the place were strong and beautiful, readily apparent to those with wit enough to really see them. The silent stone walls, the blank windows, the crenelated battlements—above all, the sheer *size* of the thing—imparted to me a kind of awe such as I'd never felt before in my life. This was not the rough keep of a mountain warlord, this was the seat of power for a great king . . . or an emperor.

And it was *mine*.

# I, Strahd

Something within my belly shivered and turned over. It was a good feeling, or so it seemed to me just then.

Captain Erig, leader of the party I'd sent ahead, stood at strict attention before the main entrance of the keep. I signed for him and his steward to come forward. With a deep bow, he formally turned possession over to me, and the steward gave up the keys and a hefty scroll with a detailed inventory of the booty the previous occupants had left behind. I gave it a quick look, noting the limited amount of food—another factor in Dorian's suicidal decision, no doubt—then passed it on to Alek. At another signal from me, Reinhold dismounted and took a flat velvet pouch from one bulky saddlebag and gave it to Captain Erig. Grinning, he accepted with another bow before handing it to a young sergeant, who vanished inside the building.

I dismounted as well, feeling stiff after so much riding. The muscles in my back and thighs ached. I ignored them, as usual, and nodded once more to Erig, who raised his hand high.

Behind us a horn was sounded, and those armsmen who were not actually on guard duty hustled into the courtyard. They stood in a half-circle on our left. All eyes were on me.

Drawing my dagger, I switched it to my left hand and held out my right to Reinhold. He removed my glove and pushed up the sleeve until the lower part of my arm was bared.

The chaplain who had accompanied Erig came forward, chanting his prayers under his breath. He held a small gold ewer of wine, which he now poured over the blade of my dagger. This done, he made the sign of his faith over it and stepped back to his place among the men.

I raised the dagger to the sky and brought it level again, pointing it briefly north, east, south, and west, then stabbed it lightly into my right wrist.

"I am Strahd. I am the Land," I said loudly, intoning the ancient epigram. It was part and parcel of the ceremony of possession. The blood welled out, dribbled down my palm, and dripped onto the muddy earth at my feet. "Draw near and witness," I added. "I, Strahd, am the Land."

\* \* \* \* \*

"Will you stay long, my lord?" asked Erig after the ritual was over.

"We shall stay for the night," I said as the chaplain muttered over my small wound. Because I was looking for it, I saw the faint shimmer between his fingers and my skin. The cut vanished. He used the last of the wine to wash away the remaining blood and wiped it dry with a clean cloth. I thanked him and rolled down my sleeve.

"Very good, my lord. We've been prepared."

Reinhold's unhappy expression was eloquent, but resigned. Yesterday, when I'd made my proposal, he'd asked, "Is it a good idea for all the senior staff to be away from the main camp at this time?"

"What? For the army to be unsupervised, or for us to have only a light guard?" I had countered.

"Both."

"I think the commanders can cope for twenty-four hours without our help, and if they can't, then we'll find new officers. As for our own protection, the enemy are dead or routed. Once the drawbridge is up we'll be more than safe."

My manner had indicated that I would not be argued out of it, so he'd accepted things. I put his present grim state down to the fact that the food was bound to disagree with him again.

Alek wore a similar low face, but for a different reason. He was now worried about the Ba'al Verzi taking this as an opportunity to go to work.

"Risky, my lord," he whispered.

I made no reply.

Erig took us on an initial tour of the keep, and I saw for myself the tremendous amount of repairs that would be needed to make it livable. But while walking through the vast halls and rooms, I resolved that this place had to have more than just the necessities. I would make it a showpiece, not only to restore its former glory, but vastly exceed it. It would be the jewel of the Balinok Mountains, the crown of Barovia, the greatest treasure of all in the long history of the Von Zaroviches.

More than two hours later, dusty and thirsty, we emerged into a neglected garden at the rear of the structure. I usually had a good head for direction, but had lost myself several times and just now regained my inner map sense. The wind had kicked up, cold and relentless, cutting hard into our flesh after the stuffy stillness of the keep's interior. I left the others shuddering in the lee of a doorway, though, and strode to a low gate facing due east. There appeared to be nothing beyond it.

# P. N. Elrod

I was almost right. I was on a sturdy stone construction that jutted out some twenty feet from the cliff face. It gave me the odd feeling of floating since there was no visual reference to connect its base to the cliff. I craned out over the edge and was just able to see how its supports arched out from the rock face.

"Beware, my lord," called Alek, coming up to me. There were two red spots high on his cheeks from the lashing wind.

I showed him my teeth in a tight smile and turned away. It was a knife I had to fear, not a push. He stood next to me by the wall.

"It's amazing," he said, finally relaxing enough to appreciate the view.

A thousand feet below, all the valley was spread before us: the army camp, the village, and thick, dark forest to the horizon. The River Ivlis and the Svalich Road cut roughly parallel paths of silver and brown running east.

"It's mine," I told him.

We heard someone shout behind us and turned. The others were pointing upward. There was a flash of movement on the tallest tower. Snapping in the wind was the banner that had been passed to Erig's sergeant. My red, black, and white colors had been raised for all to see: Strahd Von Zarovich was now the ruler of this land.

"Mine," I repeated.

\* \* \* \* \*

The evening meal out of the way, we decided to bed down in the same hall since it was the only one with a working fireplace. The other rooms were in such a poor state that their discomfort outweighed anyone's desire for privacy, including mine. This met with Alek's silent approval, and I could see that he would be difficult to get rid of.

The youngest men, Illya and Leo, were too restless to retire yet and had left to do more exploring by lantern light. Ivan, Gunther, and Victor had a dice game going; Reinhold was busy writing letters and rubbing his troubled belly. That left Alek watching me while pretending not to do so. I waited him out, until natural necessity finally compelled him to leave us. Then I stood and stretched and announced I would take a last look around before sleep. This was met with preoccupied grunts and nods, so I simply walked out the door.

Guards were at watch in the hall without. I passed a few words with them, idly and unnecessarily repeating my story, and found the way to the main entrance hall. More guards. It was not easy for one such as me to be alone. Someone was always within call, be it a soldier or servant. The others—and most especially the killer who might be among them—would have a better time of it. All were of a sufficient rank that none of the men would question their movements.

If Alek were the one, then he would wisely refuse to strike. If not, then the real culprit could hardly fail to seize this opportunity—presuming that he was unaware that he was expected.

I walked outside, into the night.

The cold was merciless, but the air was clean and smelled of impending snow. I could see nothing at first, and little more when my eyes adjusted. The sky was heavy with clouds, masking off any helpful moon or starlight. Some lamps burned by the broken portcullis, but those were much too distant to be of any use. I'd have to rely on my ears, not eyes, for any warning.

I turned right, taking it slowly. I was the lord of the castle, after all, and entitled in every sense of the word to enjoy it . . . even if I couldn't see a damned thing in the murk.

Rounding the corner tower, I heard, or thought I heard, something behind me. I kept going and hoped that it wasn't Alek playing bodyguard again. I sensed rather than saw the high wall ahead that joined the curtain wall to the keep. There was a wide gate in its center, allowing one to pass through to the servants' court and stables. The portcullis that should have been there was gone. Yet another bit of work for the restoration to come. I walked through and drifted close to the stables in the far corner of the yard. None of the attending grooms who slept near the horses noticed me.

Another turn to the right and a slow stroll through an open gate into the abandoned garden. The ground was firmer here, not as muddy. There were also plenty of alcoves to hide in, formed by the buttresses that supported the outside walls of the chapel. Some movement drew my eye up to the broken windows of that sad, holy place, but the motion did not repeat itself. I put my back to it and walked toward the overlook.

Outside the protecting walls, the wind tore at my cloak as though to steal it away. What warmth I'd hoarded in its folds was instantly dispelled. I cringed from the cold, but refused to let it best me and went to the very edge of the overlook, bumping into the low wall with my knees. Again, I felt as though I were floating, this time in a great sphere of darkness. There was no up or down, no sense of depth or distance, and yet I had the persistent knowledge that both were very great and very dangerous.

A crash. I couldn't tell how far away, though it had to be close or the wind would have obscured the sound. I thought of the chapel windows and the row they'd make if broken out some more. No other noise followed.

My heart pounding hard in my ears. I silently drew my sword and unbuckled the scabbard, letting it slip to the ground. I didn't want it banging into my legs. Next, I unhooked the throat catch of my cloak and draped its heavy weight over my left arm. The bitter wind still buffeted me, but I no longer felt it.

Within the chapel garden I heard the unmistakable sounds of combat: the ring of metal on metal, grunts, curses. I darted forward, rushing into it.

My eyes were able to see movement in the blackness, but not much more than movement. I could barely make out two or three figures milling about one another. Three, I decided, just as one of them staggered from a blow and lurched right into me.

I tried to dodge him, but he was moving too fast and we both went down. Things got mixed as we each tried to get away from the other. I couldn't bring my sword arm up, only punch at him with my encumbered left. The cloak fell off and entangled him, and I used the respite to find my feet.

Only to be knocked down again. Something hard

slammed into my left flank; it sliced through my clothes and scraped against the chain mail. I grappled and seized a flailing arm and twisted it back. The man belonging to it hissed with pain and broke away.

I rolled upright. "Stand where you are!" I roared.

Another voice called a question, but I couldn't make it out. Alek Gwilym's voice interrupted at the same time. He was to my right. He'd been the one that had first run into me, I realized.

"Beware, Strahd!"

Then there was a sharp gurgling cry very close to me, and something heavy dropped right at my feet. It thrashed and choked, then went silent.

"Strahd!"

"Shut up, you fool!" I was trying to hear where the third man had gone. His breathing betrayed him. He was to my right, between me and Alek. I bulled over, but miscalculated the distance and blundered into him. The two of us then fell over Alek, who was yet on the ground, struggling with my cloak. Cursing and punching, I found my feet and bellowed for them to be still or I'd run them both through. That brought instant order to the confusion.

"What's going on?" a fourth man demanded. He came running up from the servant's court gate. It was one of the many guards, and by the grace of the gods, he carried a lantern. He stopped in his tracks at the tableau revealed by his light, but I had no time for his gawking.

"Go to the keep! Fetch the commanders!" I shouted.

Eyebrows climbing, he started to run.

"Leave the light, blast you!"

He all but dropped it and bolted away.

44

After so much unrelieved darkness, the feeble glow of the lantern seemed like a burst of sunshine. It picked out the huddled figures of Leo Dilisnya and Alek and the very, very still form of Illya Buchvold. I recognized him by his clothes and a shock of blond hair; otherwise his lower face was obscured by some kind of kerchief. I pulled the thing away. It was soaked with blood. His throat had been cut.

I pointed at the body with my sword and looked at Alek and Leo. "Explain."

Leo's teeth were chattering with reaction. "Illya told me . . . told me you were in danger, my lord."

Alek locked eyes with me. I leaned forward. Leo cowered back, but Alek held him in place with a heavy hand on his shoulder.

"Go on."

"He said there was a Ba'al Verzi after you. That he thought . . . thought . . ."

"What?"

"Thought it might be Commander Gwilym."

"Why did you not come to me with this news, then?"

"He only just told me. He wasn't sure. That's why we went off. Then when we came back the others said you'd gone for a walk, and Alek Gwilym had left to go after you, and the guards said you'd gone around the keep, and Illya thought we could cut through to the chapel and head him off by climbing down from the windows."

"What made him think to come to the chapel garden?"

Leo gestured vaguely in the direction of the overlook. "The two of you were there earlier. He thought the assassin might try pushing you from the wall."

And so he might—after first stabbing me. "Alek?"

"I can't tell if this whelp speaks the truth or not, only that the two of them broke out one of the windows and jumped me while I was looking for you." He kept a grip on Leo and, shaking off the cloak, pushed himself to his feet. "So what made you kill the heroic Illya? Hmm?"

The young man was nearly in tears. "When he—when he turned on Lord Strahd. It was so fast. You were knocked away, and then I heard Lord Strahd, and then Illya went for him . . . and I just *knew.* He'd lied to me, to everyone, and I knew *he* was the Ba'al Verzi, and he'd used me to try to kill my lord . . ."

Now the tears flowed more freely. He was shaking from head to toe with rage and shame.

"I had to stop him," he choked out, impatiently swiping at his face. "He was my kinsman by marriage, but I couldn't let him kill my lord Strahd."

A neat strategy by the assassin: unable to get me alone, he'd have his dupe take care of Alek while he killed me, then murder the dupe to silence him. I strongly suspected the overlook was also meant to be used. Dropped over the edge, it might be days before my slashed and broken body was found. Not even the Most High Priest Kir would have been able to draw me back then.

"Why the mask?"

"Wha—?"

"The kerchief." Alek pointed to the one I'd left crumpled on Illya's body.

"I don't know. A disguise, perhaps."

"Disguise?" He spat out the word as though it had a

bad taste. "What use would that be to him here?"

"Not a disguise, Alek," I said patiently. "We've both been on enough night raids to know how easy it is to pick out a white face in the dark. He used the kerchief to cover himself, just in case a light was inconveniently near. He couldn't smear his face with ashes or mud or it'd give him away later, so he did the next best thing."

"You think he's the one, then?"

"I don't have to think." I pointed to Illya's right hand and brought the lantern close. The lax fingers were loosely wrapped around the hilt of a small but distinctive knife. Red, black, and gold glinted from its bloodstained surface. The edge looked uncommonly sharp. I gingerly plucked it up.

"Is it truly one of their blades?"

I had to be sure for myself. Putting my sword down, I concentrated on the knife, holding it flat on my palm. With my free hand, I traced out a sigil in the air above it and said a word of power. Faint at first, the blade began to pulse with a lurid green glow that grew strong and steady until we were all bathed in it, shadowless and colorless. Like ghosts.

Leo's pupils shrank to pinpricks. He made the protective sign of his faith and flinched back against Alek. I wasn't certain if he feared the magicked blade or the fact that I knew how to raise and reveal it.

The others displayed similar reactions of honest horror once they arrived and the story was shared. Ivan Buchvold all but collapsed after receiving the double blow that not only was his young brother dead, but he had also been a Ba'al Verzi assassin.

"Impossible," he said, over and over. "How could it be? It must be impossible." But the truth was there for him to see, and a later search of Illya's belongings turned up the knife's special sheath. Such things were made from the skin of the killer's first victim, and this one proved to follow guild tradition down to the last gruesome detail.

For now, though, everyone was in some form of shock or other. The others from the news of the traitor, and I from the drain of magic, or so I thought until I bent down to retrieve my sword. My sight flickered and I swayed, dizzy for a moment. Alek, ever watchful, noticed.

"You're bleeding, my lord," he said, pointing to the hand that held the knife.

I hadn't known that I'd cut myself, nor could I feel it yet. Not a bad wound, but bad enough. The seepage ran black down the glowing blade and dripped onto the ground.

"Cast it away, my lord. It's too dangerous to keep. Unlucky."

"I think not. The Ba'al Verzi failed, didn't he? I'd say that makes it very lucky for me. What's said to be unlucky is sheathing it without drawing blood . . . and that's taken care of itself."

"But, my lord, there's your side as well."

I looked down at what I thought to be a mere bruise. Illya had struck hard at me in the fight, I now remembered. His special knife had not only scraped the chain mail, but had sliced right through it. Cold air blasted against the warm blood oozing from the gash there.

"A scratch, Alek, nothing more. I've had worse on the practice field." I switched the knife—carefully—to my other hand and held the bleeding one out from my body. The blood fell freely onto the bare, dead earth of the garden. "I am Strahd. I am the Land," I said, repeating the ancient epigram. "Draw near and witness. I, Strahd, am the Land."

No one moved. Except for Ivan, whose head was bowed over his dead brother, they stared at me, looking as though the breath had turned to ice in their lungs.

Alek, the most hedonistic and least pious of the lot, joined them in making the protective sign of the faith.

# Chapter Two

## Sixth Moon, 348

"Does this pigsty have a name, Alek?"

"Renika, my lord."

It was deemed a wise policy to allow the rabble at least one good look at their new lord before civil rule was turned over to the boyars, and while I hadn't stopped at every village in Barovia, our tour of inspection had certainly covered quite a number of them. This portion of my duties was always highly abhorrent to me—I would almost have preferred to be digging ditches since the various discomforts of that task were comparable—except that we were also collecting the taxes, a benefit that no man working with a pick could ever hope to gain from his labor.

"Get on with it, then."

Alek and the two trumpeters kicked their horses to a faster pace, while I and the rest of the party continued more slowly. The men and mounts were tired, it was late in the afternoon, and this was our fourth stop today. I wasn't planning to spend the night, though, having discovered it was safer and healthier to camp on the open road, away from troublesome rats (and other village vermin), not to mention the wisdom of keeping a goodly distance between my men and the nearest tavern. I wanted this business done as quickly as possible, and any delays traced to overindulgence in the local brews was not something I was prepared to tolerate.

The horns sounded ahead of us, announcing my approach to the village. Alek had yet to lose his amusement for the work; perhaps it had to do with the fact that no matter where we went or how isolated the hamlet, the locals never failed to exhibit utterly identical behavior. First fear, then cautious curiosity, and finally emergence from the frail shelter of their homes to offer greetings. One and all, without exception, the people had managed to gather a gaggle of brats to present bouquets of flowers to me. I accepted their weeds, but that was as far as I cared to take it. If the mothers expected me to reward their offspring with a kiss or a copper, then they would just have to live with the disappointment. I'd been forced to do many terrible things in the name of duty, but one must draw the line somewhere.

Renika had apparently long known of our coming. This time, Barovia's ubiquitous wildflowers had been strung into garlands that ran from house to house all along their main street. More were strewn in our path, and a virtual rain of petals were dropped on us from the upper stories. Several musicians were thumping and puffing out something resembling a popular marching song, no doubt to honor my exploits as a soldier. Everyone had donned his or her best clothes; some of them even wore shoes.

A tiny girl, still a novice to walking, was urged in my direction, clutching her bouquet in one miniature fist. She tottered forward in her painfully clean smock, just managing not to fall over. I bent low, swept the flowers away from her, and held them high, nodding to the cheering crowd. There were actually enough people here to form a crowd. The revenue promised to be better than average.

The girl remained where she was, looking undecided, ultimately sticking a green-stained thumb into her mouth. Her mother darted up to grab her out of the way so I could dismount. In turn, one of the trumpeters relieved me of the flowers so I could face the burgomaster unencumbered. It's difficult to put on a properly stern face while so frivolously burdened. Alek was of the opinion that that was the purpose behind such presentations: to place the visiting dignitary at a disadvantage by the subtle diminishment of his dignity.

The burgomaster launched into the usual speech of

greeting and wish for my continued good health and wise rule. These preambles always concluded with an invitation to some meal or other, which I never failed to politely refuse. Had I accepted all of them, I'd have had more stomach problems than Reinhold Dilisnya.

"And now, Lord Strahd, I humbly beg your permission to allow us to honor you by letting Renika be the first village to celebrate that blessed event that ultimately brought you to this, our beloved Barovia."

*What?* I thought. *Dorian's depredations?*

"Indeed, with your permission, I would like to be so bold as to propose that the great day be made into a national holiday to be marked by all from one end of the land to the other."

"What are you talking about, Burgomaster?"

"I beg leave to allow your grateful subjects the honor of celebrating your birthday, my lord." He finished with a flourish of his arms, which signaled to the crowd to start cheering again. When the noise finally subsided, the broadly smiling man gradually became aware that I was not at all amused.

"I find it interesting, Burgomaster, that you wish to celebrate a day that means I am yet another year closer to my death."

His face went blank with utter shock. "Oh, no, my lord! That is the *last* thing I—we wish to do!"

"Then we are in accord, as it is also the last thing *I* wish to do."

Nonplussed, he blinked his eyes rapidly as his mind attempted to adjust to this unexpected turn.

"The taxes, Burgomaster," I prompted, reminding him

of the purpose of my visit.

In a gratifyingly brief time, a small wooden box with iron banding was produced and offered to my clerk of the exchequer. He unfolded his portable counting table and immediately got down to work. Chosen for his speed and expertise, he soon finished and made his report.

"Too short, my lord," he concluded.

Nothing new there, the taxes were always less than expected.

"*Much* too short," he added, significantly.

I fixed my eye on the burgomaster. "Explain."

"It's been a very difficult year, your lordship. The war has drained us . . . the harvests have been lean . . . there's been a lot of sickness . . ." Some of the crowd nodded their vague agreement to his excuses.

"And yet you wear a very excellent gold chain around your neck."

"Part of the office, my lord, it's really the property of the village."

"And enough fine wool on your back to clothe a whole family. Those buttons are pure silver, are they not?"

"An inheritance from a wealthy, but sadly deceased, relative—"

"And which of these humble hovels is your home?"

Sensing that this was not going to be a good day for him after all, he hesitantly pointed with a trembling finger, though I could have spotted it a mile away. Looking very new and freshly whitewashed, the bold structure stood out from the rest of the buildings like an over-dressed woman surrounded by her drab servants.

"Th—the public nature of my office requires that I

maintain a certain standard of living, making it necessary that I—"

"Peculate on a regular basis?" suggested Alek.

"Eh?"

"Steal the public and his lordship blind?" he bellowed
in his ear.

The crowd watched silently, their pinched faces and
worn bodies proof of a hard life of scant food and little or
no respite from their labor. This must have been rare
entertainment for them: they seemed all but nailed in
place.

"Alek," I said quietly.

With the clerk and some armsmen, he strode to and
thrust open the door of the burgomaster's house. Things
were so still that we clearly heard the squawks of outrage
and fear coming from within. Soon a scullery boy and
several servant women dodged and hustled into the
street. I was strongly reminded of the sort of confusion
one finds in a hen yard while attempting to chase down
the evening's meal.

Alek came out last and commented, "Does well for
himself."

The burgomaster was sweating freely now. A dozen
feet away you could smell the fear oozing from him.

The clerk emerged not long after. He and the armsmen
carried a number of scrolls—the tax records of Renika—
which were gone through one by one. To the illiterate
rabble, it must have seemed like some sort of magical
rite. I glimpsed more than one of them making a sign
against the evil eye in the clerk's direction.

"Much too short, my lord," he repeated. "Did it gradually over the years, but it shows up badly when compared to his predecessor's collections."

"But those were better times," the burgomaster protested.

"I've accounted for the drop in population, its recovery, and the years with bad weather, scant crops, and the recent war. Still too short."

"Perhaps out of compassion for your people, you simply lowered the taxes to ease their burdens," I murmured.

He wasn't quite stupid enough to fall into that trap. He did not instantly agree with me and glanced nervously at the silent, very silent crowd. He'd get no sympathy from that lot.

"Lord Strahd, I . . . I admit that I may have made some mistakes in my sums. I'm not as skilled with numbers as was my father, but I shall gladly make up the difference, whatever it may be."

I raised an eyebrow at the clerk.

"Clothes off," he ordered.

The burgomaster blinked some more, confused by the incongruity for a moment, then his face lighted up with understanding. "Yes, yes, of course." The compensation would begin with his own rich wardrobe.

He whipped off his gold chain of office and gave it to the clerk, then his brightly dyed cloak, then his waistcoat with the silver buttons. The clothes were heaped one by one on the table until he was down to his last garment, which the clerk told him to retain for purposes of decency. The man shivered as the summer air hit the sweat covering his pale body. He looked ridiculous, but pathetically grateful. He was more than willing to suffer some little humiliation rather than the traditional fate of a thief: the sudden removal of one of his hands.

Of course, that was the old law. *I* was running things now.

"On your belly," said the clerk.

The burgomaster winced and spread himself flat, probably expecting a whipping at this point. I might have ordered one, had I thought it would do any good, but this object lesson was for the people, not the thief.

The clerk turned to the armsmen. "Tatra."

The one so named stepped forward. He wasn't a large man, but had exceptionally strong arms, a good eye, and no objection to the work. As he crossed over, he quietly drew his sword. Some of the peasants saw what was coming; mothers clutched their infants and hid their own eyes, other people leaned in for a better look. No one said a single word by way of warning. Possibly they knew the futility of it; more likely they knew better than to risk trying.

It was over very quickly, raising a collective gasp from the crowd since it is something of a shock to see how far the blood spurts when a head is expertly severed. Tatra grabbed it up by the hair before it could roll away and held it high so everyone could see. The burgomaster, if one could judge anything from his last mortal expression—which was one of pensive worry—never knew what hit him.

Now I cleared my throat. All eyes, save two, came round to me.

"I expect my subjects to be honest in their dealings

with each other, but most especially with me. The taxes will be collected and turned in each year—all of them. *No excuses.*"

There was no need to ask if they understood; it was very obvious that they did.

"You are free to choose a new Burgomaster according to whatever custom you follow. Make sure you pick an honest one, or we'll have to go through all this again next year."

A few people, perhaps potential candidates for the office, gulped, looking unhappy.

"My collector will be back in one week. You will have that long to correct your records and make up the amount that this dolt withheld for himself over the years. Be ready."

The point made and the show over, we mounted up and rode away without further ceremony.

"That makes four out of four today," remarked Alek. "This is becoming monotonous."

"I've always thought as much."

"But this one did stand out from the rest with that birthday business."

"More like a death day, for him at least."

"Shows imagination, though."

"Didn't help him, though."

"Agreed, my lord." He brushed some stray flower petals from his shoulders and hair.

"Does the next pigsty have a name?"

"Jarvinak, my lord."

"How far?"

"Three or four miles, no more." He checked the

progress of the westering sun. "There's time. Shall we try for five out of five?"

I squinted at that bright orb myself and shrugged. "Why not?"

# Fourth Moon, 350

"Lord Sergei's party is on the final approach to the guardhouses, your lordship," one of the footmen puffed out, breathless from his run up the stairs.

"Very well."

That did not give me much time to get to the front courtyard. Of course, I could just slip out my bedroom window, tie a rope to one of the crenelations, and rappel down the wall. That only took a few seconds, as Alek and I had discovered while practicing the sport last summer with the castle guards. On the other hand, I was in my best dress clothes, which were designed for show, not agility, and the sight of me in even a controlled fifty-foot drop over the side of the keep would alarm the guests and compromise my dignity. It would not do to let people know I was overly anxious about anything, especially not this event. Instead, I quickly made my way to the spiral stairs just off my private dining room and skimmed down to the main floor.

Once the regular flow of gold and goods from taxation had been re-established, the restoration of the castle proceeded with considerable speed. Artisans, carpenters, masons, and others with the necessary skills had turned up like dogs at a feast, ready for whatever scraps might come their way. I fully exploited their combined talents, using them to turn the castle into the showpiece that I'd envisioned on that first day over three years ago. In the end, the final result exceeded the vision as each expert sought to outdo the work of the others. But some adjustments between beauty and practicality had to be made, hence the difficulty of getting anywhere quickly. It was still a castle, ostensibly designed for defense, and what eased the passage for the inhabitants would certainly aid the invader. (One result of this was that I rarely, if ever, had a hot meal. I was told that the master cook and one of the remaining engineers were working on the problem.)

Alek and a few others of my entourage were waiting in the great entry for me. All came to attention at my appearance. Some wore armor, others were in their robes of office, most were bedecked with the glitter of gems and gold in medals and badges that represented their lives' accomplishments. Next to them I must have cut something of a stark figure in my plain black garments. It was the best quality fabric, though, and contrasted well with a blinding white silk vest and shirt, both with buttons of true pearl. Carefully knotted below my chin was a neckcloth of the same blood red as the great Von Zarovich ruby that flashed from my breast.

Another footman rushed in. I arched an eyebrow, giving him permission to speak.

"Lord Sergei is crossing the drawbridge, your lordship."

At a nod from me he vanished and the party fell into

# P. N. Elrod

line: Alek Gwilym at my left, Lady Ilona Darovnya on my right. Their retainers and my own sorted themselves, and I led the way through the massive doors of the entry. The timing had worked out after all; Sergei's banner bearers were just emerging from under the portcullis. They separated, one to each side, trailed by others who merged into place with my own honor guard. The implied symbolism must have been quite satisfying to those present. Alek, now steward in charge of the castle defense, had arranged an excellent show.

A constant rumble and roll of drums filled the courtyard now, quickening the heart. The lighter voices of pipes joined them just as Sergei rode through the gate. I felt the eyes of the gathered crowd shifting between us, hoping perhaps to gain some insight to our inner feelings at this historic moment.

With Sergei, the insights must have been easy. Even from a distance, one could see each emotion flashing over his face, like summer light and storm clouds on a mountain side. He was blessed with the strong Von Zarovich features of black hair, high cheeks, and a tough jaw, but these were markedly softened by the Van Roeyen side of the family. He had Mother's warm blue eyes. By the gods, but he was a handsome man, an opinion very obviously shared by all the young, and not a few of the older, female members of the court and staff.

As he rode closer, more and more heads turned from him to me. Comparing. I endured it, for there was nothing else to be done. It was no less than I'd expected: I was doing it myself.

Younger, much more handsome, open and smiling—

everything that I was not—Sergei reined his horse and dismounted.

I was taller, I noted.

He marched forward, sweeping off his hat and gracefully dropped to one knee, a bare step short of our party. I took up that step and placed my right hand on his shoulder. He looked up then and smiled directly at me, happy, guileless, and brimming full of that which I'd long ago learned to interpret as hero-worship.

*That* was unexpected. To have it coming from a stranger was one thing, but receiving it from my own brother—even a brother I had never met—was quite something else again.

Sergei placed his right hand upon my own and recited in a clear voice the words of greeting, followed by a pledge of faith and service required by custom when siblings of rank formally face each other. I made my response and Sergei rose again, then we embraced. Witnesses to the ceremony could hold themselves in no longer and began to spontaneously cheer.

*     *     *     *     *

"Who would have thought such a thing could finally come to pass?" my youngest brother confided to me some hours later.

Introductions by the dozens, feasting, and endless talk and questions had yet to dampen his enthusiasm or energy. He looked as fresh as midsummer dawn.

"Our parents?" I suggested.

His smile faltered, then turned into a laugh. He laughed

very easily. It might have been irritating had it been for effect, or to cover up an insecurity, but in truth, it was the result of a free and innocent heart, a lightness of the soul that I had inevitably lost in my years of war and slaughter.

"I meant that we should finally meet after all this time," he said.

"We're hardly strangers."

"Oh, but reading a letter just isn't the same. 'Dear Brother: Today I went hunting,' or 'The apple crop failed,' or 'A storm knocked down many trees.' That's not how you get to know a person. You must've grown weary reading of such news from me while you were away."

"No soldier ever wearies of receiving letters from home. The smallest detail was always of great interest to me and kept my memories from fading. I am in your debt and only sorry that I did not have as much time to reply as I would have liked."

"Oh, but we understood, all of us. You had your duties to consider, and unless you gave them your full attention . . . well, the wrong side might have won the war. We missed you terribly, especially Mother, but we knew that you were needed more elsewhere. No other commander could have done so well as you."

*Possibly not,* I thought. But my passion for war and obedience to duty had swept me from the home of my childhood, never to return. I had not seen my younger brother Sturm grow up, or been there for Sergei's birth or for any of a thousand other joys that a man might take from the heart of his family. I had not even been able to attend the burial of our parents, four years past. Their deaths had occurred during the height of a particularly close and bitter campaign, and I could not be spared. I'd yet to see their graves. In some part of my mind, they were still alive as I'd last seen them three decades ago; Sergei's presence had driven home the fact that this was not true.

"I wish she could have seen this place," he said, now speaking of our mother. "It would have made her very happy to see what beauty you've wrought here and that you named it after her . . . well, I suppose she might have burst from the pride and honor of it all."

"Ravenloft for Ravenia Van Roeyen," I said. I remembered her ink-black hair and the pride and sorrow in her blue eyes when I went off to war. Sergei took after her quite a lot, not so much in exact looks, for our father was certainly in him, but in mannerisms and patterns of speech. At times I could almost hear a ghost of her voice in his own when he spoke. "A pity you were not able to come in time for the naming ceremony. Lady Ilona would have been glad of your assistance."

"I don't know if my help would have been proper, though, since I'm not yet ordained, and that won't happen until Most High Priest Kir passes on—which won't be for years and years, I'm sure. I've letters for you from him, by the way, and for Lady Ilona as well."

"How is the young whelp?"

Sergei was made a touch uncomfortable by my addressing Kir in such an offhand manner. I'd felt the same way about my teachers, once.

"Still trying to look old enough to suit his office?" I added.

He surrendered into a grin, threw his head against the back of his chair, and rolled his eyes at the ceiling. "I'd forgotten he was just a child when you first left for the wars. Yes, yes, he still works at looking older. He's grown quite a beard and that seems to help. No one dares to show him any disrespect in class, though, or he metes out something worse than rapped knuckles."

"And what did *you* end up doing?"

Sergei's jaw sagged at this bit of insight from me. He was chagrined and amused all at once. "Conjugating a hundred verbs for three different languages." He sipped at his wine and lifted the cup slightly in my direction. "Now, what about you? Did his predecessor ever punish you?"

"Old Zarak? He once put me to holystoning the floor of the classroom."

"Not really!"

"Yes, really! Said I needed more humility or some such rot. I don't know if it humbled me or not, but he got a very clean floor for his trouble. I did pay better attention in class after that."

"I just can't see you doing it, Strahd."

"Apparently Zarak could. Took a week before I could straighten my back and knees properly."

Sergei laughed again. Responding to it, even I managed to raise a brief smile to the memory of the boy I'd once been. The boy who was gone forever.

I looked at my brother across the table, where we'd shared our first private meal together, and saw myself in him, myself as I *should* have been. Not that I begrudged Sergei his own life, but that mine had been all but used up, sacrificed to the demands of duty and obligation. When possible, the eldest child always went into soldiering, the second administered the estates, and the third was consecrated to the service of the gods. Such binding tradition could be broken, but when one is raised to it and knows nothing else, one has little chance to discover until too late that there are other things in life.

I looked at Sergei and felt a hot surge of anger for my lost years and envy for all those that lay before him. Yet, I could not hate him. He was bound by tradition as well. Indeed, as I had before him, he'd no intention of breaking with it. He was pledged to the church of our god and glad of the fact. The anger eventually cooled into a kind of pity for his blindness. Someday, perhaps, he would come to understand how he'd been manipulated and feel as I felt now.

"Is anything wrong, Brother?" he asked, concerned by my change of manner and long silence.

It was pointless to try explaining it to him. He was just too *young.*

\* \* \* \* \*

Sergei's sword came down with deadly speed. I barely blocked it with the flat of my blade and at the last instant, preventing him from chopping me in half the long way.

He was strong but also knew when to break off, which he now did and thus avoided the thrust of my parrying dagger into his guts. He danced back, assumed a guard position I was unfamiliar with, and grinned like a young wolf. A less experienced fighter might have charged in, but I held away, studying him. He was prepared for an upper body attack, but only from the front; the positioning of his feet was too awkward for a really fast turn.

I attacked his left flank, changed it to a feint at the last second, and dived to his right. As I'd hoped, he wasn't able to cover himself. I ducked under his guard, slammed his sword arm back with my own, and stopped with my dagger pressed lightly against the center point of his stomach, just below his breastbone. A single sharp move would send it right up into his heart.

He saw and grinned again, nodding his surrender. We stepped apart and bowed to one another as the applause began.

*So this is what it's come to,* I thought, *twenty-five years of battle training so I can entertain the court peacocks.*

I was being unfair: our audience mostly comprised soldiers who had served with me. Their response rankled because they had probably seen that Sergei's defeat had been a very near thing. I was conscious of my hard breathing and the sweat running from my face like rain. Sergei still looked fairly fresh, and only a few minutes passed before he asked Alek to spar with him next.

His challenge was readily accepted. Alek was lean and fast, but cautious. He refused several openings Sergei offered; their first minute dragged as they tried various feints and dodges on each other. Sergei then tried a feint-feint-attack, but Alek read it correctly and countered, working both sword and dagger as the expert he was. In the years since he'd ceased to be my second-in-command and become castle steward, he'd not allowed himself to grow soft. Perhaps there was nothing more for him to do now than to keep the guards in shape and to dally with the chambermaids, but he worked his body in practice combat every day as if his life still depended on it. And it showed.

A lightning quick parry, feint with the dagger, and a return cut—Alek stopped with his blade just touching Sergei's middle.

"I've much to learn," Sergei said, unable to give up his smile.

"You're doing as well as any of my fighters and better than most, my lord."

Judging from the renewed applause, the others agreed with him.

"Perhaps one day I shall be half as good as my brother, and then perhaps I may count myself worthy of being a warrior," he said, bowing to me.

I returned the bow. It was expected of me. As flattering as any of the peacocks, but he'd been sincere. On the other hand, it was easy for me to interpret his true meaning as mockery. Surely he knew just how close he'd come to defeating me. In a few weeks, especially if he took training from Alek, he would be the best fighter in Barovia.

The sparring games had been going on since early morning, and now the sun was just beginning to clear the curtain wall of the courtyard. It was too soon for the midday meal, but I ordered the footmen to have a table loaded with food standing ready. After a series of matches, we were always ravenous. While Sergei and the others reviewed their moves and style, I strolled over and wiped at my sweat with a serving cloth, then eased my thirst with iced wine liberally diluted by water. This high up in the Balinoks, having ice the year round was hardly the luxury it was in the lower, more temperate areas to the south, but I still found it so and enjoyed it.

"My Lord Strahd!" came a woman's voice.

I finished my long drink and handed the cup to a waiting servant. The woman who'd just approached me was not immediately familiar, nor was she dressed for court show. Her motley clothes were dusty, and her eyes red and swollen from lack of sleep.

"Falov, isn't it?" I vaguely recalled that she'd been one of the many junior lieutenants in my command. Like the rest, she'd been mustered out to either settle in Barovia or return home. From the sheepskin vest she wore over her mail shirt, I concluded she'd chosen to remain in the new land and supervise flocks instead of soldiers.

She bowed. "Yes, my lord. Forgive me for coming unannounced—"

"Never mind that. What's the trouble?"

"Bandits, my lord."

"Bandits. So?" The mountains were full of them. Hardly impressive news. My men often made forays into their strongholds in much the same way the rat catchers worked their trade at the castle. One could never hope to entirely stamp out the vermin, but it reduced their numbers and kept them in line.

"It's a large group, my lord . . . led by Red Lukas."

Now that did catch my attention. The renegade had been a troublemaker for over two years, flouting my laws

with his murders and thefts. "You're certain?"

"Aye, my lord. I saw him myself. No one else around here has such a head of hair. Like fire it was."

"Where?"

"Not half a day's ride from here."

"Ah, but where will he be now?"

"The same place, I'm sure. I have some men keeping him under watch, but we're not enough to attack. We were hoping your lordship could spare some troops to help us take him."

"Take him? I've no intention of releasing troops to take him, Falov—"

Her mouth opened, then snapped shut on whatever protest she might have had.

"But I will go myself to see to his execution."

Her disappointment changed to elation almost as soon as the words left my lips. "Thank you, Lord Strahd." She didn't question whether such a clean-up job was beneath my station, as would some others of the court. Having once been a soldier herself, she could readily understand my interest in running headlong into what promised to be a good fight.

"It's like sending a giant to smash a roach," said Alek when I outlined the situation to him a few minutes later.

"It takes a nimble giant to strike so small a target," I returned. "This is hardly a midsummer flower festival. We're going after Red Lukas."

"Who is he?" asked Sergei.

Alek filled him in on a few details of the bandit's most recent crimes, which included the slaughter of at least fifty people in a farming village. The few survivors had claimed he'd decided not to burn it because others would eventually move in and provide him with more such sport the following year. My little brother was right-eously horrified and asked to come along. He whooped in a most undignified way when I said yes.

"Do you remember being that eager for blood?" Alek asked as we walked back to the keep to get ready for the expedition.

"I still am, Commander. Can you not tell?"

He glanced at me, his pale, hard eyes going bright with amusement as they locked briefly upon mine. "Yes, my lord. Now that you mention it, I can. Let's hope that Red Lukas has his affairs in order."

The cold meats laid out for the sparring gamesters were hastily packed for the journey. Within an hour, we were geared up and cantering through the pass on our way to the northwest branch of the Svalich Road.

*     *     *     *     *

Red Lukas had chosen an excellent lair. On this shoul-der of Mount Ghakis, he commanded a wide view of the road and valley below and had all of the town of Vallaki in sight. Any sortie from that direction could be spotted in plenty of time for him and his followers to either pre-pare a defense or hide. The land was more than rugged at this point, and once off the road a horseman was at a tremendous disadvantage.

"It's beautiful," observed Sergei. He'd entered Barovia from the east and had not yet seen this portion of the country. We were high above Lake Zarovich, which I'd renamed in honor of my father. Looming beyond it, with snow heavily cloaking its flanks and peak, was Mount Baratok. The angle was just right for its every detail to be reflected in the quiet surface of the lake.

Alek Gwilym ignored the scenery and peered ahead and to the left. "How far?"

"A mile as the crow flies," Falov answered, keeping her voice low.

"And as the soldier stumbles?"

"Two."

"They're closer than that to us. I can smell 'em."

We'd seen nothing since leaving our horses with Falov's people and posting the main body of troops in a stand of trees just off the road. The air was so still that any sound would carry for a considerable distance; we dared not bring the troops closer, lest the bandits be alerted.

"More than that," said Falov. "Listen."

"I don't hear anything," Sergei whispered.

"Aye, my lord. When the birds grow silent, there's usually a good reason for it."

My instincts told me it was too late for stealth. Along with the others, I drew my sword.

And only just in time.

Screaming and roaring, they burst out from their cover and fell upon us like white-hot vengeance. Alek was the closest and the first to be attacked, but managed to parry and counter. After that I lost track of him: I had troubles of my own.

Sparring practice has about as much resemblance to field combat as a sculpture has to its subject. It may look the same, but one is cold stone and the other alive and moving and reacting to you. The two men who picked me out for quarry had some battle experience, but were undisciplined. I'd rather face a well-trained soldier than such amateurs, for the latter could often be dangerously unpredictable.

The one on my left charged in first, perhaps thinking it was my weaker side. I got my blade up, moved it so his slid down its length, and before he could break away, got him between the ribs with my parrying dagger. It did not sink in as deeply as it should have, nor was I able to wrest it out for another try. He must have had mail on under his coat; worse, he didn't seem to be aware he'd been stabbed.

His partner crashed into me, knocking me over. I felt my breath go as one of his knees dug into my gut, but he'd left himself open. Even without air I was able to smash the pommel of my sword into his face. I felt bones give under the blow, and his nose spouted blood.

The first man, my dagger sticking absurdly from his side, raised his blade to bring it down on my head. With the other man on top of me, I could not possibly dodge it. Desperate, I grabbed his friend by the clothes and pulled hard, dragging him between us like a shield. The sword buried itself into the wrong skull, as far as both opponents were concerned. Not a pleasant sound, that, but better hearing it happen to another than to me.

My shield's body collapsed onto mine; I was still struggling for breath. He lent a whole new meaning to the term "dead weight." Pushing and grunting, I surged up and heaved him off, shoving him hopefully in the direction of the other man. Alas, he wasn't where I'd thought, and the ploy was a wasted effort.

Something hit my side. Damn, but it was almost in the same spot where the Ba'al Verzi had gotten me. More lost breath, but I swung around, keeping my blade up to protect my head. Good thing, too, for his return swipe would have otherwise taken it right off. I blocked it and cut forward and down, finally winging one of his shoulders.

He'd had enough and turned to run.

Honor has no place in this type of fight. One might as well question whether it is more honorable to kill a roach while it's holding still or wait until it's moving. But the fact is, a roach is a roach, and the object is simply to kill it. Five running steps and I'd caught up with this two-legged specimen. On the sixth step he was at my feet, firmly skewered in the back and shuddering out the last of his life. I didn't waste time watching him, but pulled out the blade, retrieved my dagger from his side, and turned to help the others.

Alek was nowhere in sight. Sergei had killed one man and was busy circling with another. Falov was on her knees, face white, and clutching her arm. Her attacker was on his back with a knife in his throat and not doing much of anything.

"Damn," said Falov, and fumbled for a horn dangling from her belt. She just managed to sound it, giving the signal for the rest of the men to come ahead. Better late than never.

"Where's Commander Gwilym?"

Falov pointed ahead down the road. She winced, and I

understood that she'd been wounded as well, but not badly. Sergei was still holding his own; actually, he looked like he was toying with the man. I left him to it and rushed away to find Alek.

I found another body instead. The road made a sharp turn, the outer shoulder marked by whitewashed rocks. This was necessary since the land dropped away beyond them. The man was dead from a sword cut—there are few other weapons that make just that sort of wound—but neither the blade that killed him nor Alek was anywhere to be found. There was no blood on the bandit's sword, hopefully meaning my steward was yet unharmed.

The tracks, such as they were, were too confusing to read well. Dust and grass were churned up, right to the base of the rocks. No other tracks led away up the road, Alek must have . . .

I looked over the edge and found him, lying spread-eagle on his back on a rocky shelf that slanted just like a roof. He'd slid part way to its edge and was within a heartbeat of sliding farther. It wouldn't have taken much: just beyond his feet the angle turned to a true vertical, dropping hard away. I couldn't see the bottom.

"I've got you," I said and fell to my belly, my arms hanging down toward him. "No, don't look up, I'll come to you."

His slight movement caused him to slip away by a handsbreadth. "*Don't,*" he said between clenched teeth.

I didn't bother arguing, just inched toward him. My feet were hooked over the rocks above. Pebbles tumbled ahead of me, lodging in Alek's hair.

"Don't, Strahd," he whispered. "I'll drag you down, too."

My fingers closed on his wrist. Now for the other one.

The ground under him shifted. He slipped down a little more. I tightened my grip. "Don't move, damn you."

He didn't, but the earth was not as obedient to my will. A piece of it dropped away below his boot heels. Some seconds later we heard a distant crash as it struck whatever lay below. He muttered something, a prayer, perhaps, and went still as a corpse. Useless. He slid a bit more and I went with him. My ankles and my arm were feeling the strain of holding our combined weight, and my head felt heavy and swollen from the rush of blood between my ears.

"Let . . . me go," he breathed.

I gripped all the harder. I didn't dare yell for help. Our balance was so precarious that anything could upset it.

"Let me die alone, Strahd."

"No."

"I've no wish to kill you, my lord."

"Shut up."

Another slip. My gloves were sodden with sweat. I couldn't feel my fingers grasping anymore. I felt only the pain in my legs, spine, and neck. My shoulders . . .

The rock my feet were hooked over loosened. Just a little. It sent a reaction all down my body and on to Alek. He dropped another sickening inch. All I could hear was his strained breath and the faraway tick of pebbles that had shot out from the edge and landed far below us.

Slowly, his free hand crept over to his waist. It moved as if it were detached from him, unable to affect the rest of his body by the change of position. His fingers spread and closed upon a second knife in its sheath on his belt.

"*No,* Alek."

"Better me alone than both of us."

Sweat blurred my vision for a moment. When it cleared again, Alek had drawn the knife and was bringing it up. All he had to do was stab my hand, and I'd have to release him.

"You would draw my blood, Commander?"

"Only a drop or two if it spares the rest, my lord."

"I forbid it."

"Then I must disobey."

"Alek, do that, and I'll go over regardless. I swear it."

"You must not." But he hesitated, which was what I wanted.

The rasp of breath, my heart thudding so fast that it might burst from my chest, my muscles stretched so far as to part from the bones, the bones themselves ready to crack, but I had to hold onto him just a little longer.

"*Strahd!*" Sergei's voice. Hoarse, shocked, afraid.

"Grab my legs, boy!"

Sergei obeyed. I felt him strongly seize my ankles and set himself. At the same time I was able to tighten my hold on Alek's wrist.

"Climb up or die." I told him.

Alek chose to climb. More earth broke and crumbled beneath him when he rolled over, but he gained enough purchase with his knees to thrust himself up and catch my belt. His weight dragged at me. My face was shoved into the ground for a moment, then he was suddenly gone. I heard Sergei grunt with effort and felt myself being pulled back from the abyss. A second later and the three of us were sitting safe on the road, dazed and panting like dogs in the sun.

\*    \*    \*    \*    \*

"It's not that I planned it, my lord, but the lowborn pig flipped me like a skillet cake, and over I went. I was expecting him to poke his head over the edge to finish me off any moment, until you appeared."

"You finished him yourself," I said, pointing to one of the bodies my armsmen had laid out on the narrow verge opposite us.

Alek regarded me with a hard eye. He said a lot of things with that look, mostly reproach for putting myself at risk to save him, combined with gratitude for doing it anyway. My only reply was to quirk my brows and shrug.

I'd retained a third of the men for guard and sent the rest up the mountain to look for more of Red Lukas's bandits. They'd probably be up there the whole night searching, but the exercise would do them good.

Falov was having her wound tended; she wouldn't be using her sword arm for a few weeks, but the gash should heal cleanly. My own wasn't serious. This time the blade had not been magical, and my mail had taken most of the force of the cut. The man I'd killed had not been so fortunate in his choice of armorer. In serious combat, it always pays to have the best quality protection possible.

Sergei was busy questioning the one prisoner we had. He'd succeeded in knocking out the fellow I'd seen him fighting; the man was recovered, but predictably unco-operative.

"We can leave him for Lady Ilona," I said. "I'm sure she can get him to talk."

"I'd as soon not let him within ten feet of her, Strahd, not unless he's chained head to foot."

"Be assured, that's exactly how he will be presented."

The man snarled something obscene about Lady Ilona, drawing a black frown from my brother. Sergei stepped forward as if to strike him, but checked himself, forcibly relaxing the fist he'd made.

"Why not go ahead?" I asked him. I wanted to do it myself, but was too tired to move just yet.

"He's hardly more than an animal," he said. "He can't be expected to understand such things, and beating him will hardly put him in a mood to learn."

"Kir's done a good job of teaching you, then. And it's just the sort of thing Lady Ilona would have said herself, had she been here."

Sergei turned, giving me a grateful look. "Thank you, Brother." He had truly wanted to pulp the man and felt bad at having so natural an urge. The particular dilemma of when and if one should use force always seemed to plague the soldier-priests, making me glad I'd been lim-ited to fighting. To struggle with such moral puzzles had no appeal for me whatsoever.

"There's no need to take him in for questioning, my Lord Strahd," said Falov, walking over to us, her arm in a sling.

"Why is that? You know who he is?"

"I think so. Take off that hood he's got tied on so tight,

and we'll all know for sure."

Sergei signed to one of the men, who pulled off the prisoner's head-covering. It was matted down with dirt and sweat, but the hair beneath was fiery as an autumn sunset.

"Red Lukas himself," said Alek. "And you captured him alive." He looked at Sergei with new respect.

Sergei seemed more startled than triumphant. The word quickly spread among the rest of the men, and Sergei became the focus of some backslapping congratulations for several moments. Though it was not seemly for a noble of his rank to be so treated, I said nothing. Sometimes it's better for morale to allow a certain limited familiarity. This was one of those times.

"What's to be done with him?" asked Falov.

"Immediate execution," I said.

That startled Sergei. "But I thought he was to be questioned first."

"All we were going to ask him was the location of Red Lukas. Since we have the answer, I'll waste no more time on him."

"But the customs, the laws—"

"I am the law here," I reminded him. "If you have any other objections to make, I suggest you carry them to the surviving victims of that village he wiped out."

Sergei glanced back at Lukas, who spat in our direction. It fell short.

"Alek, if you've recovered yourself, please see to things. Falov, can you entrust some of your people to carry the news around? We'll put the proof in something to preserve it for them, and they can be off tomorrow."

# P. N. Elrod

"My lord, I would be most happy to go with them myself. I don't need two arms to sit a mountain pony."

"Excellent. Be sure to take it through Vallaki and that village I mentioned so the people may see."

"See what?" Sergei asked.

"Red Lukas," said Alek. "Or at least his head pickled in vinegar."

"You're planning to parade him all around the country like . . . ? That's barbaric."

I sighed. Sergei was proving to be something of a novice to the art of enforcing domestic order. "It's necessary, Brother. Not only do potential murderers and thieves see the penalty for their crimes, but the common folk are made aware that there is one less criminal for them to fear. I think they will rest the easier for having undisputed proof that Red Lukas is dead, and parading his head through the streets is the best means I know to accomplish that."

Sergei, as I'd expected, had nothing more to say on the subject, although it was clear he was not exactly pleased with the demands of the situation. His sort of compassion was well placed for a priest, but a ruler cannot afford to be so indulgent.

*It's just as well,* I thought, *that he's destined to be ordained.*

# Chapter Three

## Sixth Moon, 350

"Sergei, I do sympathize with the need to express your personal grief, but to expect all of Barovia to do the same is unrealistic. The whole thing will be a waste of time better spent working."

Sergei planted his hands on my table and thrust his head forward. "You've told me more than once about maintaining appropriate behavior before the common folk. For you to

## P. N. Elrod

let Kir's passing go unmarked implies a lack of respect for the church and all it stands for. A public show of sorrow and acceptance of the will of the gods in taking the Most High Priest will reaffirm their faith and bolster their confidence in your rule."

I directed a long-suffering look at Lady Ilona Darovnya. She met it with a restrained smile and shook her head, meaning she was going to remain strictly neutral on this issue. She saw it as a conflict between two brothers rather than between church and state, otherwise she'd have openly taken Sergei's side.

Sergei noted the interplay and waited, watching me closely. Gods, but he was young and earnest. I might have been tempted to lose patience with him but for the knowledge that he was completely sincere in his views. His argument with me was not for personal gains—else I'd have had an excellent reason to arbitrarily overrule him—but for what he perceived to be answering a need others might have. I'd never seen anything good come from attempting to fulfill such needs, but on the other hand, he did have a reasonable political point to make. It rankled me that he knew the best road to persuading me lay in that direction.

I gave in with undisguised ill-grace; just because I'd been persuaded did not mean I had to enjoy the decision. "Very well. Make your gesture. I'll declare the first day of next week to be one of nationwide mourning for him. Like as not the peasants will use the time away from their fields to clean out their stocks of *tuika* and spend the following day struggling to recover from the debauch."

86

"Oh, *Strahd*—" he began, drawing my name out in his own expression of long-suffering.

I waved him down. "I know them better than you do. You'll have your gesture, but I doubt if one in fifty of them will observe it in the way you intend. A rich man thinks all other people are rich, and an intelligent man thinks all other people are similarly gifted. Both are always terribly shocked when they discover the truth of the world. You, my dear brother, are a pious man."

He eased back and finally laughed a little. At himself. "Yes, I see what you mean, though I *am* aware that not everyone is pious. But I tell you, this day will mean much to those who are, and perhaps, a day away from toil may allow those who aren't to become so. It may even do you some good, Strahd."

Had anyone else said that to me, I might have had him beaten, but Sergei was only at his usual gentle chiding. I let it pass. "Go on and arrange things, then. Tell my clerk to draw up something appropriate, and I'll sign it later."

Gratitude warmed up his pale face. For many, the news of Kir's untimely death had been sad and shocking, but Sergei had been stricken especially hard by it. He'd been very close to the young priest, both from the requirements of his training and the genuine friendship between them. "Thank you, Brother," he said, favoring me with a wan version of his smile before leaving.

"I just hope he doesn't expect me to wear an armband as do the peasants," I murmured to Ilona.

"I think plain black clothes will suffice," she responded. "You're more or less dressed for it now."

"I *like* to wear black."

# P. N. Elrod

"It does favor you, my lord." Lady Ilona also wore black in the form of a near-transparent veil that completely covered the sky blue of her robes. It was not a flattering color on her, and she had just enough personal vanity to be mildly annoyed by it. "Do you really think a day of mourning for Kir is that much a waste of time?"

"I suppose not, but I don't want the people believing they can just drop their tools and make merry whenever it pleases them, or we'll have no end of holidays to put up with."

"I hardly think they'll make merry on this occasion, my lord."

"You should talk to Alek, then. There's a custom in one country he's been where the relatives of the dead sit the body up in a corner and have a party with dancing, song, and drink until the wine puts them in nearly the same condition as the dear departed."

"That certainly sounds more appealing than some rites I've heard of. I may look into it for myself. Better to celebrate a soul's passage to a better place than to wallow in sorrow over their leaving. We'll all be there soon enough ourselves."

I looked away briefly and pinched the bridge of my nose. "Lady Ilona, forgive me, but I do have other duties that require my attention."

Her clear eyes clouded a moment, for she could see that my work table was quite bare, but she took the hint and rose. "As do I, my lord."

I rose too, we made our bows, and off she went. Her walk was a bit stiffer than normal due to indignation, but I didn't care: the woman knew very well how much I detested being reminded of my mortality. Kir's death had also been a singularly unwelcome reminder, made doubly unpleasant since he'd been so much younger than I. Apparently I was entering the stage of life where the people of one's youth start dropping away one by one. What was next? Watching my hands for the bulge of veins and the onset of age spots? Soon my contemporaries, like Alek or Gunther Cosco, would be huddling in shawls about the fire and shaking their heads over whoever had died that week.

By contrast, even Sergei's bright presence was a mixed blessing. I could not help loving my brother for his youth and spirit, and respecting him as a proven fighter, but those very qualities made me aware of the span of years between us. Sometimes it was most difficult for me to bear his company, knowing that all his life lay ahead of him, while most of mine was forever lost.

True, I had many accomplishments in conquest and war. I had turned Castle Ravenloft into the jewel of my vision. But what was this compared to the swift and unstoppable passage of time? Once I'd been as Sergei, unconsciously convinced that I'd live forever. Like the proverbial rich man and intelligent man, I, the young man, had encountered the hard truth of the world as it now concerned me. In these three years of peace, that truth had grown upon my soul like some parasitic plant run wild. With every passing day I felt its roots dig themselves in more deeply.

Alek Gwilym seemed to understand me best, but was wise enough not to speak of it directly.

"Get yourself a woman, Strahd," he'd once said, picking up on my sour mood.

"Your solution, not mine," I replied dryly.

"Not a solution so much as a distraction. Find some pretty flower and have a few brats with her. There are plenty of prospects to choose from right here in your own court."

"Aye, and with any number of relatives attached to complicate the balance of power."

"Then talk to Lady Ilona. I'm sure she can put you on to some orphans of rank that have been placed under her protection. You're a hero—I guarantee you'll find every one of them willing and grateful for the honor of carrying on the Von Zarovich name."

"My brother Sturm has already seen to that detail."

"But Sturm's more clerk than ruler. You've often said as much. He does fine playing administrator to your father's estates, but do you see him handling an entire country? Would any of his children have the necessary knowledge or experience to ably govern after him? Hardly, not with him as their only model. I suppose he could send his eldest to live here and learn from you . . ."

*But then I'd have the same feeling toward that child as I have toward Sergei.*

"It's different when they're your own," Alek said, uncannily reading my thoughts. I wondered, and not for the first time, whether he was truly gifted with the Sight or merely good at deducing what was on my mind.

"Different?"

"Because it is your flesh and your blood being carried on, not your father and mother's in some other vessel, but *yours*. That's the difference, Strahd. Find some pretty flower, and if the gods are smiling, within nine moons you'll be holding your own immortality in those two hands. Much better than a sword, and far more magical than anything you'll find in all those books you've collected."

I looked hard upon the books now. Despite the rough-and-ready world of camp life, I'd managed to assemble and preserve quite a number of them. Not as many as I would like; there was room on the empty shelves of my library to hold five times as many volumes as I presently possessed. Their implied knowledge and wisdom seemed empty to me, though. My mood would pass, I knew, and I'd again fill my hours with reading and magical experiment, but with the memory of Alek's words haunting me it seemed uncomfortably certain that he was, after all, right.

\* \* \* \* \*

The day of national mourning was marked in court by continuous services in the chapel. I put in my allotted time in prayer for the soul's rest of Most High Priest Kir, then spent the rest of the day in my library. No food was cooked; all the land supped cold on whatever they'd prepared the day before. I, for one, was not deprived by its absence. The cheese, bread, strawberries, and wine that sustained me were little different in temperatures from the more elaborate meals I'd had since moving into Castle Ravenloft. (The master cook and engineer still hadn't solved things.)

Sergei, though not yet ordained, was given the Priest's

Pendant to wear as a symbol of the approaching ceremony. He was much moved at the sight of it, since it brought solidly home to him that *he* was soon to take Kir's place.

"I'm not sure I'm worthy of this office," he confided to me later.

"Who of us is?" I responded, which he seemed to think a very wise answer. So affected was he that he wrapped his arms about me in a brief embrace and whispered thanks before rushing away to his room to privately mourn.

Lady Ilona presided over the chapel services. It was very solemn and beautiful in its way. When I'd been there, I saw Sergei watching her every move from his seat in the balcony overlooking the chapel. Very soon, he would have to serve at future functions, and he studied her closely, his brow furrowed with concentration. One could not fault him for such honest concern, and though he was inexperienced, he promised to make a good priest—perhaps because he naturally possessed all the humility that old Zarak's holystoning chores had failed to inspire in me.

The day of mourning came and went, but the church continued on quietly with its own ancient rituals and devotions. Until the proper period of time had passed, no ordinations could be performed, so Sergei was in a kind of limbo, unable to bury himself in any official duties to get his mind off things. With that outlet blocked, being a Von Zarovich, he made another for himself and began daily trips down to the Village of Barovia, frequently spending the night.

As a soldier, my initial idea of what he was doing there had conflicted with the sort of behavior one might expect from a future priest. It struck me as being entirely normal, though, and not worth my concern . . . until Alek reported that my brother was working among the poor people. The news about Red Lukas had been inevitably garbled, and now the popular story was that, single-handed, Sergei had captured and beheaded him and his whole troop. No word of truth on the subject from Sergei's lips could change their minds, and he was frequently subjected to a cheering welcome and a shower of flower petals. Recently, he'd taken it upon himself to see to the beautification of the church and was attempting to set up some sort of hospice for the sick.

The news was hardly pleasing to me.

"He's only practicing for his vocation, my lord."

"That's fine for a priest, but not for Sergei. When he's put on his robes, he can do whatever he pleases, but not until then."

"What harm is there in it now?"

"Before you know it, every beggar and layabout in the land will find his way to the village with his hands out and hopes high. The lad has a good heart, but he doesn't know enough yet to see when someone's taking advantage of him. Worse, the people may think he's acting in the Von Zarovich name. I can't have that."

"Why not? How could his generosity pose a threat to your name?"

I leaned back in my chair and sighed. "Suppose for a moment you were one of my boyars, and you'd just spent the last month collecting taxes from your district

and sent them in. You then hear Lord Sergei Von Zarovich is making life easier for the poor of Barovia. How
good-hearted of him, you think, until you begin to wonder where the money is coming from. Just when you
trust your taxes are to pay for road upkeep and military
protection, you hear that Von Zarovich's brother is toss-
ing it into the gutter by the bushel load. Might he not be
taking his funds directly from *your* contribution? Would
you not resent that and perhaps think your own people
deserved some similar gratis for simply being poor? You
might even consider that since Lord Strahd's brother has
so much money to give away, you might not need to
send in as much tax next year, if at all . . ."

"Yes, I see where you're going with that idea: Sergei
helps out one minor village and the whole power structure of the country collapses."

"This is nothing to be mocked, Alek, I am serious.
Should the boyars ever decide to revolt, how long do you
think *we* would last?"

"You have reason to believe they would?"

I didn't answer him right away, giving him plenty of
time to work it out for himself. He had a fine mind; it did
not take long.

"Who do you suspect?"

"All of them."

That took him aback. "I know blood oaths of loyalty
may be broken, but *all* of the boyars?"

"Or a single strong one to sway the others. He or she
can make certain promises, drop a casual word over the
wine. 'These are uncertain times, you know. The gods
*forbid* such calamity, but should *anything* happen to

Lord Strahd, I *hope* I can count on *your* support.' You know what it's like."

Alek frowned, his lips a thin line, and his eyes narrow and harder than usual. "So . . . there is still a traitor in the camp."

"Essentially. I want you to sniff him out."

"Execution, too, should I find him?"

"It depends on the circumstances. If he's smart, then a word of warning may be all that's needed. If not . . ." I opened and lifted my hand. "But tell me first."

"Of course, my lord."

\* \* \* \* \*

On the morning following Alek's departure, I was of a mind to summon Sergei for a good talking to; he'd been away all yesterday and had only just returned. I thought it best to get it over with before he took it into his head to run off again.

He came into my study looking unsuitably cheerful for a man in mourning for a dead friend. He wore a peculiar, stuffed expression on his face that he'd never sported before and seemed ready to burst from whatever was bottled up within him.

"Sergei, about these trips you've been making to the village . . ."

That was all the opening he needed. It didn't matter to him that I was still speaking; the sound of my voice alone was enough to set him off. That's when the whole dismal story came bubbling out of him.

He'd met a girl.

# P. N. Elrod

Fuming with impatience, I was barely able to tolerate listening to his drivel about her endless virtues, beauty, and all the many traits men in love attribute to their women when the fever is on them. I'd heard it before from others; Sergei's variation on the theme was hardly original, and certainly less welcome. Gods, one would have thought she was the first female he'd ever encountered, from the way he spoke of her.

My reaction was, to put it kindly and say the least, cool. In addition to the ludicrousness of a Von Zarovich coupling himself with a peasant, I was compelled to point out that he was destined to enter the service of the church as the next Most High Priest. But the moral implications, the political repercussions, the sheer idiocy of this new direction he'd taken meant absolutely nothing to him. No word from me would change his mind or move his heart. He was well and truly besotted—blind and deaf to everything but her—and to the devil with his responsibilities and the rest of the world.

We did not part on amicable terms.

The truth be told, I was furious. Never before in my life had I been more angry with anyone and less able to do anything about it. And, while I was yet in this volcanic frame of mind, my clerk announced that Lady Ilona was without and requesting an audience.

"Are you come to take his side or mine?" I demanded of her as she glided through the door. "Is it to be church and state today, or is this merely another family matter to you?"

"My Lord Strahd needs to better control himself," she murmured.

Her quiet voice had the same effect on me as a sharp rap between the eyes. I'd been pacing up and down my study, positively shaking with frustration over this new crisis, then abruptly stopped. After a few moments, I was able to speak again in a more civilized manner.

"The boy doesn't know what he's doing," I finally growled.

"They never do when they're that much in love."

Suspicion sparked in me. "How long have you known about this?"

"Sergei only now spoke to me. He was concerned about your unhappiness over his plans."

More likely that he asked her to rush over and calm me down. "And you've accepted it—just like that?"

She shrugged. "What am I supposed to do? Forbid him to love?"

"But he's throwing away his priesthood, everything he's worked for—"

"There are other ways to serve the gods, my lord."

My soldier's instinct wearily informed me I was fighting a losing battle. Until this moment, surrender had been an alien concept; the loss and emptiness I now felt were utterly disgusting and instantly exhausting. I found my chair and dropped into it, feeling tired beyond my years. "What's to be done?"

Ilona came around to face me. "Nothing at all. These things always find a way of working themselves out for the best. Trust that that will happen and don't worry about it."

"You sound like my mother."

She smiled; as a girl she had known Ravenia. "I shall

take that as a great compliment, my lord."

"This is completely ridiculous, you know that."

"I suppose it is, but there's never anything sensible in a young man's love. It exists, and one can do nothing else but stand aside. Anyway, you know in your heart Sergei is incapable of besmirching the honor of the Von Zarovich name. I'm sure the girl will prove to be perfectly lovely and suitable."

"Oh, I'm sure she will be, too. Doubtless the fortune attached to Sergei's name will inspire her to a great deal of goodness."

"You speak as if goodness does not really exist, Lord Strahd."

"I've had little enough experience with it."

"Then you'll have something pleasant to look forward to."

\* \* \* \* \*

Less than a week later, Sergei brought her up by carriage from the village for the first and last time. She had no family, having been one of the orphans protected and raised by the local church, and would now be chaperoned by Lady Ilona herself until the wedding day. It was my faint hope Ilona would be able to teach the girl enough about court etiquette so as to avoid any wretched embarrassment at public functions.

I directed to all the staff and retainers that her arrival was to be an informal event; she would be properly introduced to everyone at the dinner Sergei was giving in her honor that night. Those who could read the true meaning in this would see the wisdom behind it. If she turned out to be a total disaster, there was still time to declare her indisposed for the evening and postpone things. Sergei, the gods preserve his innocent heart, hadn't the faintest inkling about the business. He alighted from the carriage and helped her out as though she were an empress, and not a lowborn orphan jumped up from the gutter by some quirk of the gods.

I was just considering that her lack of a family was probably fortunate, in that they wouldn't be mucking about the court and being awkwardly in the way, when Sergei escorted her up the steps to present her.

Then all my disparaging thoughts fell away like dead leaves. She was, without doubt, the most beautiful girl I'd ever seen.

As she approached, I came to see that she was as beyond beauty as a river in spring flood is beyond a drop of water. I felt myself drawn into the flow, swept under by the current. Overwhelmed. I could almost hear the roar and rush of it instead of my brother's voice when he spoke.

"Strahd, this is Tatyana."

The girl made a low curtsy. She wore the simple, homespun costume of Barovia, but she wore it like royalty, and her copper-colored hair like a crown. She made me suddenly believe in the folktale of the kidnapped princess raised by peasants and eventually returned to her rightful place in the castle.

"Welcome," I whispered, barely able to make my response.

She raised her face to me. The clear skin, the great

eyes—brighter than gems—and full dark lips had come together in such a way as to make all other women seem ugly by comparison.

There was *no* comparison. She was unique. She was perfect.

I felt my heart swoop and soar at the sheer joy of looking at her. This raised a blush on her cheek, and I instantly knew I must put her at ease. I took one of her hands, and she straightened—how like a tall flower she was—and with a bow, lightly kissed her fingertips.

"Welcome to Castle Ravenloft, Tatyana. Be welcome and look upon this as your true home, forevermore."

My words seemed to go right to her heart, and her returning smile was like that first glimpse of sun after a bitter winter. All I wanted to do for the rest of my life was keep that smile on her ever after.

And then she looked at Sergei.

It was as if the sun that had favored me had been all along hidden by a cloud. Its brilliant glory now shone in full upon him . . . and him alone.

\* \* \* \* \*

Unused as I was to informing anyone about my activities, custom demanded I tell Sergei of my plan to take Tatyana for a short walk before supper. He was for it, of course, his eyes alight with the knowledge that my purpose was but to get to know her better and thus approve of her. My approval was of no importance. One might as well "approve" of the air one breathed or the true azure of a summer sky. The need for one and beauty of the other were there with or without any pompous human judgments; such was Tatyana. She was sky and earth, air and music, sunlight without shadow.

And, though the most unaffected girl I'd ever met, she also held a deep awe for me that needed be—must be—dispelled.

After ascertaining that she was ready, I called at her room, and with one of Lady Ilona's acolytes walking in escort well behind us, took her down to the main floor and outside to the south courtyard. She rested one hand on my arm the whole time, but hardly murmured a word beyond her initial greeting. Perhaps she was bracing herself for some horrible question-and-answer session from me.

Once outside I did make inquiries about the comfort of her quarters and the suitability of the clothes she'd found there. She'd changed for the evening, wearing a copper-colored gown of flattering lines, which Lady Ilona had been at some pains to acquire for her.

"Everything is wonderful, Old One," said Tatyana. "Everyone has been more than kind."

This form of address was perfectly acceptable and proper for her to use with me, considering our social stations and, unhappily, the difference in our ages. In Barovia, it was a sign of great respect; she did not know to call me Strahd. I decided not to correct her, though, concerned that it might add to her shyness with me. Above all, I wanted to put her at ease.

I paused and faced her. "I am very glad to hear it. And you must know that if there's anything else you need or want, you have but to ask. This castle and all who dwell here are your most humble servants, myself included."

Instead of reassuring her, this comment seemed to make her somewhat more disconcerted.

"Is something wrong?"

"Nothing at all. Only that I think you are the kindest one of all to speak to me so. Before our meeting, I was a little afraid of you, you know."

"Afraid?"

She opened her palms, spreading them out toward the whole of the keep. "All my life, this place has loomed over the village. When Dorian was here, we all lived with the dread of him as the elders live with the pain of their bones. When your armies came, we were in fear of what might happen to us, even as we rejoiced in our freedom. But the years of your rule have been peaceful. You've taken away our fears, and we are grateful."

That was not the sentiment *I* had heard from the village, but then what my soldiers might gather in the tavern and what a young girl might hear in the protective walls of a church are bound to be quite disparate reports.

"And what of your fears?" I asked.

"Gone as well. I've seen some of the beauty you've made here, which means that I've seen some of your soul as well, and this is a good place. You may be a fierce warrior, but there is much warmth in you, or you could not have made such things."

I laughed a little. It was good to do so. I had years of laughter stored up inside me, it seemed, and without the least effort this lovely girl was bringing it forth. "I think your tribute would be better directed to the artisans than to me."

She smiled at me. Oh, gods, how she smiled. "Now I also see why Sergei loves you so."

My good humor faded with the mention of my brother. To cover it, I resumed our walk. "Come, I wish to show you something that I had no influence on in regard to beauty."

We strolled under the center portcullis gate, and I guided us toward the chapel garden. The wind had died down with the waning of the day, and the scent of roses filled the air. She loved them, breaking away from me to dart from one to the other and breathe in the sweetness of each. With my dagger, I cut off an especially large bloom, careful to strip away the thorns before giving it to her. This brought forth another smile, making me wish the garden were a hundred times larger so I might offer her a thousand such roses.

"There's more to see," I said, taking her hand. We passed through the gate to the overlook and approached its low wall. "This is not my creation, but at the very least one may come here and appreciate it."

Hesitant from the height, Tatyana nonetheless came to the edge. The sun was behind us on its last crashing fall toward the western peaks of the Balinoks. Its golden light streamed over the valley. As we watched, the shadow of Castle Ravenloft began to visibly creep away from us to cover the land far below like a dark blanket. In its soft folds, tiny lights appeared one by one in the village as candles were lighted and cooking fires built up.

"There's the church, my home," she said, pointing. I didn't bother to look. To see the wonder and happiness upon her face was what I craved. Nothing else was important.

## P. N. Elrod

"*This* is your home," I said.

Her eyes turned to meet mine. "Thank you, Elder."

I let it pass. "No more fears?"

"None. I feel complete, somehow, in being here. Before, I was happy enough, but it was as if only part of me existed, and I never really knew there was anything else. Only after meeting Sergei did I truly realize how much more there is to the world."

I managed to keep my smile in place.

"I feel alive and real for the first time. I believe now that all the life I'd led before was but a time of waiting until Sergei came into it."

The last of the light had faded, and the castle and valley lay both in darkness.

I could hardly speak. My voice was a dry whisper, like a desert wind. "You love him, then?"

"More than the gods, more than myself, more than anything I've known, imagined, or could ever imagine. I hope you don't think it's wrong of me to love him so much."

"No, not at all."

She had just put into words that which I felt for her, myself. I turned away so she could not see my face in the emerging starlight. Along with the sharp joy of love, I was being cut in two by the razor edge of utter hopelessness, and I was unable to keep it from showing.

It was worse than any sword thrust, colder and more cruel than a blast of winter sleet upon naked skin. I could have cried aloud from the pain she so innocently gave me.

To have such raw elements tearing through my brain

and body was too much. I would have to tell her or die on the spot from the torment. I faced her and kissed her hand once more, my heart booming like a battle drum.

*What to say? How to say it?*

My throat was clogged solid with so many words that none of them could escape. In this darkness, I was a tongue-tied youth of twenty again and not the tempered warrior. I looked to her and held her eyes, and it came to me that she *knew* without having to be told, and just as swiftly, I knew she did not. Reason fighting with emotion and neither winning, such was my state of mind for this, the longest moment of my life.

The madness passed as the sheer impossibility of it overcame me. Everything in me had wanted to blurt out how I felt, everything but the small voice of doubt we all possess that causes cowards to flee and wise men to wait. I knew myself to be anything but a coward, and so it must have been some innate wisdom that insisted on silence. For me to speak now would only confuse and frighten her, and spoil any chance of making her forget Sergei and turn to me.

Sergei . . .

*No.*

And I blotted that malignant thought out before it could complete itself. To even have allowed it to lightly brush against the most distant reaches of my mind was beyond dishonor, something so shattering it was beyond evil itself.

"Elder?"

Her sweet voice brought me back from that abyss.

"Are you well?"

"Of course I am," I lied.

*Sergei* . . .

I shook myself. "Time to go in, don't you think?"

# Twelfth Moon, 350

That first night, the following day, and all the others afterward soared past more swiftly than a hawk in flight. Each revealed a new delight in Tatyana and inflicted fresh agony upon my heart. Each drove home the fact that, no matter how much I wanted her, she was not interested in me.

The idea that I was—in her eyes at least—too old to be considered a lover was first and foremost in my mind, though looking in the mirror made me doubt it. My body was as lean and tough as ever, daily sword practice made it so, and if my face was hard and had its share of weather lines, better that than the sag of loose skin. In the past, not a few lady guests of the court had given me to understand that I was anything but repellent to them and more than satisfactory in meeting the demands required by the physical art of love. But this innocent girl seemed immune or unaware of me in the way that I desired. She never called me by my name, only as "Elder" or "Old One" to show her respect for me and all the years of life I'd lived—daily proof that my doubt was only my own hopeful self-deception.

By subtle acts, I did try to play the suitor; I gifted Tatyana with jewels and fine clothes, commissioned her portrait. I even played music for her while she sat for it, and though she accepted all with deep appreciation and happiness, it was always in a way that made it clear she saw me only as Brother and not rival against Sergei. Humiliating as it was, I held fast to that small piece of cold comfort.

It was better than nothing.

As the harsh months of winter made outside activities less attractive, I spent more of my free time in the study, going through my books. Previously, my interest in the Art had been that of an experimenting dilettante; now it occurred to me that some magical spell might afford the means to draw Tatyana's attention away from Sergei and over to me. But the constant distractions of government and other duties had had their effect, so my skills were not as they should have been. Some spells were easy enough to master, others were quite incomprehensible. Those I did understand were useless in regard to my situation; nonetheless, I broke open each book in its turn and went through it page by page in hope of finding *something*.

Human desires being what they are, one would think the ritual for casting a love-spell or creating a love-philter would be more common, but my books were bereft of such things, except for a single short treatise on the subject. The writer's conclusion that love was a force that could not be successfully reproduced by magical methods struck me as being inanely smug. I tore the page out and summarily tossed it into the fire.

"Burning books for warmth, my lord?"

My dagger was out even as I pivoted to face the speaker.

# P. N. Elrod

It was Alek Gwilym, leaning against the doorway with his hands in his pockets. He looked me up and down, his eyes settling on the blade. "Good."

"Announce yourself next time," I said, with no small irritation.

"An assassin wouldn't. I just wanted to see if you could still guard your back, so please don't have your clerk whipped for keeping quiet. Anyone coming after you would have killed her as a simple precaution."

"I won't." I replaced and resheathed the dagger. He'd gotten his message across. "What is it? Another Ba'al Verzi after me?"

Alek had been gone for months on his errand. The Barovian winter had left its mark on him. His face was a touch gaunt and still red from the wind, his clothes smelled of snow, and he looked in need of a new pair of riding boots. He removed his fur hat with the ridiculous-looking but necessary ear flaps and strode over to the fireplace.

"Gods, but this feels good. We've been out in the white muck for weeks, with drifts right up to the horses' shoulders and the road so buried even the guides were getting lost. The worst part was the last mile before we made the castle. The last one's always the longest, you know." He hopped on one foot to remove a snow-sodden boot, dropped it and its mate near the fire to dry out, and drew up a chair for himself.

"Make yourself at home," I said.

"You've got true luxury here, Strahd." He stretched his long hands toward the flames. "Some of the so-called courts I've been to would murder to have something like this."

"Would they now? Who?"

"The Van Roeyens, for one."

"That's my mother's family!"

"Blood's thicker than water, but gold . . ." He rubbed his thumb against his fingers meaningfully and raised his brows.

"Which of them?" I asked wearily.

"Your Uncle Gustav."

"Really, Alek, the old boy must be over eighty by now."

"Eighty-two. But he has a houseful of poor relations, and the income from his lands is hardly up to the task. I suggest you might send him a generous Winterfest gift as a distraction."

"Ransom myself without being made captive? There's a novel way for him to obtain money without work."

"Better than having him send some of your cousins over for an extended visit. Young Vikki is almost as good with a sword as I. I'd hate to learn firsthand about her talents with a knife on some dark night."

He was right. Beyond my late mother's marriage tie, the Van Roeyens had little enough regard for me, except as a source of income by means of inheritance. Perhaps a timely "gift" would put them off and keep them at their strategic border location for a few more years. I made a note of it for my clerk to see to.

"Who else?"

Alek ran down the list he kept in his head of all the households he'd visited, ostensibly as my ambassador. The more clever hosts would have been able to correctly interpret his real mission, especially the ones with anything to hide. Ironically, the truly innocent were indistinguishable from the more careful guilty. Those who were obviously guilty were less a threat since I knew for certain where they stood.

"So the Markous clan can be trusted to stand with me as long as the Darovnyas remain loyal," I said an hour or more later. I'd ordered food brought up for us both. Alek chose tea over mulled wine, and this time it was hot. (The cook and engineer had come up with the brilliant idea of heating water right in my study by making use of the fireplace. Perhaps in another three years they'd successfully solve the soup problem.)

"And the Darovnyas will remain loyal as long as Lady Ilona supports your rule," Alek added, spearing an apple with his dagger.

"She supports her faith over her family—and even over me."

"Ah, but she is a flexible and practical politician as well. She knows you're the strongest, so here she stays—close to the core of power."

"But the others? You picked up no clue on the Dilisnyas?"

He shook his head and cut a slice from the apple. "Reinhold's belly still enslaves him. If he'd loosen his purse strings enough to properly endow his local temple, I'm sure the chaplains there would not be ungrateful; then the rest of us wouldn't have to listen to his groans after supper. He had the worst food, too: gruels and milks, fruit boiled to such a pulp you couldn't recognize what it had once been. Out of pure self-defense against starvation I'd sneak off with young Leo and raid the pantry at midnight like some thieving scullery drudge." He popped the slice in his mouth and crunched with

obvious pleasure, and before it was quite gone, he followed it up with a fat square of yellow cheese.

"What does that have to do with anything?" I had little
patience for idle stories today.

"The pantry was close to the wine cellar, and Leo had
his own key. Reinhold doesn't drink, so his stocks were
in sad need of paring down. The two of us did our best."

"And did Leo confess anything interesting once you
got him drunk?"

Alek smiled; then it turned into one of his rare laughs,
signifying he was very pleased with himself. "I wish you
could have been there. The young dog was doing his
best to get *me* drunk, so that *I* might talk. He didn't know
it, but I caught him downing a few swigs of olive oil just
before that first raid on the cellar. He put on a very good
act; if I hadn't seen his preparation, I might have believed
his every mumbled word that night."

"Did you learn anything useful?"

"That he's very smart and highly interested in the
affairs of Barovia. He had many questions about your
political plans and how the Dilisnyas will figure in them."

"Nothing unusual in that, or particularly secret."

"No, but—now I don't have proof of this, it's only a
feeling—but I don't think he shared any of this with Reinhold."

"Indeed? One wonders what he's up to, then. Is it for
himself or someone else that he is so curious? He struck
me as being rather feckless and easily led."

"Which leaves the Wachters and the Buchvolds as
possible influences. He was very close to Illya, don't
forget."

113

"And cut his throat without hesitation, don't forget."

"In your defense," he pointed out.

At the time, I'd had a fleeting hope that the need to watch my back so closely had passed with Illya's death. Alas, no. Never, for a man in my position.

Alek's information on the Wachter and Buchvold families was just as inconclusive. Well, I'd have a chance to judge things for myself, soon enough.

"My brother is getting married this summer," I said.

"I'd heard some news of it on my way up."

"It's to be a large wedding. Invitations are being prepared."

"I think I see where this is going, and I can't say I like it."

"You don't have to. Just be there when the guests arrive and have your eyes and ears open for anything . . . interesting. Have you enough people to cover them all?"

"I should, unless any have died from winter fever while I've been away. Haven't had a chance to check on things."

"Then go do so while you can."

"May I take this to mean I have additional goodwill visits ahead of me?"

"Yes, you may."

He sighed and shook his head, but voiced no real objection. I knew that, discomforts aside, he preferred being out and doing something over being tied fast to his castle duties.

"Give yourself a week to thaw out, fatten up, and look your people over, though."

"Thank you, my lord. I may even find time for a bath."

Having raised a brief smile from me, he nodded at the clutter on my table. "Another magical project?"

"Something like that."

"I turned up five new volumes for your book collection. Cost more than a few coppers, I can tell you. There's not such change left in that purse you gave me."

My eyes snapped up. "If they have true spells of the Art in them it doesn't matter." Alek had standing orders to buy any books concerned with magic for me, and he carried a generous supply of gold to pay for them.

"I'm sure they do. I couldn't read a single word of them. Made my head ache just to look at the pages."

My heart began to beat faster, but I did not let it show. "Sounds most promising. Where did you get them?"

"From the private library of some minor noble. He was selling off his grandfather's estate to pay for his wine. Seems his life's ambition has been to drink himself to death. With what he charged me for that lot, he should be well on his way by now. Let's hope you get a more constructive use from them than he."

"Indeed, yes," I murmured.

# Part II

# Chapter Four

## Sixth Moon, 351

"Lady Ilona, how can you be so blind? Sergei I can understand; he's been tottering around in a lovesick haze for the last year. But you should be able to see the folly of it."

"Whether it was a mistake on Tatyana's part or not, time will tell, but your reaction has made her and Sergei very upset. And on the day before their wedding, too."

I'd lost all desire to continue on the subject. "If they're so upset, then go and comfort them. In fact, I think you would best serve the court if you confined your concerns to the upcoming ceremony rather than this matter. There must be much for you to do yet."

"It is being seen to, my lord," she said coolly.

*That* voice again. I was hearing it more and more often, and each time it grated harder on the ear than the time before. I hated the sound of it, and the gods help me, I was beginning to hate its source, but Ilona returned my look, stare for stare, without wavering. There were damned few people who could still do that these days.

"Do you really expect me to stand to the side and condone foolish behavior in my own house?" I finally demanded.

"The girl was only being generous—"

"She had *no* right to throw away her jewels on some pig of a peasant! By the gods, those were the ones *I* gave to her!"

"Meaning they were hers to give in turn."

"Meaning I entrusted them to her care as part of the family heritage. They belonged to my mother and hers before her and so on. Tatyana might have been unaware of their true value, but not Sergei. Yet instead of stopping her, he publicly *approved* of it. The whelp has *no* idea the door he's left open."

"I'm sure arrangements can be made to get them back—"

"Of course they can, but that's not the point. She shouldn't have debased herself so, particularly before the rabble. Now she won't be able to put a foot outside the gates without some muck-covered beggar crawling all over her. Everything will be recovered, rest assured, but I'll see to it that the filth that laid hands on her is flayed alive for his insult."

"It was but a remembrance of childhood play—"

"If grabbing her and beating her head against the floor in some sty of a tavern is play, then she's well rid of the motherless animal."

"But until she comes to that realization, how do you think she'll feel when she finds out what's happened to her old friend? Do you think it will please her to hear of it? Will she respect you for causing injury where she sought to bring healing?"

My hands had balled into fists, and I was hard-pressed not to use them. Gods, but I wanted to smash something, anything or anyone, just then. Instead, I backed away and forced them open. "Very well," I said in a much quieter tone. "I'll have someone *buy* back her jewels and cause no harm to the—the . . . man."

Her lips parted for another comment, then snapped shut. She knew when she was ahead.

When she'd gone, I threw myself into the chair before my overloaded study table and spent a very long time glaring at nothing. Anger such as I'd never known before burned through me from the bones outward. I felt that if I held on long enough to the chair arms, they would kindle into flame from the heat.

Much as I loved Tatyana, today she'd exasperated me beyond all patience by giving her jewels away to some begging brute out of her past. He'd been just cunning enough to compare her good fortune in life to his own lot and then played upon the guilt he'd created in her. She'd turned everything over to him without a second's thought. It was the most idiotic and irresponsible act I'd ever heard of, but Lady Ilona was right. Any reprisal from me against the peasant would serve no constructive purpose. The damage was done.

But I was still angry.

I could talk to the girl, but instinctively shied away from that ploy. Earlier, she'd been so enmeshed in her good mood for helping her old "friend" she'd been unable to really hear me. There was no reason to expect that she'd be any more receptive now. She was yet too inexperienced in the realities of the world to understand why I was so furious over what she'd done.

Tatyana needed someone to . . . guide her. Sergei was hardly the one to do it, though. For all my talks with him, he seemed unable to grasp that generosity was a dangerous liability. Had he entered the priesthood as he should have done, his pet charities would have been properly regulated by time-honored and proven checks and balances. As it was, the income from his own lands was constantly being drained away, and I could see the time arriving when he'd be living off charity himself.

*My* charity.

Of course, I'd support him. It would not do for my enemies to see a Von Zarovich in rags and somehow contrive to use him as a weapon against me. But, while I trusted Sergei to be too loyal and smart to be turned to obvious betrayal, I knew there were other, more subtle ways to create a traitor. He was still a pious man and a stranger to deception. As went the axiom, so went Sergei; he was a sheep vulnerable to any wolf who could put on a kindly face.

And Tatyana . . . gods, if Sergei fell into some waiting trap, then what might happen to her?

After the wedding, they were planning to travel back to our ancestral lands so Tatyana might meet the rest of the family. I couldn't rely on my brother Sturm to keep things under control; from his letters to me, it was apparent that he thought Sergei could do no wrong. Bad enough, but the most intolerable thing of all was the simple fact that Tatyana would no longer be *here*. I might never see her again.

Oh, I could persuade them to stay easily enough. Their affection for me would respond to a well-placed word or two. But would that be any better? Up to now, I'd been just able to bear seeing the two of them together, even steal a moment when I could forget about Sergei and pretend that she loved me only. But after the wedding . . . knowing that tomorrow night she would be in *his* bed, knowing that she'd be finding a virgin's delight in his clumsy maulings . . . it sickened and disgusted me beyond all measure. How much longer could I continue to hide the truth from her?

*Not long.*

But I'd have to, perhaps forever.

As surrender had been, black despair was once an alien concept to me. Now I was as familiar with both as with my own features, for there they were in my mirror, gaping back at me every day.

\* \* \* \* \*

# P. N. Elrod

The sun was well down and my rooms dark and close despite the tall, open windows of the bed chamber. I paced over to them, searching for and not finding any breath of fresh air. Only very rarely on this side of Mount Ghakis did the wind drop away to nothing, and it usually meant a storm was coming. Stepping through the windows onto the courtyard overlook, I peered up at the night sky but saw no sign of threatening clouds yet.

All was quiet within the keep. I could just make out the shadow shapes of the guards on the western curtain wall. Theirs was a soft enough job these days. Castle Ravenloft was one of the best located and most nearly impregnable fortresses I'd ever seen. Alek was of the opinion that the only way it could ever be taken was from within, and it was a necessary point of pride for him that such would never happen while he was steward.

He'd returned from his latest ambassadorial tour several days ago to resume his duties, making sure all was running smoothly for the wedding. He was still not happy about the many guests that had come crowding through the gates in the last week. For all his searching and sniffing, he'd not turned up anything conclusively suspicious about any particular house and had taken this as a personal failure. For my own part, I was satisfied that if anyone was actively plotting mischief, he or she would see that Alek was there to block the plans. If they were wise, they would cancel them.

The air being the same inside as out, I returned to the study and lighted some candles. The books Alek had brought back six moons ago had proven to be highly unusual and uncommonly advanced. Most of the lore in them was quite incomprehensible, and that which I did understand was . . . dark. I suspected that the original writer of the books had participated in a number of ceremonies that would have met with disapproval from most of the magically talented. Certain diagrams, ingredients, and even the sound of the words of power made me decidedly uncomfortable, but the spells themselves were fascinating.

And frustrating. During this time I experimented relentlessly on the most simple of them and met with failure again and again. As for the more complex spells, I was unable to even translate their titles; the language was outside my magical vocabulary. The reason behind this was to prevent any overly eager apprentices from jumping ahead in their education, thus heading off a disaster before its occurrence. The popular legend I'd heard about this concerned a student who attempted to summon some form of invisible servant. When it came, the thing was invisible all right—and rather hungry. Suffice it to say, the student lived just long enough to deeply regret his precipitate act.

The candles burned low and began to gutter. The shadows jumped as each flame struggled to remain alive against the flood of melted wax. Another night was slipping away from me. My last night. My last chance to have her.

Blackness surged up and clouded my brain for a time. This had happened before and was now becoming more frequent. I had thought it was simple illness before realizing it was but another part of my growing despair. Secret and safe in some hidden cache within me, the blackness was always ready to rush forth and resume gnawing at my soul like a starved monster. It was a long-suppressed hatred toward Sergei, toward the life I was trapped in, toward life itself.

Shuddering, I pushed it back. Time was short. I could waste *none* of it wallowing in such a useless self-indulgence.

I bent over my book and tried to draw sense from it once again.

Two of the candles succumbed and went out at the same time, casting the page in darkness just as some of the words were becoming clear in my mind. Impatiently, I grabbed up the book to take it to better light. The pages were stuck together now, probably by some errant blob of wax. I parted them. Carefully. The words—suddenly crystalline—jumped out at me.

*A Spell for Obtaining the Heart's Desire.*

Gods, why couldn't I read this one before this moment? I'd gone through these books a hundred times. Perhaps the constant study was needed in order to obtain understanding. Perhaps only now was my mind able to discern the more difficult facets of the Art.

And this spell . . . *this* was the one I needed, had searched so long to find. My heart raced so from the possibilities that my chest ached.

I looked at the list of ingredients, for without them it was pointless to start. *Bat's wool, ground unicorn horn . . .* yes, yes, I had those.

The candle flames flickered again. A curl of smoke drifted into my eyes. I blinked them clear and resumed reading.

*Bat's wool, ground manticore spike . . .*
That wasn't right. I started over.
*Rat's skin, ground manticore spike . . .*
On the fourth reading I saw that it was useless. The spell's protection was too strong for me to break through. The last candles danced, flickered, and went out. I was in total darkness. I didn't bother trying to replace them. What was the point?

*Heart's Desire.* More like heart's breaking. It was hopeless. The answer to all my problems, the cessation of all my agonies, was in my hands, but I was utterly unable to use it. I might have to study for years before—

Hopeless. Hopeless. *Hopeless.*

It was too much to bear. I blundered over to the study table and slammed the useless thing down with all my strength. I wanted to slam other things, break them, tear them apart, tear the whole keep apart starting with my idiot's collection of magical studies.

Blindly, I scrabbled for the offending volume. I'd begin with it.

"That's a very old book. You should handle it more carefully."

The voice—coming from everywhere and nowhere—took me cold. My back hairs shot up, but long training overrode the initial shock, and I dropped to a fighting crouch, dagger in hand, before the last words were out.

"Who's there?" I thought it might have been Alek's voice. Only he would have grit enough for such a prank, but I wasn't sure.

"You ought to know." Tatyana's voice now, yet not her. It was behind—no, in front of me. "You called me," she continued, the sound moving first one way, then another. "I heard your hate. I am here to give you your Heart's Desire."

"Stand still!" My tone was rather too harsh. Even in my great anger earlier, I would not have spoken to her so. And as for what she was saying to me . . . "Tatyana? Show yourself!"

Sergei laughed, in such a way as he'd never laughed before. "You could not tolerate the sight."

It was then I knew this to be an illusion born of magic. Whatever spoke to me was using their voices, hoping to frighten me by their very familiarity. But I was no trembling child to fear a noise in the night. I was—

The laughter grew, filling the rooms, filling my head. I clapped my hands over my ears, dropping the dagger. Whatever was with me would not be vulnerable to such an insignificant weapon.

I was dealing with something far beyond my experience in magic and needed no wise teacher to tell me it was deadly. Yet it wouldn't have come without some type of summoning on my part, which meant I had a portion of control over it. Dispelling it was no problem; I knew how to do that easily enough, if I chose.

"Strahd," Ilona now. Whispering. "You called me. Don't you want your Heart's Desire?"

"Don't you want your Heart's Desire?" Tatyana sweetly echoed.

"Or will you let her go to your brother?" asked Sergei.

"Will you let me go to your brother?" Tatyana questioned mournfully.

Gods, it knew *exactly* what to say to me.

"Will you let her go?" Alek demanded.

*No . . . she will be mine,* I whispered in my own mind. I couldn't *not* at least *think* it.

They heard me. And laughed.

"What will you do to get her?" Alek again.

I refrained from answering, but it accurately picked up on the question in my mind: what might be required from me in turn?

"Nothing beyond your means or skill, Strahd." I would have sworn it was Alek's voice, but for the fact that he'd never spoken to me with anything remotely like the contempt I heard now. "Shall we begin?"

I gestured vaguely toward the table, wanting to buy more time to think. "But the rite . . . I've not . . ."

"Nothing beyond your means or skill," said Tatyana in a tone that only an expert courtesan could use without insult. I felt her hand—or something like her hand—caress my face in a feather-light touch. I even smelled her scent on it.

"Nothing beyond your means or skill," Sergei sneered, and the hand slipped down to close upon my throat. It was much larger now and smelled of battle-sweat, blood, and oiled leather.

I grabbed for the hand. It was gone as if it had never been. "What are you?"

The voices merged and separated around, above, through me. They took on weight with no substance and pressed upon me. My heart . . . pounded . . . labored. My blood seemed too chill and thick to push through my veins, and I cried out against it. The voices laughed at my pain, and in that sound they seemed to assume a single, huge shape.

I was in total darkness. The shape was darker.

It writhed and twisted and pulsed without rhythm— pleasure from pain, pain from pleasure—and it murmured of things still darker than itself, things I knew and things I did not, things that should never be said and were said anyway, and with each word it grew and grew, until the room was filled with its presence, and the sheer bulk of it pressed me down so that my knees crashed into the floor, and I was pushed flat, and the weight ground at me with pressure so great I couldn't scream, not even in my mind.

Then it was gone.

I rolled on my back, clawing at my chest where iron bands yet seemed to squeeze upon me and felt . . . nothing. No broken ribs, no burst heart—

Not yet. But the next time. The thing would return and crush me into—

I *knew* it now. Knew what it was. We were old, old friends.

*Death* was in the room with me.

My heart turned leaden; it would collapse in upon itself by its own heaviness. It labored hard against my breastbone. Futile effort in the face of the inevitable.

Death stirred around me like an ocean's tide.

I fought to drag in one more breath.

Death washed over and . . . receded. For the moment.

"Have you come for me?" *If so, then take me and be damned.*

Nothing. I waited for many terrible, slow heartbeats. Then:

"I have come . . . on your behalf," it answered, using all the voices at once.

This was some last trick. A final taunt before dragging me into the Abyss.

"You have fed me well," it continued.

Gods, but wasn't that true. All those years of war. How many had I killed in the cause? What did it matter now?

"You are due your reward."

*Yes,* I thought bitterly. *Another death for Death. What other fate was there for a blood-steeped warrior when there were no more battles to fight?*

"Your reward, Strahd Von Zarovich," it emphasized.

*Reward?*

Then the voices assumed a secretive tone. "You hunger for your brother's betrothed, for your lost youth. I shall remove the rival from your path, and you shall age not one day more . . ."

Sergei gone, time removed as an adversary, Tatyana turning to me as I'd dreamed a thousand times over. My Heart's Desire. It must be a lie. Had to be. *Could* Death lie? Why not? But why should it even bother? What was I if not one more mortal to fall spiraling into its bottomless maw?

" . . . if you do as I tell you."

There it was. The parley, the bargaining, the trade. What did it want of me? What could Death possibly want from *me?*

"Nothing beyond your means or skill," Tatyana said clearly.

The iron bands about my chest eased. I sucked in air, gasping, coughing. It had pulled back, but was not gone.

It was waiting for my answer. I had no way of knowing for how long.

*Not long.*

It waited. Silent. I could hear nothing but the pant of my breath and the tiny creak of my own joints as I sat up.

It waited. One minute. Two. I wiped sweat from my brow. My skin was colder than stone.

It waited . . . then began to draw back. I felt it going. Going with my only chance. My last chance.

*Tatyana.*

Going.

"What must I do?" I whispered.

It stopped.

Turned.

And laughed.

\*   \*   \*   \*   \*

My fingers were shaking and so icy I could hardly feel them, but I managed to strike flint and iron, one against the other, and the tinder caught on the first spark. I lighted a fresh candle from the brief flame, then used it to light others.

The study looked the same as before. Felt the same. There was no sign that anything had been in here with me. It was gone; but I sensed—or imagined—it hovering close by, like someone listening from the next room.

The shaking subsided after I downed a healthy dose of *tuika*. More potent than wine, it warmed the belly and soothed the nerves. Much as I disliked dealing with the

Barovians, I had to acknowledge that they knew how to make a good brandy.

With restored light and vision, the reality of what I'd just been through should have faded like a dream upon waking, but not so for me. It *had* happened, and I had listened to the thing with a fearful eagerness. Some of its instructions made no sense, but ofttimes in magic, one must perform rituals with no discernible purpose to them. It's a foolish practitioner who ignores them or discounts their importance.

This was dark magic. I was on the threshold of true necromancy, yet oddly calm about the fact, as though someone else were about to make the crossing for me, as though I would reap the benefits and someone else would pay the price.

There would be a price. No bargain was without one, but I knew I'd be able to pay it. And cover for it. A bluff here, a lie there, a blatant misdirection; it was hardly different from the statecraft I was presently engaged in with the other ruling families.

But the benefits—to not age one day more was one thing, but to have Tatyana . . . she was worth *any* price. If Death had wanted my very soul, I'd have given it up for her. She would turn to me and smile and laugh for me alone. She was springtime and summer rain, autumn color and winter stillness. And by tomorrow night she would be mine.

The harsh scrape of metal on stone jolted me from my dream of love. Very close. From the bedchamber. No, just beyond it. I glimpsed a man's shape moving away from the open windows.

# P. N. Elrod

One of my swords hung on the wall by my bed. It was in my hand and I was through a window in a few short seconds. I was in time. He'd gone but five yards along the courtyard overlook and, hearing me come out, stopped and turned to look at me.

Alek Gwilym.

The wind had kicked up, herald of the storm to come. It flowed strongly down the flanks of Mount Ghakis, and Alek had to brace himself against its growing force as it gusted into the keep. His own sword was out and probably the source of the noise that alerted me: its edge must have brushed against the wall or walkway. He held it angled across his body as though wary of an attack. High clouds began to choke off the starlight. There was just enough illumination left for me to see the guarded expression on his face.

"My lord?" And there was a new note of cautious doubt in his voice. "Forgive me, but I came to tell you—"

I strode close to him, my own blade held ready. "What?"

He flinched. I'd *never* seen him do that before, not once in the eighteen years I'd known him had he ever been like this. Afraid.

He knew. He'd heard everything.

And he would talk.

As though someone else guided my arm while I stood idle in mind and heart, I made a fast cut to his head.

Just as fast, he parried and dropped back a pace.

"No, Strahd! Do not—"

Another cut. Another parry.

"*Strahd . . .*" His mouth moved, but the wind carried

off his words. Its whisper had gusted to a roar, obscuring the ring of metal on metal. None of the watchmen would hear us or see us in the dark. We might as well have been in the middle of a desert for all the help either of us could expect.

I struck again. Alek retreated. He was backing his way toward the corner turret. Someone would be there. I feinted right, then circled to that side to cut him off.

"Don't do this—"

I lost the rest of what he said, but took his meaning. He did not want to fight me. No matter. Neither of us had a choice. That's what I told myself, anyway.

On my next attack, he parried, then countered full force. This was no practice match with blunted blades to stop just short of their mark; this was as earnest and deadly as any battle we'd ever fought.

Lightning flashed over the shoulders of Mount Ghakis, instantly followed by the drumbeat of thunder. The sound pounded through me, quickening my blood, stirring my muscles to greater speed and strength. The battle fever was taking me over. With savage joy I embraced its heat.

Alek recognized it in me, then gave in to it himself. This time, he didn't wait for my attack. He whipped in, pushed me back, and when we were clear, a parrying dagger was in his other hand.

I went for another head cut. Sword block. Struck lower. Sword and dagger. Dagger swipe to my belly. Drop back. Leg cut. Dagger block. Chop to the dagger hand. Sword block.

More lightning. Fat drops of rain spattered hesitantly over the walkway and, meeting no resistance, increased to a deluge. Water clawed at my sight. I barely got my blade up in time to block an attack launched when I blinked. My hold on the sword was loose from the rainwater and my own sweat. The leather soles of my boots slipped on the wet stone paving. Alek had little better balance, but he wore gloves, and that was a major advantage for him in maintaining a solid grip on his weapon.

He used the advantage, doing a quick lunge and twist, trying to take the sword from my hand. I went with the motion instead of fighting it, but my arm was pushed wide, and Alek seized his one opportunity and drove in with his dagger.

I didn't feel it. Not at first. Only something tugging at my clothes. Nothing more until the next flash of lightning revealed the abrupt stain of red on my white shirt. I'd not worn my chain mail; there was no need to, after all, here, safe in my own rooms.

*You would draw my blood, armsman?*

*Only a drop or two,* he'd answered.

More than that, much more, was welling from me now. The pain shot through me like a sudden, unquenchable fire.

He broke off, staring, perhaps in shock. Not that he lacked a stomach for slaughter, but he'd struck down his lord, the man he was oath-bound to protect. The man who'd betrayed him, who was repaying all his years of loyalty with death.

And was receiving death in return.

*No.*

But no denial would heal it or stave off the outpouring

of my life. My knees were going to jelly, and my flesh felt both hot and cold. This was a bad wound, worse than any I'd ever had before. It was also my last. I knew the signs, having seen them in others; I was going to die.

As Alek hesitated, I made one more strike. It was a dishonorable gesture of pure vindictiveness; it should have also been impossible for me to complete. A terrible frailness had seized my whole body, blurring my sight, slowing my arm, but somehow my blade found solid flesh and bit hard. He cried out once and dropped his dagger to clutch at his belly. He'd not been wearing mail, either.

My strength was swiftly draining away; I used what was left for a final push and turn, then yanked the blade free. It fell from my nerveless fingers and clanged dully against the paving stones next to Alek's dagger.

He grunted and gasped and sat down, still holding his sword. He could yet finish me, but made no move to do so. Instead, he let go his weapon and sank forward onto the walk, as though settling for sleep in his own bed.

Pain kept me from going out entirely; I couldn't breathe very well. Somehow I'd lost my feet and now lay curled on my side, the stones pressing hard against my joints.

"Don't you want to live, Strahd?"

Not Alek. The voice was too clear in my head, undistorted by wind and rain, but it sounded like him. And Alek heard it, too. I saw his wincing reaction.

"Don't you want to live?" asked Tatyana.

"Live?" Sergei.

"Live?" Ilona.

## P. N. Elrod

"Yes . . . damn you . . ."

It laughed in all its voices. "You know what to do."

And, so help me, I did.

My legs were gone, but I could use my arms to crawl. Rain spattered into my eyes and stung my back through the thin fabric of my shirt. I was soaked and cold and more than halfway to death . . . and moving ever closer—but Alek lay between us, and in him was my last hope.

His breathing was shallow, and there was a yellow-gray cast to his skin that's only found on the dying. His eyes rolled toward me. Blood welled up in his mouth and spilled from one corner.

"Didn't have to, my lord," he murmured.

I said nothing.

"I'd have helped you . . . no matter what. This . . . did not . . . have to be."

"I'm afraid it did."

He choked and coughed and finally cleared his throat. "Should have let me die on the mountain . . . spared me from seeing this."

"Alek—"

His near hand came up and clutched at me. He sucked in another precious draught of air. More blood spilled from his mouth, obscuring his words. "Traitor in . . . the camp . . ."

A reproach to me? Or was his fading mind spewing out an old memory?

"Ba'al Verzi . . ."

What did he mean?

" . . . sleep." His grip on me relaxed, and he drifted off to briefly dream his last dreams. He was nearly gone.

What did—but there was no time to waste on his mutterings. With every beat of my heart I, myself, was weakening.

I found his second dagger in its belt sheath and pulled it out. He still lived, but was too far lost for awareness. He couldn't have felt it as I dragged the edge firmly across his throat.

Blood. A whole fountain of it.

Life. If I dared to take it.

As my own life ebbed, I didn't dare not take it.

I drank. Deeply.

And lived . . . again.

\* \* \* \* \*

The rain washed away all trace of evidence that might have otherwise inspired awkward questions. Gallons of fresh cloud water poured upon us, diluting the blood, preventing its stain from fixing permanently to the stones. It washed everything clean again, the excess flowing in waves to butt against the wall and swirl down the drainage holes to the gutters, then to the keep's storage cisterns far, far below.

I stood up and threw back my head, letting the rain plaster my hair from my face. It was glorious. My death wound was gone. A hole remained in my shirt. That was all.

Alek Gwilym, valiant soldier, trusted officer, loyal companion—for eighteen busy years my only true friend—was dead by my hand, but I was unable to regret or even mourn that death. I seemed beyond such mundane

141

thoughts this night.

The first part of my pact was sealed. The bargain was begun, the healing effect of Alek's blood had proved it so. I felt . . . different. My heart was pounding from all the exertion, but I wasn't the least bit fatigued. Quite the opposite.

I felt young again.

Leaving Alek, I rushed back through the windows, got a candle, and peered at my image in the bedroom mirror. I looked the same. Time had not reversed itself. Disappointing, until I recalled the voice's promise that I would not age one day more. Well, this was as good a time in life as any for aging to cease; I was still very much in my prime.

The flame gave a slight gold sheen to my skin, but I could tell I was very pale, even ill-looking, though I felt better than I had in years. The sickly effect would probably pass soon enough.

There were other things to think about, anyway.

With little effort, I pulled Alek's body inside and bundled it ignominiously into the closet, making sure the doors were locked, particularly the one leading to my private dining room. There was to be a small wedding supper for the immediate family there tomorrow—the servants would be in and out of the place all afternoon. Alek deserved better, but it couldn't be helped. Later I would think up some story to account for his death, but not now. Avid anticipation of what was to come left me too agitated to concentrate or feel anything but suppressed excitement.

There was no question that I wouldn't see things through. In a few more hours Tatyana would be mine.

\* \* \* \* \*

I awoke, sluggish and stiff, very late the following morning, and only because my servant took the liberty of violently shaking me to consciousness. My snarl of protest got the apologetic response that he had feared I was unwell, a conclusion readily confirmed by me in the barber's mirror a little later. I looked positively ghastly in the searing, bright daylight and ordered the curtains drawn. The sun was out as if the storm had never happened, and there was entirely too much of it for me. No one else seemed to mind it or the overbearing heat, and I found their cheerful attitude about the weather extremely annoying. I kept to my rooms, hardly able to move from bed to chair, as enervated now as I'd been energized the night before. Only in the late afternoon did I begin to feel like my own self and was able to tolerate a few necessary visitors.

Reinhold Dilisnya, Victor Wachter, Ivan Buchvold, and all of my former staff officers took turns trooping in to pay their respects. I took particular note of Ivan's behavior toward me, but despite the scandal about his brother, Illya, nothing seemed to have changed. He looked older, of course; they all did.

Wives and children were brought in and introduced, as if I had any interest in them. At least Reinhold understood me enough to leave his family at home. Rubbing his fretful belly, he looked like he would have preferred to be with them.

His brother Leo was no longer in the keep, he told me. The young man had fallen ill and asked permission to leave, which I found to be rather curious. When one is not feeling well, one is not usually inclined to go traveling. And in this case, Leo was perfectly aware that Lady Ilona, with her unquestioned reputation as a healer, was present to deal with all kinds of infirmities.

Very odd.

It could have had something to do with Ivan's presence. Leo might not have been comfortable around the brother of the man he'd killed and chose to leave rather than . . .

*Forgive me, but I came to tell you . . .*

Purposely not glancing in the direction of the closet, I uneasily wondered what it was that Alek had not been able to say; why he had come secretly to me by way of the overlook walkway instead of more directly, using any of the other entrances to my rooms.

Impossible now to know. Perhaps later, when there was time to think, I'd figure it out. The restlessness was beginning to return to my mind, jangling my thoughts, preventing me from concentrating on much of anything for more than a few moments at a stretch.

I'd been vaguely hungry, but nothing the kitchen or cellars offered looked or smelled appealing except for my morning cup of beef juice. That was all I had to sustain me through the whole interminable day, but instead of increasing, my initial fatigue wore off as the sun began to sink behind the mountain.

My last caller was Gunther Cosco, and had I been able to stomach anything, we might have enjoyed toasting each other's health as in the old days. The years of peace had not completely destroyed his good looks, but time and drink were having their way with him. His skin sagged, and I noticed he kept his hat on to hide the receding hair and the brown spots starting to appear high on his forehead. He served as a reminder of what might still be in store for me if I wavered. But soon I would complete the ritual and put that possibility behind me forever.

Guests having gone down to the main floor or the chapel, I dismissed the servants and saw to my own dressing. Unlocking one of the closet doors to get the proper clothes, a frisson of shock went right through me like last night's dagger thrust.

Alek's body was gone.

Heart in my throat, I searched all the closets and double-checked the other locks. No visible tampering. My servant had no key of his own. He was trustworthy, but not so much that I would allow him easy access to the gems and other family treasures I kept here. I was one of two people who knew the locks and in what order to safely open them. The other had been Alek Gwilym . . .

Far, and yet not far enough, I heard the laughter of familiar voices. *His* was one of them.

He must have been part of my payment to them, a portion of the bargain that had not been quite clear to me. I tried to shake the voices from my head, wondering what else I might have overlooked at the time.

Time . . .

There was none to spare. I shrugged the problem off as something to be dealt with later and got dressed for the wedding: white silk shirt, red neckcloth, stark black trousers and coat, and the Von Zarovich ruby on my breast. All the others would be decked out in peacock finery and revel in it; I had never shared their taste for garish fashion and would not go in for it now. Knowing what was to come, I deemed their frivolous dress to be . . . inappropriate.

From the massive strongbox that had held the ruby, I also withdrew a small bundle of elaborately embroidered fabric and tucked it into a pocket of my coat. It seemed to weigh no more than a feather. But, insulated as I was by the layers of cloth and thread, I still felt the cold, dark magic pulsing from it as though it lay right against my bare flesh.

\*  \*  \*  \*  \*

Sergei was done up in his gaudiest uniform, a soldier who had never really served. At least he had refrained from loading it up with assumed honors as had some of the vain fops that were visiting the court. Other lords rewarded their servants with these trinkets, but I held the opinion that such things were to be earned, not given as bribes. The only bauble on Sergei was the Priest's Pendant, which he would have to ceremonially give up just before walking into the chapel.

In his chambers, he greeted me with a broad smile and an embrace, and readily accepted the apology I'd prepared for him. How easily the words flowed from me, how happily he lapped them up; yesterday's incident over Tatyana and the jewels was forgiven and forgotten just like that. He *still* didn't understand.

No matter.

I went through the motions and said the right things. He babbled back in turn, displaying his nervousness for the approaching event. I watched him and looked hard into my heart, searching for a single vestige of warm feeling for this young man. Nothing. For all the fact that we shared the same blood, he was no different from any other strutting fool I'd ever encountered. No different, except that he was about to marry the one woman I loved, could ever love.

"I wish you had someone like Tatyana," he enthused at me.

*Oh, but I will.*

I took out the bundle of fabric. "For the groom, I have a present," I said, handing it to him. "It's magical and quite old. Well suited to the day."

Sergei's constant smile faltered when the red, black, and gold hilt seemed to leap from the wrappings. He went still as stone, gaping at the thing.

Yes. Sergei was most definitely a sheep, vulnerable to any wolf who could put on a kindly face.

"I see that you recognize it," I said. "The time-honored weapon of a Ba'al Verzi assassin. The sheath is made from human skin, usually from the weapon's first victim. The carvings on the hilt are runes of power."

Had our roles been reversed and Sergei the one offering me such a gift, I'd have had my sword out and been backing toward the nearest door and calling for help. All he could do was stare with blank shock.

One should never store a blade in its sheath lest tarnish or rust set in, and this knife had not been out since that night I'd taken it from Illya. But as I removed it now, the blade was as perfect as ever. It gleamed like a mirror in the candlelight and was razor sharp. The runes had their share of preservation magic as well as evil power.

"Legend has it that it is bad luck to draw such a dagger unless you can give it blood," I went on.

Sergei's lips parted, but plainly he could not think of anything to say. This was something quite outside his limited experience.

The Ba'al Verzi.

Deception was their greatest weapon. Your oldest friend, your most faithful servant—by the gods, even the mother that bore you could be a Ba'al Verzi.

Even your own brother . . .

I smiled warmly. "I'm generally not superstitious, but I think this time it's better not to tempt fate. Don't you agree?"

Moving swifter than the eye could follow, swifter than thought, I struck, driving the short blade up under his breastbone and into his heart.

No man dies in an instant. For what seemed a very long time, he met my hot joy with a look of hurt astonishment, then slowly, slowly, doubled over, silently falling into my arms. I felt the life thinly cling to him for a few seconds more, and then . . . it just wasn't there.

I eased his inert weight to the floor and worked the knife free of his body.

"Drink of the blood, first from the instrument and then of the chalice."

Thus ran my instructions.

After last night's business with Alek, this draught was nothing for me. Taking care not to cut myself on the blade, I licked every drop of blood from the dagger, dried it, and left it on the floor. Then I opened up Sergei's tightly buttoned uniform. It was a small wound, seeming hardly large enough for the amount of blood that had poured out. With his heart stilled, the flow had slacked off, but there was yet much to be had. I put my lips to the wound and drank.

Alek's blood had been taken out of fevered necessity, Sergei's as an inseparable part of death's ritual, but its taste was . . . satisfying. Alek's had kept me alive, Sergei's was the fulfillment of appetite. It was the sweet savory one keeps to brighten up the end of a dull meal. There was perverse warmth to be found in his cooling life; it renewed my energy and spirit, and I felt strength such as I'd never known before, tearing through my veins like heat lightning.

Without, I heard the laughter of guests and clatter of servants, the whisper of long skirts and the tap of dress boots; within, I heard the beat of my own racing heart. My fingers discerned the very warp and weft of Sergei's garments; I smelled the soap he'd used, and the sweat, light upon his skin, and the difference between wet blood and that which was already beginning to dry. It was as if I'd spent my whole life with my senses heavily wrapped in the thickest of cotton bandaging, and only now had it been stripped away, freeing me.

*Free.*

One more thing to do, though. A bluff here, a lie there, a blatant misdirection . . .

I found my feet, stooped, and swept up Sergei's body, aware of its weight, yet able to ignore it. Raising it high, I balanced it a moment—one-handed—then let it fall. It landed with a bone-jarring thump, sprawling in a most natural and satisfying manner.

His eyes were still open. They were the same blue as his uniform, the same blue of our mother's—

*Free.*

I knelt and closed them.

"You were supposed to have been a priest," I whispered. "Why didn't you just do what you'd been born to do?"

The thudding commotion I had just made drew attention, and Sergei's personal servant came through the door, but I'd heard his approach and threw myself over my brother's body, as though overcome by grief. I looked up and, in a fair imitation of one of my own rages, imparted the bad news to him. Like Sergei before him, all he could do was stare until my bellowed orders at last penetrated his skull. Then he departed quickly enough to summon help.

Easy. Very, very easy.

I tasted blood on my lips and felt the stab of sudden worry. What had the man seen? Horror at his master's death would account for most of his shock, but what else . . .

Mirror. There was one just over there. Sergei had been preening before it when I'd come in.

Yes, there was blood on my mouth, my face. Bad, but if I cleaned it off, anything the man said could be discounted. A bluff here, a lie there . . .

There was a basin of water on the table below. I scrubbed my face, cleaned my bloodied hands, dried off, then checked in the mirror.

Clean. No need to fear—

I was so pale. Paper white. Whiter. My very image was fading as I watched. My last sight of myself was of a man utterly consumed by surprise, utterly ludicrous, utterly laughable with his popping eyes and hanging mouth.

Myself, Strahd Von Zarovich.

Faded—

Fading—

Gone.

# Chapter Five

## Sixth Moon, 351

"My Lord Strahd?"

*Gone.*

"My lord?"

The reflection only. I ran my hand against the mirror's surface and left behind finger streaks.

"Lord Strahd!"

I turned toward the intrusive voice. Tatra, a lieutenant now, stood just inside the door with several of his men. They were in their dress uniforms, boots shining, swords polished and held ready, and looking quite grim as they stared from Sergei's body to me.

"Where's Captain Gwilym?" I asked in a shaken tone. This time I did not have to dissemble for my lies.

Knowing I wouldn't like his answer, Tatra retreated into discipline and stood at attention. "No one has seen him today, my lord."

"Then find him. He's in charge of security. I want to know how he managed to let a Ba'al Verzi into the keep." I pointed at the knife, where it lay near Sergei's body.

Tatra and the others recognized it and made the protective sign against evil.

I . . . dropped back a step, feeling ill for a moment. Just as well. I was too close to the mirror, and they mustn't see . . .

"But my lord, isn't that the knife—" Tatra caught my glare and chose not to finish.

"You think there's only one blade for the whole filthy guild? The one I took from Illya Buchvold is still locked away. This one . . . this one is . . ." I looked up, as though pouncing on a new thought. "Find Ivan Buchvold."

Tatra was a smart man, else Alek would not have made him his second-in-command. As I'd hoped, he made the connection between Illya's death and Sergei's. It was a very logical conclusion: a brother for a brother. His face set, he snapped a go-ahead to two of the men, and they obediently slipped away.

The familiar act of giving orders restored some of my own self-discipline and got me to thinking again. There was much to do yet. In less than a minute, I had everything in hand and my men on the move. With any luck at all, I'd be able to take advantage of the natural confusion and find someone unable to account for himself during the time of Sergei's death. Ivan Buchvold would be ideal, but if not, then Alek Gwilym would do just as well.

Alone once more, I glanced at the mirror.

Empty.

I moved farther from its cold brightness. It beat upon me like too much sunlight. *What have I done to myself?* Perhaps I'd given up my soul for Tatyana after all.

And then I heard her voice shearing through the stone walls, raised in a cry of disbelief and despair. It cut right through me. *Someone's told her.*

Yes. She would have to go through the fire as well, but she would be the stronger for it. In time, she'd realize her love for Sergei had been a child's infatuation for a pretty toy. In time, I'd make her completely forget him. But for now . . .

I left two men guarding the entry to Sergei's rooms and made my way to the chapel. Crowds of guests slowed me; their faces, pinched with worry, sorrow, fear, and curiosity should have annoyed me, but did not. I was as distanced from them as a bird is from the ground.

Just at the chapel doors, I was told that Tatyana had run outside into the garden. I was thankful for that, instinctively knowing that I'd not have been able to go into that holy place.

The dark magic was upon me.

I'd changed.

But it was worth it. She awaited me.

Soon . . .

# P. N. Elrod

The day's warm air had turned chill, and mist was beginning to rise from the damp earth like restless spirits of the dead. Such thought was fancy only, but I did sense something else . . . stirring . . . all around me, like a wind that one feels only in the mind.

Magic.

Necromancy.

I'd done more this night than kill my brother and drink his blood. More had happened to me than had been promised. That business with the mirror was yet another price for me to pay, a price that had not been mentioned.

No. Not really. I'd ignored the possibility. There is a precise language to be used in such bargaining. Had I been more on guard and less eager to take what had been promised, I could have asked and gotten an answer.

Too late now.

One of Tatyana's chaperons hovered near the gate I'd come through. She was pale, but calm, and offered me an apologetic look, saying Tatyana would not let anyone near her.

"She'll see me. Where is Lady Ilona?"

"Lord Dilisnya was taken ill. She was called away to see to him, some time ago."

"Fetch her."

She left, and I slowly approached Tatyana.

The candlelight within the chapel was more than sufficient to overflow the stained glass windows and spill out into the night. Tatyana was huddled in a pool of color from one of them, her white gown catching and holding gemlike shades of green, blue, gold . . . red.

I looked down at her. If I'd had to kill a dozen brothers,

drink a river of their blood to have her, I would have done so.

She made no move, not even to wipe at the tears making salty trails down her cheeks, her throat . . .

Kneeling next to her, I put out my arms and knew the totality of joy as she at last sank into my embrace. I'd never before had patience for weeping, but now, as she clung to me and gave vent to the terrible grief raging in her young heart, I had only tender concern for her pain. She needed someone to hold her, and I was glad to do so. While I had seen much death in my time, she was still very much a child to it; perhaps between those extremes we would find a place of comfort for us both. My strength, my love—all that I had was hers to draw upon.

"Why, Strahd?" she whispered.

*It's happening.* This was the first time she'd ever used my given name.

"Why? How could this have happened? Who . . .?"

She clung to me more tightly, doubled over from the weight of her sorrow. If I could have spared her from this, I would have. Her sobs were such as to break her in two, but there was nothing to be done about it now.

"I cannot say," I murmured, not sure she understood the muted syllables, but knowing the droning sound of a familiar voice might help. "Whoever did it will pay." *Has paid.* "I promise you."

Above her weeping, I heard the winds within me rise. They tugged at my thoughts, trying to draw me away from the bliss of holding her. I put my back to them, shutting my eyes against them and the thickening mist.

But Tatyana straightened and shook off my arms.

157

She glared up. The stars were still visible, for the moment. "Why?" she screamed skyward. "Why did this happen? How could you do this?"

She wasn't addressing me, but the gods themselves. I tried to take her back, but she only pushed me away and got to her feet.

"Was it so wrong for us to love? Is that it? How could you have let us love each other so much and then do this?"

"Tatyana—" I reached for her, wincing as I felt the raw agony coursing through her body. "We cannot question the will of the gods in these matters."

"Who else, then?" she snapped. She avoided me and, pacing in a circle, still looking up, raised her hands high. "Tell me! How could you have let this happen? *Tell me!*"

Then the burst of anguish passed, and she dropped to her knees. I went to her, gathering her easily into my arms as before.

"Tell me," she said faintly.

"Hush," I said, rocking her. She lay quiet for some moments, then moved again with fresh energy.

"Lady Ilona." Her eyes were fever bright. "I must get her."

"She's been sent for."

"She must—must bring him back."

I grew cold all over. "What are you saying?"

"She's a great healer. And I've heard that sometimes . . . oh, Strahd, she'll have to try. She'll have to bring him back. This was but a testing of our faith. He *will* come back! I see it now!"

So did I. All too clearly. Ilona might possibly be able to

do it, but I could not allow that.

"Tatyana," I took her head in both my hands and looked into her eyes. Ravaged as she was by her emotions, she was still perfect, still the most beautiful girl I'd ever seen or ever would see. "Tatyana, please do not get your hopes up. Lady Ilona will do her best, but you must know that it might not be. I've seen her fail more often than succeed."

"But she will succeed this time. I know she will."

"No, you do not. None of us do. Remember when they tried to bring back the Most High Priest Kir? He died and remained so because it was the will of the gods. No one was able to bring him back."

"No! That has nothing to do with Sergei! He was murdered, and that was done by the will of some mortal, not by a god. Lady Ilona must try. Otherwise I shall join him. I can't live without him—and won't."

"Tatyana!"

She stopped raving and met my eyes.

"Listen to me, sweet girl. Listen to me!"

My voice sank to a gentle whisper, which somehow broke through to her and kept her looking at me.

"Sergei is dead. He will not return. Not even Lady Ilona and all her people can change that. You must accept it."

"But—"

"Accept it!"

Her great eyes clouded for many moments, but I felt a palpable link forming between us in that time. I'd touched her in a way more intimate than any joining of flesh. She would be mine.

"He is gone, but I am here for you. I will always be here

for you. You will turn to me and know my love."

She blinked, her brows coming together in puzzlement. "Strahd?"

*Yes . . .*

Now her hand came up. It was the same caress I'd felt last night in my study, only instead of a phantom sent to tempt me, this was the fulfillment of the promise made.

*Heart's desire.*

Oh, yes . . . by the gods, yes . . .

Her eyes cleared, and awareness flooded them. "Strahd." This time she said my name in a different way, the way one lover speaks to another.

"I'm here. I shall always be here for you."

*Heart's. . .*

Now I raised her to her feet. Her face tilted up to meet mine. As I'd done in countless dreams before, my lips closed softly over hers.

*. . .desire.*

She returned my kiss.

*Heart's. . .*

Her arms went around my neck and her body pressed close, breasts and hips against me.

*. . . hunger.*

We broke off at the same time, but for different reasons. She to stare at me with all new thoughts, new feelings, and I in near-pain for the swift beating of my heart. But, along with the ecstasy of holding her, having her, I sensed the intrusion of other, alien forces at work around us. The mist had risen high and the stars were gone. I could see within the garden well enough, but not far; the chapel walls were lost.

Found.

Yard by yard, the mist was retreating. It was not natural, for it moved in a slow spiral as though we were in the vortex of a vast, gray whirlpool.

"Strahd." She drew my attention back to her, pulling me down for another kiss.

I ran my hands through her thick russet hair, stripping away the virgin's veil of her gown. Tonight I would be her husband and she my wife. Tonight would be the first of thousands yet to come. Tonight I would teach her more about love than she had ever dreamed or wished. No woman before her or since would know of better . . .

My lips brushed over hers, then moved on to her cheek, her chin, and finally down to the hot silk of her throat. She sighed at the touch, her breath coming sharply with that first surprised awakening of true pleasure.

"My lord Strahd!" Someone called from the gate, his voice muffled and flattened by the mist.

*Not now, not now.*

Her body melded to mine, and she threw her head back. I supported her easily. She was so light, like a swan floating over its own reflection as it glides on the water.

"Lord Strahd, come quickly!"

Tatra, vainly trying to call me away from all that I'd worked for, given everything for . . .

"Murder, Strahd!"

. . .murdered for. I ignored him. Tatyana's heartbeat was as fast as mine. I felt it rushing through her like the rolling thunder of a summer storm.

# P. N. Elrod

"Betrayal!"

He was blundering around us in the mist.

*Damn him!* I roared in my mind.

Tatyana cringed and stiffened in my arms. "Strahd? What . . .?"

"Hush, he'll go away. I'll send him away."

She shook her head. "No, what are you—?"

"Hush, it's all right."

Now she was fighting me. I released her, and she stepped back to gain her balance. Her breath came hard, like a spent runner's. Her hands went to her throat, where I'd begun to kiss her in earnest.

"Elder, what—?" Another shake of the head, as though trying to awaken from a heavy sleep. "No, we must not do this."

I held my hand toward her, palm up. "It's all right. This is as it was meant to be."

She wavered between taking my hand and remembering the illusion of a lost love. "But Sergei . . ."

"He's gone. You will accept it and turn to me."

"Old One, he's *dead!* How can you say such things to me?"

"Because you are free. Both of us are free. Tatyana, beloved, I can give you—"

But her face crumpled as the fact of Sergei's death overwhelmed her once more. "No!"

Her grief would have to run its natural course—I saw that now. Any forcing on my part would only drive her from me. It would take time to bring her around. But I had time. I had more time than any man ever before me.

I could wait. And would.

"Strahd!"

Several voices now, raised to bellow out my name like the rallying cry they had used on the battlefield three years past. This time the shouts came from the chapel, along with the cries and screams of women and children and the crash and ring of weapons.

What in the name of all the hells was going on?

Tatra suddenly staggered out of the swirl of mist. His uniform was torn and bloody, and half of his dress sword had been broken away.

"Betrayal, my lord," he gasped. "Dilisnya traitors killing everyone."

"Where are the men?" There were two of my own guard for each armsman from the visiting houses.

"Too sick to fight. Poisoned, I think. The Dilisnyas are cutting them down. Some of us got outside. They can't find us here in this murk."

One of the chapel windows shattered, and we ducked as shards of color rained down. Someone was trying to club his way out using a chair. The screams were louder, more clear now. My hand went to my sword, but Tatra stopped me.

"Too late for that, my lord. There's been long planning in this. You must try to escape while you can."

I started to snarl a reply to such a cowardly course, then looked at Tatyana. She had to be kept safe.

"Are the stables free?"

"I don't know."

"We'll find out. Run ahead. Gather up any of our own that you find. If the stables are held, we'll make for the gate."

"Yes, lord." He ran off.

"Come, Tatyana." I took her hand.

"No." She pulled away. "I'm staying here with Sergei."

This was no moment for foolishness. I grabbed her arm and started dragging her from the garden. The mist had drawn back, and the walls of the keep were visible again, the stars returning. Their light cast a silvery glow almost like daylight, but Tatyana stumbled as though she couldn't see.

"*No*, Elder." She balked and tried to shake away. "I will stay with him."

"For how long? You think they'll let you live?"

"I'm hoping they won't."

Now she did wrest from my grip. I lunged to catch her again, but she shied away and ran. I called her name. She seemed not to hear.

She darted through the low gate leading to the overlook.

*No . . .*

"Tatyana!"

I was right behind her, but she had the speed of a young deer. I snagged the trailing hem of her dress, but she tugged free with hardly a pause and made the low wall.

Up, in one light bound.

I clawed and caught only air.

Gone.

The mist had cleared from most of the mountain, but the valley was still hidden. Tatyana's frail figure dropped, spinning, into that roiling white cloud. Tattered fingers of it stretched toward her like something hungry and, arms spread wide, she plunged headfirst into their grasp.

She shrieked the whole way down.

Sergei's name. My name. Neither of us. I couldn't tell. I couldn't hear for my own scream. It bounced off the walls of the keep and was swallowed whole by the mist below, vanishing even as she vanished.

Then . . . silence.

Then . . . laughter.

*Its* laughter. With all their voices. *Her* voice.

I screamed again to drown them out, beating my hands against my ears, but it was inside my head as well and nothing could stop it. I fell away from the wall, fell to my knees.

The blackness returned, greater than ever, covering me, covering the world, never to lift. Ever. I'd not known true despair until now. It weighed upon me, heavier than the mountain, smothering and crushing me into something less than dust.

"A Von Zarovich groveling?" the voices mocked.

No. Just a man like any other. A man who has lost everything, who has nothing left. Nothing. A man broken by unspeakable pain.

The agony was so great I did not feel the first arrow when it slammed into my side.

The second caught me in the back, knocking me flat onto the ground. Pushing to my feet, I stared, uncomprehending, up at the towers where the shots had come from. Archers stood ready at the crenelations, their bows full-drawn and aimed directly at me.

More men crowded into the overlook. All in the Dilisnya colors. All poised to shoot.

And, one after another, they did.

I braced and took the arrows, welcoming them, knowing for myself the madness that had seized and driven Tatyana. It would end now. I would trade this small pain for the obliteration of the larger. No hell could possibly hold worse suffering for me than this.

More arrows. Their searing shafts were *nothing* compared to the pain filling my heart. But they were too slow. I had to speed along to my death, even as she had. Grabbing one of the arrows, I wrenched it from my body, roaring from the burning shock. Blood rushed from the wound. Not as much as I would have expected. I pulled out another.

Some of the men fell back; the bolder ones held their post and loosed more shots at me. I faced them, encouraged them, and drew out the shafts one by one. Broke them in half. I was like a beast in a trap, gnawing off one of my limbs to free myself.

Finally—

—weakening . . .

*To age not one day more. Very well, then. Let me die now.*

On my knees again. The archers cautiously approached.

Weaker. . .

Hands and knees. The earth and paving spattered with my blood . . . with Sergei's . . . with Alek's . . .

I'd taken enough shots to kill a dozen men, but still lived. Not right. Not . . . natural.

*No.*

Laughter for my realization.

*To age not one day more.*
I wasn't going to die. Not tonight, not ever.
Laughter for my anguish.
A thousand nights, a thousand years lay before me.
Without her.
Alone.
Laughter.
One of the bastards kicked me. I rolled with it. Landed on my back. Stared impotently up at their grinning faces.

How dare they? How dare anyone? I was a Von Zarovich. But I was nothing to them, only another kill— perhaps more difficult, more stubborn than the rest, but that made for better sport. They laughed, their voices unknowingly joining the vile chorus in my mind.

Laughter . . . for my newborn rage.

I was looking at dead men. I could not die, but they would. Before another hour passed, I'd send them wailing on their way to rotting hell. All of them.

All except the traitor behind them. For him, something special.

Who . . .?

The one who'd kicked me now passed his bow to another man, then removed his helmet.

Leo Dilisnya.

\* \* \* \* \*

The pale marble walls of the main dining room were splashed and stained with blood. Except for that and an unwonted disarray to the place settings on the long central table, the room still looked prepared for a celebration. The candles on the three chandeliers high above were all alight and seemed to strike sparks from the faceted crystal around them. Lying, as I was, on the cold floor, with no strength left to do anything but stare up, I had ample opportunity to study their bright beauty.

Illusion. Nothing was beautiful anymore. Beauty had died when she'd—

Before carrying me here, rough hands had ripped the arrows from my body. I moaned in spite of myself and clutched at the many wounds dotting my chest and belly. They burned like coals thrown out from a fire. They had also stopped bleeding. So far, no one had noticed.

One man had been detailed to guard me. More stood ready over the other prisoners: Ivan Buchvold, his brother-in-law, Victor Wachter, and Victor's nine-year-old daughter, Lovina. The girl clung to her father like a limpet, too stunned to cry. The men bore expressions startlingly similar to hers and were much the worse for wear. Both had marred their fine clothes with blood and sweat, indicating that they'd had a share in the fighting.

Which seemed to be over for the time being. I heard no more clamor within the keep. The place was numb with that strange silence exclusive to a battlefield when the battle is over.

The double doors at the south end of the room were thrown open. Accompanied by guards, Lady Ilona and Reinhold Dilisnya were shoved in our direction. Ilona kept her feet; Reinhold, his face gray with illness, dropped right down and curled up like a dog. Ilona went to him, held her hands above his shivering form, and

bowed her head in prayer.

I turned away, gritting my teeth to keep from crying out. The next time I looked, Reinhold appeared to be asleep.

"Lord Strahd?" Ilona knelt next to me. Her age was showing this night. I wondered what terrors she had seen. She reached out.

"Touch me not!" I snarled.

She jerked her hand back. "My lord?" Then she got a really good look at me. If the changes within were visible to anyone, they would be to her. In that awful, unutterable instant, she saw and understood. Her head sagged.

"Spare it for others."

"Oh, Strahd, what have you done?" She somehow knew I was not a victim, but was myself responsible for what had happened.

"Everything and nothing."

I'd never seen her weep before. The sight of it now should have moved me in some other way than toward contempt. "My lady needs to better control herself," I murmured, mocking her words to me. That struck me as being quite amusing, and regardless of the pain, I was laughing.

Her eyes fixed on my open mouth.

I knew what she was looking at—I felt their sharp, new points well enough with my tongue.

"If I could help you, I would," she whispered.

As if I cared much now for the soul I'd given up. "Tell me what's going on."

She hesitated. Wise of her. In dealing with what I had become, it would always be a good idea to be as cautious as possible.

"Where's Leo Dilisnya?"

More hesitation. Leo may have been the architect of tonight's slaughter, but he was still like her—still human —while I was not.

I let my eyes slide to the other prisoners. "Tell me, and I can help save them."

Yes. That was her weakness. She knew it, too. She also did not question my ability to succeed at an apparently impossible task. "I want your word on that, Strahd Von Zarovich."

"You trust me to keep it?"

"As a point of honor, you would. You've not lost that, have you?"

"I don't know. Perhaps we'll find out."

It was as much a guarantee as she would ever get from me now. She reluctantly nodded. "I don't know where Leo is, but he'll be here soon. The guards said as much."

"What of my people?"

"Dead, or poisoned and dying. The guests . . . all dead . . . those loyal to you, anyway. Where's Sergei? And Tatyana?"

I laughed again, because I was no longer able to cry.

Ilona shivered and made the protective sign of her faith.

"Don't!"

She froze. "I am sorry for you, Strahd."

"Save it for those who need it."

She stared for a very long moment, pity, horror, compassion, and disgust playing over her face, turn on turn.

It was of no importance to me. I glanced toward the

others. "Just keep silent, Lady."

A nod, a rustle of skirts as she rose, and the harsh pressure of her immediate presence lifted from me. Some of my strength came trickling back. But my throat was so raw. I needed . . . something to drink.

The smell of blood positively filled this room. Most of it came from the walls and floors. Drying there. Useless and maddening. The guard next to me . . . he'd picked up enough from my talk with Ilona to be uneasy and had put some distance between us. Reinhold was closest, but his scent was somehow wrong. Tainted.

Leo again. All those years of Reinhold's sickness made perfect sense now. How long had Leo been planning this? How long had he been gradually poisoning his brother?

No matter. It would end tonight.

The doors swung open again, and Gunther Cosco was pushed through. He'd lost his hat, and strands of his thinning hair stood comically out from his head. He was as white as Reinhold except for a slash of red dribbling down one side of his once-handsome face; he'd taken a cut. He'd have a very bad scar—if he lived long enough for it to heal.

His guards didn't seem to see him as much of a threat and left him alone. He drifted in our general direction, but said nothing, and did not meet our eyes.

Flanked by some of his men, Leo Dilisnya came in. He still wore the humble livery of an archer—his disguise for a crucial time—but had draped an ostentatious gold chain of office around his neck. He'd traded his bow for a sword, and it and the elaborately trimmed scabbard also set him apart from the ranks. Our guards came to attention, and Victor and Ivan stood up. He passed them and Gunther by, though, and stalked over to where I lay.

"Hail, Strahd, Lord of Barovia," he said softly, by way of greeting. "Not for long by the look of you. Thought you'd be dead by now. What are you waiting for?"

Coughing like a dying man, I murmured, "An explanation?"

"I'm surprised you haven't gotten it from Reinhold already. Oh. Yes. He isn't in any condition to do much talking, is he?" He prodded Reinhold with the toe of his boot, getting no reaction. "Looks better than he did before. Is that your doing, Lady?"

Ilona said nothing. She sat by the wall, holding Lovina.

Ivan Buchvold, hovering between stony madness and violent grief asked, "Why, Leo? My poor Gertrude did you no harm . . . our children . . . how could you?" Tears spilled from his eyes. "How could you?"

"And my Oleka," Victor added. "And our children. Your own sisters, Leo."

"Half-sisters," he returned. He waited for them to respond and got only puzzlement. He prodded Reinhold again. "Half-brother, too, for that matter."

"What do you mean?" asked Ilona.

Leo cocked an eye at Gunther, who was leaning wearily against the table. "Why don't you tell them? You were so damned eager to tell me."

"And don't I wish I hadn't," Gunther replied sullenly.

Leo laughed. "You think I wouldn't have done this otherwise? Your 'great revelation' about yourself and mother made no difference to me, old man. It only gave me additional reason to put this lot out of the way in the end. I've been working on this for years, since before the end of the war."

"Ba'al Verzi," I whispered, only just loud enough for him to hear.

He showed his teeth and came over, dropping on his heels next to me. "So you see the truth of it? Took you long enough."

Alek's last words made sense now. Even as he lay dying by my hand, he'd tried to warn me; the Ba'al Verzi had only been asleep for these three years—asleep and waiting for the right moment to strike again.

*Beware the Ba'al Verzi, the great traitor who will take all for himself.*

"You should have died that first night we were here," said Leo. "Then Reinhold would have taken up the rule. After a decent interval, he'd have passed on from a bad belly, and I'd have stepped in, as was my right. If that bastard Gwilym hadn't turned up at the wrong time, quite a few people here might yet be alive. Where is he?"

"I don't know," I answered truthfully.

"We'll find him. Mind you, I certainly took the both of you in with my playacting then, babbling about my loyalty to the great and noble Strahd. I wish you could have seen your faces. All I had to do was think of what poor Illya might have said, add some convincing tears, and you swallowed it whole. Maybe he'll rest more easily in his grave now that—oh, excuse me—assassins are burned and their ashes scattered. That's what Strahd's men did to the body, didn't they, Ivan?"

Ivan was swaying on his feet one second and flying at

Leo the next. Both rolled right over my legs, ending with Ivan on top, fingers locked around Leo's neck. Men rushed in and eventually separated them.

Ivan was beyond sanity. His mouth hung wide as if to yell, but the only noise he made was a hoarse, panting grunt. The veins at his temples stood out from the skin like blue cords. Six men were holding him down and having a hard time of it.

Not for long. Leo spent some bad moments choking and retching, but recovered and drew his sword. He stood over Ivan, eyes blazing.

Ilona hugged Lovina to her breast so she wouldn't see.

Ivan gave out with a long, animal-like scream that only ended for lack of breath. Leo wrested his blade from the body and wiped it clean on Ivan's clothes. Rubbing his throat, he signed for the men to take the body out.

The scent of fresh blood blossomed into the room, sweeter than any perfume.

I opened my mouth and sucked in a ghost of its flavor where it floated on the air. Not enough. I hungered, I thirsted, I craved more with a keenness that diminished all previous wants to the point of nonexistence. Nothing else mattered but that I immediately answer this overwhelming need. Ignoring the fiery shards of pain lancing through me, I turned over.

Pushed the floor away.

Stood.

Worried despite my obviously poor condition, my guard came around to face me. A man as badly torn up as I was should be dead. Not standing. Not stepping toward him.

Smiling.

His eyes peeled wide open, and he raised his sword to strike. I knocked it away. The weapon spun from his hand and clanged against the wall, close to where Ilona huddled with the child. Victor, ever the soldier, instantly dived and grabbed it up, dropping into a fighter's crouch. The remaining guards were only just turning to see what was making the commotion.

If my man had had less fear and more wit, he might have been able to escape; I wasn't all that fast. But he froze. I moved in, seized his shoulder, and spun him around like a doll so his back was to me. Tore off his chain coif. His bared skin stank of iron and rust, damp leather and very old sweat. No matter. A man doesn't turn away from rotten bread when he's starving to death.

Legs flailing, hands clawing futilely to loosen my grip around his waist, he might as well have been wrestling a tree. He screamed, but I heard nothing, deafened as I was by the roar of his rushing blood. Other screams, other yells of fright and anger. They were no more than buzzing flies to me.

I took from him all that I could take, emptied him as a bird empties nectar from a flower, until his struggles slowed and stopped and his limp weight hung heavily in my arms. He'd provided enough to dull the agonizing edge of need, but I still hungered.

The battlefield silence was gone, replaced by an altogether different sort: the silence of waiting. Dread reigned on one side of the room, joyful anticipation on the other. Leo's men were stricken motionless, all their eyes on me. These were hard men and heartless, chosen by him for just those qualities, the kind of men who had no qualms about murdering inconvenient children as long as it didn't put them out too much.

They were about to find out the true cost of this job.

I lifted the guard's body high and threw it across the room to a knot of men. Some were able to react and dodge; the rest went down and stayed that way.

One of the archers nocked an arrow, drew, and released as smoothly as if he were on a practice field. It went sharp and deep into my chest. When I'd caught my balance from the blow, he let fly with a second shaft, striking just below the first. He had good training, excellent self-control; the best archers always do. He was starting on his third shot when I reached him. Hardly feeling it this time, I pulled the arrows from my body and plunged them into his own and with little less force than if they'd come from his own bow. He thrashed and went quiet.

Leo's men scattered in a wide circle around me. Some made for the doors and temporary escape. Temporary, only. I'd sworn that none of them would live out this night, and I would keep my word.

Hacking wildly away at two men at once, Victor shouted my name, like a war cry. The fighting rage was on him, turning him into a fiend with a sword. He had a dead wife and children to avenge, and another child to protect.

Ilona also shouted my name, for a different reason. She was behind Victor, trying to drag Lovina out of harm's way. There was little chance of her succeeding; they were running out of space.

One of the men got a swift cut in his side and reeled back. I was there to catch him. As if snapping kindling wood, I broke his back, dropped him, and got between Ilona and chaos with the fallen man's blade in my hand.

Just in time. Another brute, the size of a draft horse, closed on us. He was either fearless or a fool. Seconds later he was dead, his head rolling toward his fellows.

That marked their ultimate rout. The ones at the back were already through the doors. The rest hurried to join them, crowding themselves, getting in each other's way in their haste to leave.

My laughter followed them out.

I turned back to the others.

Victor had killed his second man and was hunched over, catching his breath. He looked up at me, looked around at the bodies, in particular the one with the torn-out throat, but said nothing and made no other move.

"Come here, Victor," I said.

Sword in hand, but held down and away from him in a nonthreatening manner, he walked across to me. The floor was slick in spots from the blood. He avoided them as though they were no more than rain puddles and somehow kept his eyes on mine at the same time. He was afraid, but not giving in to it. He saw me as I was, as Ilona saw me, but I was still his liege, his commander.

"I want you to wait here until my return," I told him.

He nodded. "Yes, my lord."

"Good. Now bolt the doors behind me."

*　*　*　*　*

179

# P. N. Elrod

Following in the wake of the panicked soldiers, I made my way to the front courtyard. Two men had been posted to defend the entry, and though aware that something had gone wrong in their master's plan, they knew nothing more. They fought me as though I were an ordinary man like themselves, and like ordinary men, they died. I smashed one into a wall, the other I took and squeezed dry like a piece of summer fruit.

Those of their companions who had paused to watch now took to their heels, heading for the gate or the stables. If any of my own people survived, I did not see them, only the bodies of those who hadn't: guards in my colors, guests in bloodied silks and velvets, sprawling or crumpled, cut down as they'd run or stabbed as they lay helpless and dying from Leo's poison.

I did not see him among the men, but caught a glimpse of some riders going over the drawbridge at full gallop. I couldn't be sure if he were among them, but if so, it was all right. There was no place he could hide from me, no place of sanctuary for him anywhere. Sooner or later, I would find him. For now, I had to stop his men.

The blood I'd taken gave me more strength than I'd ever imagined, more than enough to call upon the darkness within and use it.

Part of my mind insisted that I could not do it, that I was too far away for the spell to work. But I'd changed. The old limitations no longer applied.

Quitting the steps, I bent and scooped up a handful of courtyard earth, closing it tightly in my fist.

*I, Strahd, am the land.*

Letting the knot of dirt drop, I said a word of power and

the portcullis crashed down and closed off the keep. Another word, and I'd sealed off the towers that held its lifting mechanism.

The men were trapped inside now, with me.

Some of them might just be able to push it up again and escape, but they would not be given that chance.

Striding over, I weighed into them like a fisherman in an overstocked stream. I still had the sword I'd taken from the guard I'd killed, and I put it to full use. They fought and screamed and died. Cutting or stabbing, their own blades passed right through me as though I were a wraith with no substance or nerve. It didn't take much of this to send them running back to the false safety of the open courtyard. There they milled around like sheep, holding their distance from me, afraid to separate from one another. A few broke off into groups and disappeared back into the keep, perhaps hoping to find a hiding place.

Like their master, they would find no sanctuary, for I knew every stone, every corner; this was my home.

My home . . . and their graveyard.

*    *    *    *    *

Three hours of it and I hadn't found them all, but they were cowed enough to go to ground and stay there. Most were barricaded in some of the rooms in the keep, alternately cursing and praying, for all the help it would do them. After their butcher's work among the guests, they couldn't possibly hope any gods would bother to listen to their frantic pleas for aid.

181

# P. N. Elrod

I'd left them and was returning to the main dining hall when a tired figure lurched from an alcove and all but dropped right at my feet. It was Gunther Cosco.

"Forgive me, my lord," he whispered.

He had no weapon. I put mine to one side, knelt, and lifted him into my arms like a baby. He seemed to weigh no more than one as I approached the doors and called to Victor. He opened them right away and I swept in.

Things were much as I'd left them: a room of blood and bodies, the stink of death and fear. Lovina was asleep in a corner; Ilona stood near Reinhold, who had not moved. I brought Gunther over and eased him onto the floor, then backed well away.

Giving me a guarded look, Ilona went to him.

In hard silence, Victor took in my torn clothes and the blood that drenched me from head to toe. He'd took it in and accepted it. He was a soldier and knew firsthand the filthy business of killing.

"All has been quiet, my lord," he reported. "But Lord Reinhold . . ."

"Dead?"

"Lady Ilona did all she could. He never woke up."

I nodded and watched her work with Gunther. She looked exhausted. After a time, she stood and stepped away, motioning for me to come.

Someone had ripped a hole in his belly, not enough to slay him outright, but he was dying now.

"Forgive me," he said again.

"For what? Your son?"

"Yes. If I could have done things differently. . ."

I started to agree with him, but Ilona caught my eye

and shook her head.

Irritating woman.

"Never mind, Gunther. It's not your fault."

His hand moved feebly, indicating his wound. "Had his men hold me down. Could have made a clean kill, but didn't. Wanted me to bleed. Said you'd finish me yourself. Doesn't know you as I do."

There seemed no answer to that.

"Did he escape?" he asked.

"Yes. I'll find him, though. I've sworn it."

Eyes glittering, he said, "Good."

And died.

\* \* \* \* \*

It turned out Tatra had made it to the stables after all. He and eight of the men were the only ones left out of my own guard. During my grim hunting game, I'd found them there and put them to work getting a carriage ready and horses saddled. They were nervously waiting in the courtyard by the time I returned with the other survivors in tow.

He'd picked the largest conveyance, which happened to belong to the Dilisnya house. I wasn't sure whether that would be a help or a hindrance to them with Leo on the loose, but it would have to do. I took him and Victor to one side.

"I formally release you and the others from my service," I said to Tatra.

This surprised and, I think, hurt him. "But my lord—" he began.

# P. N. Elrod

"I ask that you attach yourself to Lord Victor's house, to protect and serve him as loyally as you have served me."

He glanced at Victor Wachter, who was looking at me with sad understanding. "Very good, Lord Strahd."

I gave some last orders to him, this time framed as a polite request, and sent him off. Several minutes later, Tatra and two men reappeared from the keep, carrying the bodies of Reinhold, Gunther, and Ivan. They took them to one side of the courtyard and lay them down.

Victor shut his eyes, his grief catching up with him. "Oleka . . ."

"Ashes," I said curtly. "At midnight tomorrow you can begin saying your prayers for the dead." That was when I expected to have all the other bodies laid out along with a mountain of wood and an ocean of oil. The funeral pyre would be visible for miles.

"You're not coming, are you?" he asked.

"There's work yet to do. None of you must remain, or you could be caught up in it. This night I want you to ride fast and get as far away as you can. Do not stop for any reason and, as you value your life and soul, do not ever return to this place."

He demanded no explanations. "Yes, my lord."

"Tell Lady Ilona I said good-bye and . . . that I hope she never sees me again."

He nodded.

"I now formally release you from my service."

Though he must have seen it coming, this hit him like a physical blow; but there was nothing else either of us could really do. He held out his hand to me.

I looked at it for a very long time, thinking, and finally shook my head. "No."

He seemed to know why I chose not to touch him. A sensible man, he also did not offer any pity or condolences.

"Like Lady Ilona, you need say nothing of this." My eyes wandered from him to take in the rest of the keep.

"But, my lo—Lord Strahd—"

"Nothing. Now get out of here . . . while you still can."

He and his new men mounted up and rode toward the gate, the carriage following. A word, a gesture to empower it, and the portcullis raised itself just long enough for them to get through, then slammed down once more, locking me in with the dead . . .

. . .and those that were about to die.

# Chapter Six

## Sixth Moon, 352

Head down, I held fast to the rock face like some impossible spider and let my eyes roam this section of the mountain once more, hoping to find some trace of her passage. It was a sheer drop from the castle overlook a thousand feet above, and this would be the spot where her body would have first touched earth. Touched . . . and shattered.

# P. N. Elrod

I shook that thought from my mind. It had haunted me constantly during my initial searches. I knew what to expect. In my former life, I'd dealt with the horrid aftermath of death in countless forms: bodies hacked to pieces, burned black, in quiet repose, skeletal from decomposition, or bloated from watery immersion. For all my love for her, I could not delude myself into assuming Tatyana would be exempt from the normal course of nature.

By this time, she would have gone to bone, perhaps with some tatters of her white silk wedding gown clinging to them along with remnants of her thick russet hair. I still needed to find her, though, to at least lay those bones to rest. Enough of that former self remained in me to want to make some memorial to her, for in so doing, I might be able to find some peace within for myself.

The night after her death had been the beginning of my search, and I'd been down here nearly every night since then, going over each stone, peering into each crevice. No trace. Nothing.

Perhaps whatever had taken Alex Gwilym's body from a locked closet had seized her as well. I did not like to think about that possibility, yet it hovered on the edge of my mind like a wisp of poisonous smoke.

When autumn set in with its cold mists, I kept up my search, moving farther down the cliff face to the wooded areas below. I'd been through them already, but as the trees and bushes lost their leaves, I'd hoped to discover anything that might have been missed earlier: a thread of silk, a seed pearl broken off from her dress. On clear nights I was able to cover a vast amount of ground, but as always—nothing.

The winter had been especially harsh; the snow and ice made footing too treacherous even for me. During the worst of it, I shut myself up in my study and resumed magical experimentation, this time with greater success than I'd ever known before. The results of my work now stalked the halls of Castle Ravenloft. They were not company, but I'd wanted servants, not diversion.

Spring came, with its shortening nights and icy rains. I'd extended my search far beyond the area below the overlook, with the idea that some animal might have found and dragged her body away. I also questioned the shepherds who dared to keep their flocks this close to the castle. Had any of them found a maiden's body clad in white? None had, and by the way that I'd questioned them, I knew they spoke the truth.

I moved sideways now, hands and booted feet finding solid holds on the smoothest planes of rock—yet another power granted to me by my "pact with Death," as I had come to call it. Since then, I'd heard no more taunting voices. Sometimes I wondered if I should be thankful or wary over their absence. Most of the time I ignored the silence, having other cares to occupy me.

Like my constant need for blood.

For the last year, Leo Dilisnya's men had fulfilled that need. Singly or in terrified groups, I'd captured the lot, taking them down to the cells far below the keep, and successfully kept most of them alive in that time. By trial and error, I learned just how much to take to feed myself, yet not kill. Not that I harbored any thoughts of mercy for them; the idea was to enforce my own self-discipline. I could have drained each to the dregs and still hungered, but that would have quickly deprived me of a larder. Hence, I made myself break away before it was too late for the subject.

Of course, when I was very hungry, this was not so easy to judge.

As the men grew weak from their blood loss and confinement, they died. Not a few went mad. But I had no pity for them, for had I not myself seen to the disposal of their own victims? How cheerfully they had carved into the guests under my protection, no doubt thinking of the fine rewards coming to them from Leo. Most had not waited, and looted the bodies as they worked. I discovered this early on when one of them got the idea of braiding his torn garments together into a rope and hanging himself. Out of necessity, I had to deprive the rest of their clothing and thus found the stolen gold and trinkets. I let them keep their treasure, allowing them the opportunity to fully contemplate its true importance and price.

My trips to the dungeons to throw them food and drink would often yield up another corpse to be removed, which I did without complaint. When that happened, I left off my search for the night and carried the body away to my working room. There, by methods set down in detail in my books, I was able to put new life—of a sort—into it. Garbed again in my colors, they took the place of the slaughtered servants and armsmen, guarding and maintaining that which they had come to despoil.

It seemed only just.

My climb brought me to a craggy outcrop and a glimmer of white caught my eye; I clambered over to it, trying to suspend my hopes, but failing. It proved to be not a pearl or a diamond, but nothing more than a bit of quartz caught in the moonlight. I started to cast it away with a curse, then pocketed it at the last second. There was a slim chance I would have found it again on a future search and only repeated this present disappointment.

If I even bothered to continue.

I'd spent much of the last year crawling all over this face of Mount Ghakis like an ant searching for crumbs; little wonder if my discouragement began to outweigh my desire for solace. My fear that she'd been taken away as had Alek was looking more and more likely now, and if I wanted her back, perhaps another pact was called for. The question was, what else might be demanded of me in sacrifice? I'd lost everything already, at least everything ordinary humans placed a value on. What I had received in return . . . well, there was little point to any of it without Tatyana.

Secretly, so far back in my mind as to hardly be there, was the thought that if I was able to put her to a final rest, I would join her, to be her husband in death as I'd not been able to be in life. Splitting my heart with a staff of wood, cutting off my head, stranding myself in the sunny dawn—something could be arranged with or without help from others.

Death was not beyond me, if I chose to reach for it.

This night's search was coming to an end, though. I could scent the change in the air. Turning, I scrambled up the rock as easily as another man might walk over level ground. A trivial task now, and really too slow, but I only wanted to gain some extra height. Some thirty yards up, I summoned and gave in to a now inherent ability to change my very shape. My body began to shrink: arms closed in, fingers grew long, even my clothes melded to my flesh, turning into the softest of black fur. It was painless and freeing, and once the process was finished, I launched into the open air, catching the sky with my wings.

The wind was greater than I'd estimated; it had more impact on this form. Fingers stretched to their limit, I struck a steady beat with them and rose high, fighting the downdraft from the face of the cliff. Along with my shape, my vision had altered. I could see very well, but all color had been washed away; I still wasn't quite used to it. This was balanced by a considerable improvement to my hearing, allowing me to know within the smallest fraction the distance of any given object from me.

I spiraled up and up, first the cliff swinging into view, then the valley. Stars glowed hot above, cool darkness reigned below, and I soared carelessly in between, master of the air.

The overlook came level now, but I avoided it and sped toward the front of the keep. I'd made a small opening in an inconspicuous place above the doors and squeezed through into the front entry. Keeping this form, I flew swiftly through the rooms to the hall stairs and in a reverse of my ascent, spiraled down again. This passage was in total darkness, forcing me to completely rely on my ears to keep from hitting anything along the way. Near the bottom, I located another minute chink in the masonry and pushed my way in.

It was a long crawl for a creature of my size, a dozen feet or more, but shorter than the other way, which called for me to cut through the chapel and use the high tower stairs instead. The chapel was long desecrated and therefore safe for me to enter, but I still didn't care to go into it. The memories hanging there along with the dusty wedding decorations were too painful to face just yet.

I emerged into a vast chamber that housed the crypts of those who had lived here before me, and of a few who had died since my own occupation. Despite these quiet neighbors, this place was not silent. The heavy air was filled with the sound and motion of thousands of other bats, who had long ago established a sanctuary in this spot.

In the past, there'd been some talk by one of my engineers about destroying them, but I chose to let them live on, unmolested. The insect population in Barovia was legendary, and the bats were very necessary to maintain control over their numbers, especially in the late spring, when the sting-flies were rampant.

They were another reason why I did not use the high tower: it was their own particular entrance. Easy-natured animals that they were, I preferred to hold aloof from the colony and spare myself from their wild rush indoors by that route. I'd tried it once, entering with them beneath the eaves of the cone-shaped roof, then half-flew, half-tumbled nearly four hundred feet down to the crypts. It wasn't an experience I planned to repeat. The bats were gregarious, I was not—though I didn't mind their company, nor they mine.

I hovered in place and, with a sudden surge of inner

strength, resumed the shape of a man again. There was no light of any sort here, either, but I hardly needed it. The clustered bodies of the bats shed enough warm illumination for me to pick my way around the crypts and piles of guano. A few of the creatures knew me, perhaps recognizing one of their own in some way. They flapped down and lighted on my shoulders and arms, greeting me with joyful chirps and twitters. Two of the more spoiled ones landed in my open palm, allowing me to stroke their backs with the lightest touch of my little finger. Their fur was so soft as to hardly be felt. The ones on my head playfully tickled my ears and tugged at my hair.

But it was very late. I had no time to spare for socializing.

With a gentle shake to tell them to flutter back to their roosts, I made my way to the right and down some steps to my . . . tomb.

To be honest, I didn't know what else to call it. My bedroom and study were several stories above this place and were, for all practical purposes, where I lived. This was the place where I died. I'd never really held a fear of death itself, mostly a loathing of its attendant aging. As age had been eliminated for me, only death remained, measured out in palatable doses that lasted from sunrise to sunset. I'd resigned myself to it, having little other choice, and had come to welcome the soothing forgetfulness that encompassed my brain. It was better than sleep. No nightmares.

No dreams at all.

As might be expected of one who spends a portion of his time in death's embrace, I had a coffin. Any bed would have served, I suppose, but since it was already placed here and ready, it seemed a shame not to put it to use. It was excellent protection against intruders, human or otherwise. Though the chances were very slight of anyone finding his or her way down here, I knew most people aren't overly anxious to open up a coffin. On the other hand, anybody bold enough to get this far would hardly quail about going a bit farther, though I had allowed for that, making sure, by many different means, that no one could get close enough to disturb me.

But the primary advantage for resting in a coffin was that once the lid was lowered, I was safe from roaming insects and curious rodents. I could control and use such creatures, but didn't care to have them creeping all over me. It is a rare craftsman who likes to sleep with his tools.

The box itself was a brilliant example of the coffin maker's art, all smooth black wood with a highly polished and waxed finish, marred only by its brass fittings. When it had been commissioned years before, I'd specifically ordered them to be made from gold. The artist had promised to rectify the mistake. I was still waiting.

It rested, without dignity, right in the dirt on the floor— another problem that would likely never be corrected. The special black marble purchased for the finishing of this room and the construction of my crypt had been held up by some tariff dispute that had yet to be settled. Two years ago, I'd received a cringingly respectful notice from the owners of the warehouse where the marble sat, undelivered, inviting me to pay a nominal storage fee. I dutifully sent money and added a note that I'd be only too happy to reward them well if they could arrange a speedy delivery of the goods themselves. Again, I was still waiting.

That a man such as myself, with my dislike (while I lived) of all reminders of death, should have been so concerned with the disposal of my remains, may seem odd. The fact is, I suffered an occasional fit of practicality and had made arrangements during those brief periods, secure in the knowledge that I was the only one who would see that they were done correctly. Death, as I had come to know a thousand times over in battle, was an all-too-easy encounter for a soldier, or anyone, for that matter. Better to prepare for the worst then try to forget about it than put it off only to realize too late your survivors were going to botch things.

Of course, in all that time I had never once conceived that my coffin would be put to such an intermittent use.

The sun was coming. There were some stained glass windows facing east in another part of the crypt, so distant as to make the penetration of true light into this section impossible. But I was not about to take any risks. Yet another good reason to have a solid bit of wood between me and destruction. I raised the lid, stepped in and lay flat, lowering it as one pulls up a comforting blanket against the chill.

Silence . . . then oblivion. The sun was up.

\* \* \* \* \*

One year ago, my officers of the exchequer, ignorant of the terrible happenings that had taken place at Castle

Ravenloft, had seen to their tasks as usual. However, when they brought the taxes in a few days after and found the drawbridge raised and no one there to answer their hails, they grew decidedly uneasy. That evening, the wind carried the small sounds of their encampment over the walls to me.

I climbed up to the battlements of the curtain wall to have a look and was not a little surprised to find them settled between the gatehouses, cooking supper. They were a prosaic tie to a life I thought had been left behind. Now I came to realize I was yet ruler of Barovia, with responsibilities and duties to perform.

With *some* changes.

Roused from my many griefs by the needs of command, I quickly realized the officers could not be allowed to come inside the keep. As former soldiers, they'd recognize the brown patches staining the grass and earth of the courtyard as blood. That was alarming enough; but one side of the courtyard was still piled with the remains of the funeral pyre I'd made for my slain vassals and servants. They'd know something very serious had gone wrong here, and to not answer their questions about it would only invite morbid and—no doubt—highly erroneous speculation.

However, giving them the truth was an equally unwise move. I had no wish for anyone to return and plague me with hammer, stake, and holy symbols under the mistaken impression they were doing me a favor. My present existence did not look wholly enjoyable at the moment, but I wasn't ready to give it up just yet.

Several ideas came to me on how to deal with this situation, including having them join Leo's men in the dungeons. That had a certain neatness to it, but was quite bereft of honor: they were sworn into my service, and I, in turn, was sworn to protect them. My change from life to unlife had not negated that pledge.

After a period of long thought, I decided not to confront them at all. Returning to my study, I drafted a simple document instructing them to leave the tax money at the gate and consider themselves honorably discharged from my service. I invited them to seek employment with Victor Wachter and gave permission to their commander to dispense twenty pieces of gold to each man—twenty-five for himself—out of the tax money, and record it in the ledger. Rather trusting of me in a way, but the man had been with me long enough to know my supreme lack of tolerance for thieves.

Closing it with my personal seal, I tucked it into a pocket, assumed the form of a bat to fly over the wall, and landed in a stand of trees close to their camp. A man again, I crept in close, waited for the sentry to look the other way, and tossed the scroll among them. It happened to strike the commander squarely in the face, which woke him instantly and caused no small alarm and confusion for some time thereafter.

When they finally settled down, read the thing, and discussed it thoroughly, most of the night was gone. But in the end, they obeyed my final orders, albeit with extreme puzzlement; it was for the best, whether they knew it or not. They'd have a bit of a mystery to plague them, but better that than the truth.

The procedure of writing out my orders had worked so

well, I continued to employ it for all future business, public and private. It spared me from having to deal directly with people, something I had never relished, and afforded them a degree of safety from me. Despite my ample larder in the dungeon, in those early days I was not yet sure of my ability to control my new appetite. The wisdom of this was proved out by the occasional death of one of Leo's men when I forgot myself and overfed. Vast powers were mine to command, but arrogance and over-confidence had been the downfall of many others before me. Until I learned to master myself, I was my own greatest enemy.

But, ready or not, the first full moon after the summer solstice was on the rise, meaning it was time to take in the taxes.

*  *  *  *  *

By written orders, given first to the local burgomasters and spread by them to all the boyars, I made it known that they were to bring their collections to the Village of Barovia or to Vallaki, whichever was closer. There, they would turn the money over to the burgomaster, who would see to its final journey up the mountain to the castle. I made several copies of the order in my own hand and with all the official seals; I expected no trouble. My initial year of occupation—along with its judicious and much-talked-about executions—had inspired a new spirit of honesty in the land, after all.

As far as I could tell from my distant view of things, all was going smoothly. Upon awakening the next night, I went straight up to the east curtain wall and noted a number of new wagons and carts cluttering the narrow streets of the village below. There were also many more lanterns burning than usual, indicating a temporary rise in the population. The innkeepers and merchants were probably reaping a hefty benefit out of it, which they would have to account for next year, but for now all was good profit.

The night following the full moon, I looked down from the west wall and saw with approval that my orders had been carried out. Several chests stood waiting to be picked up, a task I could delegate to my silent servants as soon as I lowered the drawbridge and raised the portcullis. Summoning arcane power, I did this, adding to it a mental call for the things to trudge forth from the keep.

Wanting to supervise the task myself, I went across the bridge as soon as it was down to have a look around. This turned out to be a fortunate move on my part, as I discovered. Contrary to my instructions, someone had lingered behind.

This both angered and intrigued me. People ignored my orders at their own gravest peril. Danger aside, this was the first intrusion in a year of isolation, and I was interested in testing my self-control. Here also was my chance to speak with another person and determine if the changes in me were too obvious to go unnoticed. I discounted the opinions of the wretches in the dungeons; they had ever and always been a source of food, and I'd never bothered to conceal my true nature from them.

I paused halfway across to study my visitors: a mountain pony cropping grass just beyond the guardhouses and, standing close to it, a figure huddled in a traveling cloak. The cloak's hood was pulled well forward, for even in the summer the nights can be chilly this high up. We faced each other without speaking for a moment or two, then the pony must have caught my scent, for its head jerked up with a squeal of alarm and it tried to break away from the rope holding it to a tree.

I'd had similar experiences with the horses that had been left behind last year. The animals either adjusted or didn't. Those that could not tolerate me I eventually set free near some of the farms in the valley.

The pony, while not at all happy about my presence, eventually calmed down—if standing stiff-legged, trembling, and covered with sweat may be considered calm. Its owner turned toward me again, discovering that I had come in rather close.

She was a sturdy woman of thirty years, wearing the ubiquitous black clothes of mourning. The Barovian custom for females to wear black for five years after the death of even their most distant relatives lent a universal drabness to their dress. From the look of things, the woman's bereavement was a recent one, as the dyes had not yet faded in washing. The stark color suited her, though, as it did so few of her sisters. Her cloak was of fine wool, held at the throat by a brass pin with bits of glass set into it. Neither wealthy nor poor, she seemed to belong somewhere in between; probably a villager, as she looked too well-scrubbed for farming or herding sheep.

"Greetings, sir," she said, dropping into a passable imitation of a court curtsy.

# P. N. Elrod

"Were you unaware of the orders issued to the burgo-masters?" I demanded, forgoing further preamble. "You should not be here."

"I know that, sir, but it could not be helped." Her accent was slightly different from the local one and words came smoothly to her. She'd had some education, then, and was accustomed to dealing with people.

"Explain your presence. What caused you to disobey Lord Strahd's commands?"

"I am Dagmar Olavnya, Burgomaster of Immol, a village several day's ride south of here—"

"I know where it is."

Rather than being intimidated by my manner, she merely nodded and accepted the information. She'd probably taken me for one of the minor servitors of the castle, someone with a rank fairly equal to her own. "I was on my way to the Village of Barovia with Lord Strahd's tax money when we were set upon by thieves—"

"Who stole it all."

She did not miss the heavy sarcasm of my tone. "Half was stolen. They would have taken the other half if not for my brothers. Both were wounded trying to drive the men off. You can send someone down to the hospice in the village if you don't believe me. The oldest is still unconscious, and the youngest isn't able to speak yet because of the stitches, but he can nod and shake his head to questions."

I came near enough to stare right into her eyes. She stood her ground and met my look, but her firmness wavered after a moment. With hardly any effort on my part, my mind touched hard upon hers. Touched . . . and subdued. "Do you speak the truth, Dagmar Olavnya?"

"Yes," she whispered.

She was a fine-looking woman, and I had never been immune to the effects of beauty. It would have been regrettable to have had her whipped to death, as had proved necessary for the last burgomaster who had given this same story. It was good to know she was not the liar he'd turned out to be.

Removing my influence, I allowed her to awaken on her own. She blinked once, then resumed her tale as if there had been no break. "I came here to tell Lord Strahd of this crime and ask that he give Immol time to replace the missing half of the tax."

"Why not take it back from the thieves?"

"They ran off into the woods. An army could not find them now, much less myself and two wounded men who won't be able to ride for at least a week. Even if I went alone, I'm not skilled with arms."

"And if you were, you'd go after them?"

She started to answer, then turned it into a sigh. The first indication that she could smile played once over her face, like the gleam of light that comes and goes on a swift stream. "Perhaps not alone. That might be foolish."

"Very foolish," I added, with something like a smile trying to tug at my own features. Then I crushed it and the thought behind it and stepped away from her.

"Will you see that Lord Strahd hears my story?" she asked.

"He already has."

She had a quick mind. While some of the peasants, and not a few of the nobles, might have gawked and

# P. N. Elrod

asked for an explanation, she understood right away, instantly dropping into another curtsy and staying there.

"Forgive me, my lord, I did not know you."

I waved a hand at her, which she did not notice since her head was bowed. "Get up Burgomaster Olavnya."

She did . . . just in time to see the first of my servants stepping off the drawbridge. I was used to their looks by now, and though the stench was very bad, I had no need to breathe. But both of these qualities struck Dagmar— unprepared as she was—as a single heavy blow. She reeled back against her pony, her mouth opening for what should have been a hearty screech, but she seemed too much shocked to remember how.

Her pony supplied enough noise for them both. He gave out with a near-human scream and did his best to tear away again. My horseman's instincts came forth, and without thinking, I stepped in to keep him under control. If he got away in this part of Mount Ghakis, he'd be wolf food before dawn. I seized his bit and extended my will over him as I had done to his mistress, but with far less subtlely and greater strength. He instantly went quiet, though his trembling continued.

Dagmar had slipped over to the tree, her attention torn between the waiting servants and me. If I read her expression correctly, she was trying to decide which of us was the greater terror. I could have soothed her like the pony, but now seemed as good a time as any to give the peasants a tangible reason to keep their distance from the castle. Being a fearful and highly superstitious lot, it wouldn't take much.

"They won't hurt you," I said, glancing from the pony

to Dagmar.

She eventually found her voice, though not very much of it. Had I still been human, I might not have heard her. "What are they?"

"Dead."

Now her eyes focused wholly on me, as though she'd made her decision. "They serve you?"

"I am their master," I confirmed.

Her self-possession, of which she had a fair quantity, failed. She made the sign of protection against evil, but it was more a reflex action than anything else. Without true faith behind it, it had little power over me. In this case, the spiritual buffeting was negligible and easily ignored. I threw another silent command at the things, and they began lifting the chests and carrying them into the keep.

She remained frozen until the last of them had stalked back across the drawbridge.

"They said you were a devil," she murmured, watching the things go, her eyes seeming twice as big as normal. It made her look very young.

"Perhaps they were right." I withdrew myself a few yards upwind from her; the scent of her fear was just a little too tantalizing.

"What will you do with me?"

"Nothing."

That is, if she was very, very lucky. I hadn't fed tonight, and even across the space between us, I could hear the call of her blood. Another provocation from a different kind of hunger was the fact that it had been a long time since I'd lain with a woman. My appetite had changed me so that I was now finding myself as vulnerable as a new-bearded boy, and many times more eager than what was considered acceptable. I had to keep control of myself, or Dagmar would find herself unwillingly fulfilling both needs at the same time.

Turning from her, I dug my hands into my pockets. My fingers closed over the piece of quartz I'd found the other night. I clenched it tight, grinding its rougher edges into my palm. The pain was good. Distracting.

It also reminded me of Tatyana and my long search for her. I'd have to forgo it tonight in favor of other errands.

"Tell me about the thieves," I said, my voice somewhat harsh. "Tell me everything you remember, where and when, how many, their weapons . . . everything."

Dagmar had a store of courage in her, else she wouldn't have come up the mountain alone and against my orders in the first place. She drew upon it again and managed to give a fairly complete account of her misfortune.

"You were overmatched. Your brothers must have fought very bravely."

"They were soldiers during the war."

"Their commander?"

"Lord Markous."

He'd been one of the wedding guests. "A good man." Now a dead one.

"He trained them well."

"And it served them well." I paced up and down, working out times and distances in my head and concluding the trip wouldn't require me to stay out for the day. I'd speculated about journeys that would take me out of the sanctuary of the keep, but had never really planned anything. Though this one had been thrust upon me, I was suddenly looking forward to it. I'd shut myself away for far too long, and whether she knew it or not, Dagmar had caused me to realize the fact.

Pacing finished, calculations finished, I had but one more detail to see to.

"I shall have to insist you remain here for the rest of the night," I said. "It is too dangerous a journey down to the village in the dark, and the accommodations of the castle are, at present, limited." I was being diplomatic, thinking she wouldn't care to be in close quarters with the servants.

"There is plenty of moonlight. I can find my way back."

"Can your pony outrun wolves?"

She glanced at the shivering creature, then at the unrelieved blackness of the surrounding forest. I recalled that even the brightest noon sun had difficulty penetrating some of its more dense tangles. Though I could have commanded all the wolves in the area not to molest either of them, it would be better for her to stay here. Traveling over Mount Ghakis during the day was hazardous enough, at night she could lose her way . . . fall. . . . No. I would not have that happening again.

"Come over here." She followed me to one of the guardhouses. I pushed the door open. It was dusty inside, and we disturbed some birds nesting high above, but the space was dry and enclosed. "There's enough room for you both. The wolves of Mount Ghakis are ferocious, but I've yet to hear of one who could break through a handspan of oak. Have you food enough for the night?"

She nodded. "And water."

"Very well. Stay here. I may be back before morning, or I may not. Either way, you'll return to the village tomorrow." Again, if she was very, very lucky.

"Yes, my lord." There were questions on her face, but something within her may have warned of the folly of asking them.

She got her pony, leading him into the guardhouse, and I walked away into the darkness before I might forget myself and change her luck for the worse.

As soon as the road made its curve to the north, I took on wings, climbed high, and traveled east toward the village, leaving behind all the great switchbacks, covering several hours of travel in a fraction of the time. Flying more like a bird than a bat, I held my wings out and coasted on the air with little effort.

Yes, I had shut myself away for far too long. The air was clear and cold, with just enough wind to force me to work, and the labor felt good. It exhilarated and charged up my imagination with the potentials awaiting me. Tonight I would dance with the stars; tomorrow I'd race along the forest carpet with my brothers, the wolves, or flow like smoke into secret places never touched by a man. A fresh restlessness had come upon me; it was time to give up my constant brooding, and to explore.

\* \* \* \* \*

Once past the village and the ancient gates of Barovia, I paid strict attention to landmarks; just because I had mastered the art of flying did not mean I was used to reading the details of the ground. That which is familiar at eye-level looks totally different a thousand feet up. The castle was always at my back and would serve as my best guide for the return trip, but I needed to keep track of landmarks so as not to miss the spot where Dagmar and her brothers had been attacked.

About five miles past the gates, the Old Svalich Road and the River Ivlis made a gradual push to the north to go around a high spur of Mount Ghakis. It was an out-crop of equal height to the one the castle had been built on, and it might have also made a fine spot for a fortress. In fact, I had sent an architect and a party of engineers to see if just such a project was feasible and learned what previous generations had learned: the rock wasn't stable enough to support any structures. Faults riddled the summit, constantly breaking off boulders that littered the narrow pass at its feet; some of the stones even crashed down with enough force to splash into the river itself.

It was here that half a dozen men had burst, shouting, from the trees north of the road to trap Dagmar's party against the river. The fight had been vicious but short; the thieves were interested only in whatever money they could take—that, or Dagmar's brothers had made them think twice about the risks of taking aught else. They'd fled down the Svalich Road, boldly using it as though they had as much right to do so as any law-keeping citizen.

Drawn by the smell of dried blood lingering in the air, I found the place. A great patch of blood stained the dust of the road. One of the brothers had successfully killed a thief here. The body had been dragged off the road and interred in a hasty grave, I noted. Once Dagmar had reached Barovia, the burgomaster had sent people out to investigate, and they'd performed the burial, probably without benefit of any services—something that suited me well enough. I dropped down here and stretched into a man's shape again.

The grave was shallow and currently under excavation by wolves, who were enthusiastically digging at the mound of earth in hopes of an easy meal. They broke off when they sensed my approach. A pack of eight or nine adults, they now crouched and whimpered, anxious of my temper. I said a few words of encouragement and had the lot of them fawning at my feet, like hunting hounds looking for a scratch behind the ears. I indulged only a few and invited the rest to continue their digging. When they reached the body, I ordered them away. Whining unhappily, they obeyed, perhaps worried I would deprive them of their banquet.

I wrested the body from the hole and laid it out flat. He'd been a young man, and the earth clinging to him did not improve his already rough features, but I wasn't interested in his looks so much as the latent knowledge that might still be taken from him.

That would require the dark magic, but I'd performed the ceremony often enough, and carried the necessary components with me.

A drop of blood . . . a bit of flesh . . . a scant amount of bone, combined with the right words of power and he rose as one of mine, a new servant brought back for a specific task.

When he stood once again, empty eyes staring at nothing, the wolves fled silently into the forest. As their master, I could call them back if needed, but for now they could follow their instincts and leave in peace; their help was no longer required.

"Seek out your former companions," I told the thing.

It did not move very fast, but then, his friends had not gone very far. They'd made their camp less than a mile down the road from their crime and had taken no pains to conceal it. Outwardly, they looked no different from any other travelers; something they may have cultivated as cover.

In my time as a ruler, I noticed that those who, by circumstance or inclination, made their living from theft and murder were not especially gifted with a surfeit of brains. There were many exceptions to this, but for the most part thieves thought of little else beyond their next meal or the gratification of some immediate want. They were cunning enough to learn the skills needed for their work and to hide themselves either in the wilds or amongst the other men, but beyond that I found them to be rather naive. They always seemed horribly surprised when the consequences of their actions caught up with them.

The surprise of this particular band was all the more intense, though, since it was one of their own who walked in on them. To be fair, the fact that he was dead had the most striking influence on their reaction.

They'd posted a guard to watch while they slept, and he must have been on the verge of nodding off himself when he saw my servant emerge from the darkness beyond their fire. He gave a jump and caught himself, as though having second thoughts about what his eyes told him. Then, when the apparition failed to vanish before his now wide-awake mind, he let out a yell that carried all through the valley.

The rest of the band were jolted from their rest and on their feet and ready to fight before they had quite sorted themselves out. My servant stood motionless among them, and I derived much amusement watching the fools as they suddenly discovered his presence.

Their initial astonishment was soon replaced by the instant revulsion most people have for the dead—particularly for those magically animated. Their reaction was violent, and it made full use of their weapons. While their target was not at all fast, the damage he wrought against them bare-handed was appalling. He crushed the head of one man with a single blow, another got a broken arm when he strayed too close in his attack. The others learned caution, but had given themselves over to fear—a sign that they'd already lost the battle.

The watchman had backed out of the melee entirely. I could see he was preparing to risk the perils of the forest over this threat. He got only as far as the edge of the clearing before I swept him from his feet and slammed him into a convenient tree.

My servant, who was keeping the rest busy, was coming to the end of his usefulness. Of the two men left, one was either unconscious or too injured to move, and the other looked ready to bolt despite the fact that he was close to finishing off his former friend. He'd severed one arm at the elbow, restricting its ability to fight, but perhaps was unnerved because the arm continued to crawl toward him. That action appeared to alarm him more than anything else.

I might have found continued amusement in his frantic attempts to avoid it, but the night was passing. I canceled the magic that animated the corpse so that it collapsed back to its natural state of nonmovement, then stepped in and saw to the temporary disposal of the last able man.

Later, when they awoke to find themselves bound and helpless, with me standing over them as their judge, I saw to it that they made up for their late mischiefs in the fullest possible measure. Any other time, they'd have been put to the sword—the standard fate of a thief in this land—but as final arbiter of my own laws, I could make changes as I saw fit. Besides, such scum were beyond any honorable death from a blade. Instead, I raised the nearest struggling man up and, with the greatest of pleasure, tore into his throat.

And fed.

His blood raced through me like wind and fire, like the hot rage of battle, with its delirious blending of terror and joy.

When I'd finished with this one, I seized another who was screaming and fighting to get away and did the same to him, drinking deeply until nothing was left.

No need to ration myself, no need to take care not to kill, tonight I'd sup on the lot of them, adding their strength to my own.

\*　\*　\*　\*　\*

# P. N. Elrod

Some time after the feasting, I saw to my other work, deriving an unfamiliar satisfaction from labor that in the past I would have delegated to my lesser troops.

I'd found the stolen taxes on the bodies, along with a number of other monies, indication that they had been at their trade for a goodly time. I left the latter scattered about the clearing along with the bodies, free to any passing scavengers, whatever their interest.

As far as the money was concerned, one might liberally interpret this as being wasteful; I'd gone to such trouble retrieving Immol's tax that it might be thought I had sore need of the funds, but not so. This half of their paltry due was nothing to me. All I cared about was the fact that someone had boldly dared to take it, defying my authority. The armies I'd commanded were gone now, but I would always uphold the legacy we'd brought to this land, namely that I was lord and law here, and I would not suffer any incursions against me, whatever their form.

So it was that these thieves, now beheaded (the heads impaled on tall staves of wood to keep them out of reach of the wolves), would serve as an example to others who might think of taking up their base trade. I rammed the poles firmly into the earth next to the road, then, on a leather jerkin stripped from a body, carefully printed my warning, using blood for ink. It would do until the village burgomaster, under the orders he would soon receive, put up something a little more permanent.

I hung the garment from a crosspiece tied to one of the poles. It read:

# I, Strahd

"Thieves beware. I, Strahd, walk the land."

Making my way to the banks of the Ivlis, south of the road, I bathed the stink of my work from my face and hands, careful not to fall into the deadly stream, myself. (I'd learned from books of necrological lore that running water was no friend to me, but could only really be harmful if I were foolish enough to let my heart be immersed.) I finished my ablutions and took to the air again, beating my way back to the castle.

On her journey home, Dagmar would pass the place and perhaps shudder. Or perhaps not. She'd already seen my castle guards, and they were far worse to look upon than these harmless relics. She was a strong spirit.

Since she'd last seen me walking down the road, it seemed best to return from that direction, just in case she were watching. I could have saved myself the trouble; the door of the guardhouse was shut, and when I pressed an ear to it, I heard the steady breathing of one who is fast asleep.

Her pony—damn the beast—sensed me once again and made enough commotion to wake her. I heard her gasp of alarm, then soft movements as she got up and came to the door to listen. It made me think of some staged farce where two players unknowingly mirror each other's actions on each side of a door. I straightened and stepped back, then called to her.

She eased the door open, a knife in her hand. The woman had courage as well as spirit.

"My lord has seen some trouble?" she asked, putting the knife away. The moon was only just past its full, and it still rode high in the sky, shedding more than enough light for her to see clearly. My clothes were not in the same orderly state as when I'd left her.

"Not really. I found the men, avenged your brothers' injuries, and took back Immol's taxes."

"So fast? But they were miles to the east."

I waved a hand with vague unconcern. "I have my ways."

"Magic?"

"You could call it that."

She started to make the protective sign, but caught herself this time. She didn't quite smile. A pity. I would have liked to see it. "I thank you, my lord. All Immol thanks you."

"You're welcome."

And at that point, she did finally smile, and I was not disappointed. As I'd suspected, it was most charming.

"The tales they tell of my lord are true, then," she added.

I raised one brow. "What tales?" Village gossip was bound to be unkind.

"That he is a brave fighter for those in need."

Yes, perhaps. Once upon a time. Her flattery was more than a touch obvious, but not unwelcome. Vanity aside, I realized Dagmar was definitely interested in me, or else she would have asked leave to go back to her broken sleep by now. When I made the suggestion for her, she politely declined and, while watching me closely, indicated sleep was the last thing on her mind.

*Well, well,* I thought. Despite the other stories she'd doubtless heard and the walking horrors she'd seen herself, she was still willing to keep me company. Women had always amazed me with their ability to ignore a man's drawbacks so long as they found him attractive. On the other hand, men such as I once was suffered from the same malady; but in Dagmar's case, there were no drawbacks.

"You're in mourning," I stated. "May I ask for whom?"

"My mother's oldest sister. A fever took her last month."

"That is too bad. You have a large family?"

"Very large."

"A husband?"

"He died eight years ago," she said in a tone that settled things between us.

I had never been one to deny a lady anything reasonable, and this particular request stuck me as being well within my scope. I'd fed well, so she was in no danger from me there—at least for this night. And, unless I was very wrong, one night was all either of us really wanted.

The moon settled behind the mountain peak, throwing a shadow like a black velvet blanket over us both.

# Part III

Part III

# Chapter Seven

## Sixth Moon, 398

*I've left it too long,* I thought. *The bastard will be dead by now.*

And I meant the epithet in its every sense, for literally and figuratively, all its varied meanings applied to Leo Dilisnya.

Nearly fifty years had passed since that night of death, when he'd made his attempt to seize the rule of Barovia. Those men he'd left behind in his haste to escape had paid

# P. N. Elrod

heavily for their crimes, but it was past time that their master faced justice. If he still lived.

Now that I'd been moved to take action, I had little tolerance for further waiting . . . but found myself forced to do so, anyway. I paced up and down in the antechamber, hands clenched behind my back one minute, balled into fists and swinging in the air the next.

*I've left it too long. Where have the years gone?*

For gone they were, never to be retrieved. Not that I had much need to care about time in regard to myself, but, busy in my keep with dozens of fascinating projects, I'd forgotten about time's effect on others. So it was that, when I finally took it upon myself to visit the head of the Wachter family, I was unprepared to find Lovina Wachter was not the fragile-looking child I'd last seen, but a solid, energetic woman in her middle fifties. Indeed, there was no connection between the old image in my mind and the reality standing before me.

She extended her hand. "Welcome, Lord Vasili."

I briefly touched the tips of her fingers with my own and bowed. "You do me much honor, Lady."

After inquiries to my health and to whether I needed any refreshment—which I graciously declined—she asked me to be seated. We were in the receiving hall of the Wachter home, and it had changed little from those days when her father had been my host. Tapestries of old battles, gently faded, covered the walls; the same furniture, built to last generations, cluttered the floor. There seemed to be a lot more flowers and pillows than I remembered, but that was probably Lovina's influence. As she took her own seat, she started up almost immediately, as though having a sudden change of mind. She half-turned, dug under the cushion, and pulled forth a colorfully dressed doll with button eyes and a sewn-on smile.

"I see my granddaughters have been playing here again," she said ruefully. Decades ago, her obliging husband had taken on the Wachter name so that it might be continued. Obviously this branch of the family tree had been fruitful. She finally settled herself with the doll in her lap and absently stroked its yarn hair. "Now, sir, may I ask why you have requested to see me?"

"I am here as an envoy for Strahd Von Zarovich," I said without the usual formal preamble required by an official visit.

Though the appearance of a messenger from Castle Ravenloft was something she must have been expecting, she went absolutely still at the announcement. Her eyes went first glassy, then hard like blue diamonds as they focused on my own. I kept a bland face and hoped she had not remembered me; more likely it was my name alone that had inspired her reaction. The reputation of the castle and its now infamous lord had grown darker with each passing year. I had personally done nothing to correct the stories and rumors as it had been my experience that when one denies a falsehood, people then and there determine it must be entirely true. Lovina was not demonstrating fear, though—I'd have smelled it—but something resembling avidity . . . or hunger.

Lovina looked at me minutely, taking in every detail, from my well-tailored traveling clothes to the carefully made and slightly dusty riding boots. I had put myself to some trouble over my looks, and trusted she would find nothing out of the ordinary about me. My hair was combed to hide the points of my ears, and I'd even managed to cut my nails down to an acceptable length since, in certain social situations, it was considered rude to wear gloves.

Scrutiny over, she gave a stiff, seated bow. "Then I am the one who is honored, sir."

"My lady is very kind. Lord Strahd sends his warmest greetings to you and your house and, if it may not be considered too late, his condolences over the death of your good father. He is remembered as a great man and a valiant fighter."

"Thank you," she said, somewhat taken aback. Victor Wachter had died some twenty-six years ago. I'd have sent a message then, but Lady Ilona had still been alive, and it had not seemed . . . appropriate. "I hope that Lord Strahd is enjoying good health."

"He is, Lady. Remarkably so."

I could almost see her adding up sums in her head and working out that Lord Strahd was in his nineties. Ninety-two to be exact.

I drew out an oilcloth packet from my coat and opened it. "Here is a letter you wrote him and a letter of introduction for myself, which he was generous enough to pen in his own hand."

She took both sheets of parchment and read the introduction right through. As the head of an important house, she would know my writing well enough by now from past documents. This one told her that I was Lord Vasili Von Holtz (I had combined the given name of my great-grandfather with that of his wife's maiden name) and that she was to consider my voice the voice of Strahd in all matters and render me every reasonable assistance for my errand. The bottom of the sheet was properly stamped, and it carried a wax seal impressed with the Von Zarovich coat of arms. She studied it all at length, making me glad I had prepared things so fully.

"I have heard the Von Holtz name, but am not familiar with it," she said.

"We are an old house and, though loyal to Lord Strahd, have not been as visible in our service to him as have others." This was a diplomatic way of informing her I was not going to give a lecture on Vasili's personal genealogy. "However, the honor has fallen to me to make up for it, hence my journey here. Lord Strahd was very interested in your news."

She looked over her own letter as if to refresh her mind. It was tantalizingly brief, stating only that she was certain she'd located Leo and asking if Strahd was as anxious as she to bring the man to justice; she was prepared to cooperate with him to that end. "This sounds rather pompous, doesn't it?"

I made a gesture indicating that the thought had not occurred to me.

"What exactly is your errand, sir?"

"I am charged with finding and executing Leo Dilisnya. Here—" I gave her another sheet of parchment, "—is his death warrant, signed by my lord Strahd."

This inspired another study. "You will kill him?"

"If you but direct me to him."

She apparently decided I was more than capable of performing the task. "Do you know why he is condemned?"

"I am acquainted with the facts. It has been many years, but Strahd has never given up his hope of finding and dealing with the traitor."

This was true, though if I had not let myself get distracted, it wouldn't have gone on for so long. To be fair, in all that time the trail had grown quite cold. Barovia was not that large a place, but somehow Leo had managed to bury himself very thoroughly. It was logical to conclude he'd readied a sanctuary in case his coup failed. The only thing I was certain of was he hadn't escaped the country. Since the night of his betrayal, the borders of Barovia had been, for all purposes, closed.

Lovina set the parchments to one side. "Lord Vasili, before you were born, my mother, sister, and brothers were butchered by Leo Dilisnya. My aunts and uncles-. . ." She broke off to put a hand to her mouth, then turned it into a fist and forced it away again.

"How much do you remember of it?" I asked, softly.

"Everything. They say you can sometimes forget bad things from childhood, but this has always been with me. Sometimes I can still hear their screams. Can you understand a memory like that?"

"I believe so, Lady."

"My father and I would have also died but for the intervention of Strahd Von Zarovich. For that debt, and to see justice finally served, I wrote this." She tapped the paper, then stared beyond my shoulder as if into the past. "My father was . . . haunted by Leo for years. His wife and children killed, and he unable to save them, he spent the rest of his life searching for Leo and died thinking himself a failure because he'd not found him. I promised father I would continue his quest. This year has seen the fulfillment of that promise, not, I regret to say, by my active efforts, but by accident. But no, surely it must be by the will of the gods. They've heard my prayers, and this was their answer."

And surely they must have been testing my nearly nonexistent patience. "Lady. . ."

She obligingly snapped back into the present. "But before I tell you more, we must have an agreement."

"Lord Strahd will not be ungrateful," I said cautiously.

"I don't want money. I want my family avenged."

"Then it is not enough that Leo simply be put to death?"

Her eyes glittered.

"You want him . . . punished."

She licked her lips and nodded. "Can you promise me that?"

"My voice is the voice of Strahd," I said truthfully. "If Leo still lives, he shall receive all that he deserves."

"And more?"

I smiled. "Yes, Lady."

\*   \*   \*   \*   \*

Lovina took me to her study and, on a beautifully painted map of the country, pointed to a spot on the flanks of Mount Baratok overlooking Lake Baratok.

"This is absurd," I said, forgetting myself. "It's barely a three day's ride from Castle Ravenloft. He would not be such a fool as to live so close to—to Strahd."

229

# P. N. Elrod

She stiffened, her lips thinning at my lack of manners. In this case, she had the superior ranking and was entitled to a more respectful behavior from me.

Lord Vasili bowed slightly. "Forgive me, Lady, but I—"

"Never mind. Look at this map." She pulled out a detailed rendering of Baratok itself. It bore the name of every village and valley, cliff and cleft. She indicated a small rectangle representing a building of considerable size perched high on its northwestern spur, right at the border.

My spirits sank. "A monastery? You're certain?" From my point of view, Leo could not have picked a worse place for me to find him.

"I saw him. This month I was invited as a guest to their Festival of the White Sun. I was introduced to some of the residents who live there. They have students, artists, scholars—he was one of them, going under the name of Henrik Steinman."

"And you recognized him after all these years?"

She'd expected some doubt. "Yes, I was but a child then, but there are certain sights, certain images that are burned into my mind. I remember Leo standing over us and my being too afraid to look at his face, so I fastened my eyes on a gold chain he was wearing. Hanging from it was a pendant in the shape of a roaring lion. It had ivory teeth and ruby eyes worked into the gold. Steinman was wearing that pendant. He'd had it remade into a broach, but there cannot be another like it."

"If that is so, why keep something so identifiable? And why would he wear it if he knew you would be there?"

"I couldn't say. Perhaps he'd forgotten, or he may have thought I was too young to remember."

"Or it may be the wrong man."

"Then that is something you must determine for yourself, but *I* know the old man I saw was Leo."

And I was hoping she was mistaken. A monastery . . . the thought of even going near one, much less entering it, made my belly churn. Leo had most certainly realized the exact nature of my change that night. What better place of protection could he find from a creature like me than a house of holiness? It was also the very last place in Barovia where I would look for him.

"How long has he been there?"

"Several years, on and off. As a visiting dignitary, part of my duties included exchanging greetings with the lot of them, and I used it to ask questions. He was vague, of course, and I could not appear overly interested in him, or he'd become suspicious. I put the same general inquiries to a number of people to cover myself."

"Good. What do you mean 'on and off'?"

"Residents are not required to stay and may come and go as they please. I got the impression he'd bred a family somewhere."

"How delightful," I said, my sarcasm matching her own. "Just what Barovia needs: another crop of traitors like himself. You don't happen to know where they might be?"

"I wish I did," she said with an expression that would have made her gods think twice about blessing her with the information. "For then would my family be perfectly avenged: a wife for a wife, children for children . . . with Leo watching, of course."

"Of course," I agreed. It was the polite thing to do.

# P. N. Elrod

For the sake of appearance, I had traveled to the Wachter lands by coach, resting in the safety of its dark interior by day, and cantering along on one of the horses by night. It was a great black conveyance, bearing my coat of arms on the doors. These alone were enough to inspire either instant fawning service from the locals or their disappearance altogether whenever I passed through a village.

Lovina offered me hospitality readily enough, but I turned it down in favor of an immediate start on the last portion of my journey. The fact that it was well after sunset was of concern to her, and I had to give assurances that darkness was a decided advantage to me on this errand. She took this to mean that I had some subtle scheme in mind and was not planning to boldly present myself to the abbot of the monastery, which was essentially correct. In fact, avoiding contact with all members of that order was a most desirable course for me to follow.

My horses were still fresh, having rested during the day and not been driven far that night, so I instructed her grooms to hitch them up to the coach again, including a saddle for one of them. It was my habit to ride with the horses rather than to drive them, the seating being considerably more comfortable. The men wondered how I managed to brake the coach, but my story that I never went fast enough to justify its use seemed to satisfy as well as amuse them. As it happened, I could control the vehicle's workings as easily as the gates to my castle, and by the same magical means, but they had no need of such knowledge.

I oversaw their work, still impatient, but only became really irked when several barking and baying hounds objected to my presence. It was a relief to mount up and be off.

The coach rattling behind me (empty but for my baggage and a long, light-proof box), I guided the horses back onto the Old Svalich Road and followed it northwest for several miles, stopping short where it forded a broad river. Past the ford it turned due west, but my goal was on this bank, a rougher road that paralleled the path of the water and would take me north toward the monastery. Lovina had given me careful directions to follow and clear and detailed information on the lay of the land, readily answering all my questions. My final query, though, startled her somewhat.

"Have you a crypt or a place of burial here?" I already knew the answer from my past visits decades ago, but "Lord Vasili" did not.

"Yes," she said, her wonderment extremely plain on her face. "We have a cemetery just south of the main house."

"With a mausoleum?"

"Yes . . ."

"And does it have room left for additional occupants?" She nodded.

"Excellent." I managed to avoid explaining myself on that one and left soon after.

The road made a steady climb and leveled. I now skirted the edges of Lake Baratok, the source of the river, with the water on my left and the mountain high and brooding on my right, passing the occasional hut of a fisherman or hunter. No lights showed, though I did catch movement when a shutter was cracked to allow those within to peep out. The road was in good condition, indicating traffic was not unknown here, but for anyone to be using it after dark was highly unusual. I supposed if I went knocking on one of the doors and asked for lodging, it might even be given. This was a corner of the country I'd not been in for a very long time, after all. The peasants closer to my castle had, with justification, become a tiresomely cautious lot over the years and never voluntarily opened their doors after the sun went down.

But I was not planning to seek out sustenance just yet. In fact, when I arrived at the monastery, I *wanted* to be hungry.

Within an hour, I was approaching the source of the lake, a fast-flowing river that began as a spring deep within the mountain. Some long-ago builder had constructed a stone bridge here with an arch high enough to put it out of reach of the heaviest spring flood. The monks maintained it since it now was their only real link to the rest of the country. There was another road on the north side of the monastery, but that was no longer used: it led only to a dead end at the border.

When I took the coach over the bridge, the trees thinned briefly to offer me a glimpse of a vast building perched on a steep tier of rock nearly as high as that of my own home. On her state visit, Lovina had gone up by way of a series of switchbacks carved into the rock, which had served the monks for centuries. The horses and coach could manage without too much trouble, but it suited my plans to leave them here at the base of the cliff, where they were less likely to be noticed. Guiding the horses into a stand of pines, I dismounted and listened with all my senses to the woods around us.

Almost immediately, the wolves began to howl. They knew me. All the wolves of Barovia did.

The call of their many voices was too much for me to ignore. Before another minute passed, I had joyfully assumed their form (the horses, fortunately, were well used to this) and thrown back my head to join the chorus. My four-legged brothers heard me and rushed from their places in the shadows to give greetings. Soon I was surrounded by their slightly smaller but no less shaggy forms, the mated leaders rolling onto their backs and licking my muzzle to show their respect. Others crowded in, whining, tails tucked down, also hoping for some scrap of attention. On any other night, I might have given it, but not this one. I rose high and changed back into a man again and, by means I knew but could not readily explain, instructed them to guard the coach until my return.

Now it, the horses, and most importantly, my box were as safe as could be expected, given the circumstances.

I delayed just long enough to obtain some necessary items from my baggage and, with these tucked securely into my clothes, wasted no time in taking on the shape of a bat.

Wings lifting me above the trees, I got my bearings and began to beat my way up to the white building on the cliff. The air became colder and the wind more pronounced, but these were nothing compared to a gradual but unmistakable external pressure pushing against me. So far I was successful in fighting it, but the closer I came to my goal, the greater my dread of reaching it. I swung far out from the face of the cliff, so that once I was actually level with the monastery, I was still a quarter-mile distant. Circling wide to the east, I lighted on the forested ground and, panting, resumed my own form once more.

Panting, I say, not because I needed to breathe, but because of the awful aura of the place. Even this far away, I could feel it thundering all around me like a great drum. I sprawled, helpless for a moment while I gathered my strength and wits to resist it. Having always possessed a strong will, I was able to do so, but not without expending quite a lot of effort.

It would not get any better for me unless I acted. From my pockets I drew out a special tinderbox and a censer holding a piece of dry dung. With the help of one, I set fire to the other and waved it in a specific pattern before me while uttering the words of power.

Not many seconds later, the pressure decreased dramatically and was soon gone altogether. I sighed and rubbed my aching temples, then put away the tinderbox and shook the censer empty, shoving it into a pocket while it was still hot. I wasn't sure how long the spell would last and had to assume every second was precious. A bat once more, I flew as fast as I could toward the sheer walls of the monastery.

\*　\*　\*　\*　\*

Crouched in a deep shadow in the angle of a staircase, I tried to make myself small; for a man of my height, this was no easy task, and I chafed at the discomfort. Little wonder I caught the attention of a lone monk as he padded down the stairs. I'd been hoping to find such a creature. He glanced into the patch of darkness, must have seen something of me, and stopped cold to stare. I gave him no chance to do anything else, but launched up and swept him right from the steps like a leaf in the wind.

He was young and still new to his vocation, otherwise I might have had some trouble with him. As it was, I got only a negligible crack in the shins from his foot before swinging him around and locking my eyes on his. My inner desperation must have lent greater strength to the mesmerization, for despite the depth of the shadows I was able to quickly subdue his will to mine. Make no mistake, I was getting desperate. This place was far larger than I'd expected, and I had only the vaguest idea where the visitors resided. I needed an ally to help me, and though I very much would have preferred someone other than a holy man, there was no time to wait for anyone else to come along.

"Henrik Steinman—where is he?" I snarled.

The young fellow's pupils were but pinpoints, even in the dark. Looking blind, he pointed without hesitation up the stairs he'd used. Deeper into the buildings. Exactly where I did not want to go.

"Take me to him. Quickly!"

I released my grip on his shoulders, and he complied with gratifying speed. If not for my long legs and unnatural strength, I'd have been hard put to keep up with the little man. The training for monks is highly rigorous; even an acolyte often has a surprising store of energy to call upon when needed. This one was not even breathing hard when we reached the top of several long flights and trotted down a lengthy walkway on the north wall of the building. I was concerned we might be spotted by others while out in the open, but I saw no one else. It was past midnight; perhaps everyone was in bed.

The walkway, which was part of the curtain wall, overlooked a vast number of structures in the keep. Some had an obvious use, like storage or shelter for livestock; the purpose of many others I could not readily determine, nor did I really care. All I wanted was to find Leo and get out again before my protective spell wore off.

On our right, the walls dropped at least a hundred feet straight down to a narrow ledge that dipped away at a sharp angle. Several yards beyond this chasm the rock resumed again at the same level as the foundations. It may have been a naturally formed defense, as was the case for my own castle, or not. Between their prayers and ceremonies, the monks must have had some free time, and cutting away whole sections of a mountain might have been just the sort of activity they'd enjoy—so long as it could somehow be said to serve their god.

Winding out from the monastery was the north road, which had once led to the Dilisnya estates. It lent some credence to Lovina's story, for Leo's initial choice of escape might have taken him in this direction, back to his home territories. But it also provided an excellent reason to discount her claim, for Leo would know I'd look this way first and try to cut him off before he could reach safety. He may have gambled on my lack of men and the burden of responsibilities to slow me down, for that was how things had turned out. In either case, the one factor he could not have known was that the dark magic that had changed me had also changed the land. It must have been a dreadful surprise to him to reach the borders and find them . . . closed.

In other lands the boundaries are marked by rivers, mountains, or by an invisible line on a map in the possession of whatever lord had claimed it. In Barovia, the line was less commonplace and highly visible to all. By day or night, stretching up to the limits of vision, the edges of my realm are marked by a great wall of mist. Mile after mile, it rings the entire country without break, following the contours of peak and valley, impervious to the hottest summer sun or the fiercest winter wind. It was a familiar sight by now, but still disturbing. I was there at its birth nearly half a century ago, when it rose from the earth itself to flow in a slow spiraling dance around me and my beloved Tatyana. From that moment, the mist had expanded out to the borders of the lands I'd conquered and there stopped.

I knew back then, in the same way that I knew how to talk with wolves, that Leo would never escape Barovia.

The borders were closed. No one would cross them. No one did. No one could.

Including myself.

Years ago I'd made an attempt to do so, plunging into the heavy air like a reckless ship entering a fog bank. I walked in a barren land, bereft of tree and grass, and

## P. N. Elrod

somehow, no matter how far I walked, I always found myself turned and emerging from the mist into Barovia again. Once, I'd even tied a piece of thread to a tree on the edge of the border and, by the means of this child's trick, tried to stay on a straight line after I entered. Futile. Instead of coming out on the other side and into the next land, I found myself standing a bare twenty feet from my starting point, both ends of the thread stretched taut where they vanished into the gray air.

The mist was magical, of course, and its nature occupied a good part of my many studies over the years. If magic could create it, then magic might also dispel it, but in all that time I'd not been able to discover the right incantation.

Yet another distraction from dealing with Leo.

The monk made a turn toward the keep and went down another flight of stairs. The buildings here had many windows and more doors than the others, an indication that they were used as habitations, but what I found truly striking about the area was the lighting. Iron poles had been erected at intervals along the alleys. They were about ten feet tall and each terminated at the top with a brightly glowing ball. The light, I knew, would shine day and night forever, or until the magic cast on them was canceled or destroyed. Some of the priests had gone to considerable trouble over this. But, living as they were, so close to the border, they may have found the extra light a comfort that more than justified the effort of its creation.

Much to my disappointment, my guide headed straight toward this area. I had no choice but to follow.

He led me into the alleys, and though they were laid out in an orderly pattern, crossing one another like latticework, it was their very regularity that confused me. Each door looked exactly like its neighbor, and only by means of the names painted on them could one determine the identity of the tenant. Without help, I might have wandered here all night looking for Steinman.

The monk came to a halt before a door bearing that name. My first thought was to let him continue with whatever errand he'd been on, but if my quarry were not at home, I would need the priest's assistance again. Besides, I had come hungry; he had other uses.

"Stand to one side and do not move," I told him.

He obeyed.

It never occurred to me to knock; I simply grabbed the handle and began to push, then arrested all movement. There was no need to announce myself to the old man by barging through the door. He might start screaming for help out of sheer surprise, and what I needed to do required that we be undisturbed for a short period. No sense in having him in hysterics and making enough noise to raise the . . .

Never mind.

I let myself relax—quite a feat, given the circumstances—and the burden of a solid body was no longer mine. I floated upon the wind like a wisp of smoke or a tendril broken away from the border mists. A spin and dive, and I was pouring under the door, flowing silently into Steinman's room like creeping death.

Resuming shape, I caught the barest glimpse of a windowless chamber before staggering and stumbling

# P. N. Elrod

into something that felt solid but was not. It seared my skin and tore into my lungs like acid. Instinctively I raised my arms to ward it off, but touched nothing but air . . . air that was . . . poison. I gagged and clawed at my throat, but what was choking me had nothing to do with breathing.

Every corner from floor to ceiling was filled with half-visible tracings that grew brighter as they pulled at me. The room itself was under heavy protection, or I'd have sensed the threat and been wary of entering. Signs, sigils, holy symbols from a dozen different worships covered the walls. They'd been placed there by true believers, weaving a grasping net like a spider's web, and I'd blundered right into it. My own protective spell had been severely weakened, and when it was gone . . .

*Too late.*

The onslaught of the latent magic in this chamber was too much. My inner strength was insufficient to hold it off. Like a garment whipped away in a tempest, so went my spell, leaving me enfeebled and naked before the raw forces around me. The initial shock was too great to bear; I fell to my knees—right into the fiery white center of a holy sign painted on the wood floor.

It was like sinking into burning quicksand: the more I struggled against it, the harder it dragged on me. Other magic was at work as well, pushing my limbs this way and that until I was flat on my back, my arms and legs stretched to their limits; I was helpless, unable to fight by gesture or word.

No voice of darkness held me this time and mocked my innermost desires. This was a different sort of force than that which had come to me decades ago. I was bound by sheer impersonal power now, not struck immobile by pain, though there was pain enough.

And as I lay there, straining against invisible bonds, I felt myself thrown back to that moment in the dining hall, my body weak and torn by many wounds as Leo Dilisnya came to stand over me. It seemed to be happening again, for a man of his height and build came near and peered down. He was not the old man that Lovina described, nor the young one I remembered, but rather the young one with only ten more years of life imprinted on his pale face. Was this Leo's son?

He stared for a long moment, then said, "Hail, Strahd, Lord of Barovia."

I knew for certain, then, for never would I forget the mocking timbre of his voice. Lovina had been right. Despite appearances, this was Leo Dilisnya.

"I've waited ages for you to come," he continued. "It took Lovina long enough to get you here."

Could she have been his—? No, impossible. She'd have sooner strangled one of her own grandchildren as help Leo. His dupe, perhaps? That was more likely.

He made a gesture, muttering words I almost recognized. The unseen bonds holding me grew stronger, snaking over my limbs, sinking in and freezing fast like a tree root clutching hard at the earth.

"Stop," I whispered, hardly able to speak for the pain.

He paused and smiled. "That's good." He walked over to one corner and lifted up a long pole that I first took to be a walking staff. It was carved with words of power that glowed to my heightened sight. They writhed all down its length, moving as he moved. One end was blackened, charred by fire for strength. It came to a very sharp point.

"How you do stare," he said. "But what else is there for you?"

"How—?" I asked, hoping he would explain himself.

He was more than willing. "Did you think I spent all this time skulking in holes in dread that the terrible Lord Strahd would find and kill me? You must have. Arrogance was ever a failing with you. A good ruler should not hold too much of that quality. It clouds his judgment."

"Waited . . . for me . . . to come?"

"There's a difference between waiting and expecting, Strahd. I've had years to prepare for you. I put it to good use, to good work, studying the Art. I'm as much a master as you, now. What have you done? Frightened a few peasants with your walking corpses? Drained the blood from any wenches that took your fancy? Yes, I've kept up with gossip about 'the devil Strahd.' Devil, indeed. You've wasted yourself. If I'd had your abilities, I'd have put them to more profitable use."

Had I been in a strategically better position, I might have offered an appropriate return comment to that.

"I suppose you pictured yourself just walking in and smothering me like a candle. What had you to fear from one old man, you thought? All you expected to worry about was getting into this place. It's that arrogance again."

My eyes fixed hard on the ceiling as I tried to concentrate. It was also painted with symbols, glowing with the force only true faith can impart. Leo could not have put them there, I was sure. His faith was in himself; he had none to spare for the gods. However, he was an expert at lies and must have spun a pretty tale to the many obliging holy people who had done the work. He'd have been careful to choose the ones with equal shares of belief and naivete, avoiding those who might ask awkward questions about such an elaborate project.

They'd been thorough; there was not a single niche in all the room that offered any respite for me. Very well. Do without.

He poked me in the ribs with the staff. I ignored him, but could concentrate for only a few seconds. The destructive spell latent in the wood was too disruptive to my thoughts. "None of that for you, now. I can tell when you try to summon magic, so don't even bother."

My summoning wasn't magic, though, but something older, more dangerous. Had it worked? I tried to sense it, but there was so much power running through the room, I couldn't tell.

"You should have died that day we entered the castle. It would have been so much better. I've always wondered . . . how did you know?"

I said nothing.

"No harm in telling me now. Who warned you?"

"Alek," I grated out.

"Yes, of course, but who warned Alek?"

*Keep him busy.* "Soldier . . . named Vlad."

His brows pinched. "Vlad? But I'd killed him."

"You—?"

"He overheard some things he shouldn't. I *thought* I'd

247

killed him, anyway. There was so much going on during that last battle I must have gotten careless and rushed things. So he lived long enough to . . ." He shook his head with disgust. "All my plans thrown off and spoiled because I was in too much of a hurry to see the job through. Well, Lord Strahd, the death I'd planned for you is fifty years late in coming, but catching you up at last."

Had it worked? I thought I felt movement beyond the door, but it might have been only wishful thinking.

"Trying for . . . the lordship again?" I gasped out, wanting—needing him to talk.

"Oh, yes. I'd never given up on that. You've been a help to me, did you know? You crept about Castle Ravenloft with your stinking toys and stayed out of sight, so it was easy enough to spread rumors about you. Nothing really awful, of course, like the truth of what you'd become, but the sort of stories to keep the fear alive. Have you heard them? My favorite is the one about how you murdered your brother, drove his bride to her death, and then killed all the wedding guests the same night. That's quite a lot of work for one man, don't you think? Laughable, but the peasants believe it. They say the mists at the border are part of your punishment, to keep you imprisoned until a hero comes along to slay you and set the people free."

"And you are to be . . . that hero?"

He smiled. The magic played around his body like glittering smoke. *That* was what had slowed his aging. He must have used some sort of masking spell on himself when he'd talked to Lovina, insuring that he appear to be just what she'd expected: an old man. He might have

even used the lion-shaped broach to jog her memory—
or implant one. Such experiments were theoretically
possible. If so, then he was as powerful as he claimed
and thus extremely dangerous to me.

"How will you do it?"

"I don't think you need to worry about that. You'll be
dead—truly dead—after all. So will Lovina and her
brood. They're the only other threat to me here." He
raised the pole and placed the point against my breast.
Shutting his eyes, he murmured another spell.

"Beware, Leo."

He broke off without rancor. "Of what?"

"The land . . . changed . . . with me. You have the Art.
You must feel it."

He paused to think. "Must I?"

" 'I am the land.' Remember?"

"I recall watching you perform an old rite. The symbolism was obvious enough, but don't expect me to believe
there's more to it than that."

"I am the land. Destroy me and—"

Leo laughed. "I destroy the land? That's like saying the
tree will die when you kill the bird nesting in it. Really,
Strahd, you're not that important."

"The magic makes it so. You must realize."

He was not convinced, but that was to be anticipated.
All I'd wanted was some time, and he'd given it to me.
The door was slowly, soundlessly drifting open. I strove
hard to look at Leo and not the small dark figure coming
up behind him.

"You must . . . realize . . ."

"You never were a liar, Strahd, so there might be

something to it, but then you'd say anything right now. I suppose I'll just have to find out the truth the hard way." He lifted the pole and set himself, but before he could plunge it into my heart, the monk seized a fistful of Leo's hair with one hand and, with a hard pull to expose the neck, smashed the other into his windpipe.

Leo gagged and dropped like a stone. The pole clattered over my knees and rolled away.

The power holding me . . . diminished.

Not by much. I was still held fast by the great symbol on the floor, but without Leo's additional magic pressing on me, I was able to find the strength to fight it.

Free the arms . . . push with the elbows . . . twist and heave: I squirmed like a dying insect to the edge of the circle. It was exhausting. The lines making up the symbol seemed to drain me, drain my will to fight. They covered every inch of my body, anchoring me to the floor. As I tore up a portion of the pattern and moved, it replanted itself all over again. The lines cut and burned, razoring into my flesh, sinking in down to the bone, yet not drawing blood. Each motion made it worse, but lying still made it no better, and I dared not lie still.

Half desperation, half exasperation prompted me to throw another silent command at the monk, who stood unmoving over my writhing form. Responding more slowly than my other servants, he finally stooped, grabbed my wrists, and dragged me clear of the circle.

It was enough. I crawled, but it was on my own. I was free only of the symbol on the floor, though, not from all the others. And Leo had recovered enough to cough out a word and augment it with a protective gesture.

Whatever magic he used struck me with sufficient strength to almost knock me back into the symbol again. Had I been standing, it might have worked. Instead, the buffeting hitched me up against the monk, nearly sending him over.

No magic would work for me here, but something more basic might. The staff was just within my reach now; I grabbed it.

It was like holding a live coal. The agony shot up my arm and lanced into my brain. Ignore. Ignore and . . .

Unbidden, the old drills of training returned to me. A soldier I'd been, and a soldier I would remain, despite the passage of years. The staff was a fighting weapon in my hands, and I knew well how to use it, despite the pain. I swung it hard to the side, slamming it into Leo's arm before he could form another spell, then rammed the blunt end into his belly. He doubled over, and I raised it one last time, cracking it down on the back of his skull. He dropped and moved no more.

My *hand* . . .

I shook it loose and the staff clattered away. There was a black and smoking scar where I'd gripped it, and the stench of scorched wood and meat clogged the air. I could hardly see straight for the pain. All I wanted was escape before I succumbed. By getting away from this deathtrap of a room, I might ease some of the pressure. The door seemed impossibly far away, though. I crept toward it, inch by inch, the weariness so great that it was beyond me to even silently command the monk's help.

And then I crept over the threshold.

Past it.

# P. N. Elrod

*Free.*

It was like stepping from an ice cold lake into freezing winter wind. Both will kill: the difference lay only in the time needed to do it. It was enough of a respite for me to recover a bit. I hugged my injured hand, braced my back against the wall of the building, and tried to ignore the unfamiliar feeling of fear that prickled at my mind. My presence in the monastery alone was not going to destroy me—before that happened I'd dissolve into mist and let the wind carry me to safety—but there was a good chance I would be noticed. Those holy people capable of doing so would certainly have sufficient training and knowledge to successfully deal with me. I had to leave, quickly, but not without Leo.

*If* he were still alive. I hoped so; after this, I would not get another chance at him.

*Bring him to me,* I told the monk, whispering the words into his mind.

A pause, then a grunt, and he was pulling Leo's limp body from the room. I glanced fearfully at the other doorways and windows, suddenly worried we might be watched. They appeared to be empty, but I wasn't disposed to trust anything in this place.

Leo still breathed, albeit hoarsely and with difficulty. He was partially conscious, but that was of no matter to me, not if I could get to him. The monk dragged him closer, closer, until my own hands reached out, and I fell on him as a man dying of thirst falls on a pool of water.

*This* was the reason I'd not fed before coming. I wanted him dead, but I'd promised Lovina he would pay for his past crimes, and I preferred to keep my word. For this man I'd planned something very special.

Hauling his head back much the same way as had the monk, I bent over his throat and bit hard. No need to worry about causing him pain. Pain for him meant an added boon for Lovina. His blood rushed up, but long practice prevented me from wasting a single drop. I enjoyed the deep drink, reveled in it, took strength, heart, and hope from it. My hand stopped hurting as the blackened flesh went red, then pink, then assumed its normal pale tone. Whole again. The hideous pressure of the monastery, pressure that weighed on me from all sides, did not lessen, but I was better able to withstand its sickening effect.

Toward the end of my drink, Leo fully wakened.

I drew back so he could see me. His eyes fastened on my lips, my teeth. I licked at the blood there and took much joy at the change in his expression, turning from bewilderment to utter terror when he realized it was *his* blood I was so freely drinking.

He choked on his rising bile and struggled feebly, a pointless exercise, but instincts die hard. I held him easily and resumed my meal, this time with his fear adding a piquant flavor to the blood. It lasted until the very end, when his laboring heart finally fluttered to a stop, and he lay unmoving in my arms.

The look of absolute, wide-eyed horror and revulsion frozen on his face would doubtless prove very satisfactory to Lovina when she saw it.

I rose, still rather shakily, and fixed my eye on the monk, ordering him back into the room again. He obeyed, though I questioned his ability to find what I wanted without my direct supervision. Ah, well, I'd just have to trust to luck. There was nothing, not even the promise of finding Leo's spellbooks, that could persuade me to enter that hideous trap again.

The fellow emerged with an armload of scrolls and tomes, some of which bore protective holy signs. I discarded those and scrabbled quickly through the rest as he made a second trip for more. Pocketing a few that looked promising was the work of but a moment. Fortunately, these were small; Leo had probably made them that way so as to more easily carry them when he traveled.

"Any others?" I demanded.

The monk, impassive through all of this, shook his head.

"Take me to the south wall."

He started off immediately. I hoisted Leo over one shoulder and followed, up more stairs, of course. Without magical protection around me, the climb was considerably harder than before. My feeding helped, but it wasn't the same as a spell. A soldier may have plenty of strength to use his sword, but without a shield to ward off an enemy's blows he wears down that much faster.

We reached the curtain wall. I peered over the edge and grimaced at the long drop into darkness. To a bat, it was nothing, but I needed to remain in human form for this last part.

"Return to your business," I ordered the monk. "Forget everything that's happened from the moment you saw me tonight."

Without so much as a blink to indicate he understood, he turned on his heel and marched off. Before he was quite out of sight, I was tying Leo's wrists tightly together with his own belt. This done, I looped his joined hands over my head and one arm. This put all of his weight on my left shoulder, but I'd just have to put up with it. Carefully, conscious of my need to maintain balance, I eased over the edge of the wall and began to descend.

It was anything but simple. His weight constantly pulled at me, threatening to pluck me from the wall each time I lifted a hand or foot to move down. Despite my ability to cling to the smoothest of surfaces, I slipped more than once, always with my feet. I might have fared better without my boots, but it was too late now to remove them.

Halfway down the cliff and needing to take a rest, I briefly considered dropping Leo, but decided it might prove too injurious to his corpse. I wanted to have something identifiable to present to Lovina; also, if the damage was too great, my final plan for him would be impossible to carry out. The delight I would take in that compelled me to put up with the present inconvenience a little longer.

One hand beneath the other, palms flat to the stone, boots scraping and sliding when my attention wandered, I went down another ten . . . twenty . . . fifty yards. Leo's body shifted with each move, tugging this way and that. The leather knot of his belt dug into my shoulder, rubbed the thin skin over my collarbone raw, made my neck ache from the strain. All my muscles felt it, fought it. I wasted energy cursing him.

Another hundred yards. Rest. I could probably drop him from this height without . . . no. It wouldn't do. He

255

had to pay. Fate had taken away the one woman I would ever love, but Leo had deprived me of nearly everything else. All of it would have been lost but for my change. Had that not happened, he'd have killed us anyway, including Tatyana. Her death had been bad enough, but had things gone differently and she'd lived, the treatment she might have gotten from his men . . .

My old anger—for this was not a new idea to me—gave me strength to finish the descent.

For all those that had died that night in my name, he would pay. For what might have happened to my beloved, he would pay dearly.

Most dearly, indeed.

My feet struck a ledge, then shards of rock, then level ground. I pushed his arms over my head and let him fall. It was wonderful to simply lean back on the base of the cliff and wait for the trembling fatigue to work itself out of my limbs. When I was ready, I sent forth a call for my horses to come to me. Almost instantly their guards, the wolves, began howling. Soon the lot of them would be here, and I could start back to the Wachter estate. I wouldn't make it tonight, but not long after sunset tomorrow Lovina would see my return.

Leo's body had rolled a little way off, ending face up. Something had changed about him. Walking over and looking close, I beheld the ravaged features of an old, old man. He looked much like his father, Gunther, now.

The magic had left him.

\* \* \* \* \*

A day and a night later I stood with Lovina and looked at an unmarked square of stone set in the wall of the mausoleum she'd mentioned. This was a new structure, no more than twenty years old and with only two occupants in it, honored retainers of the Wachter house. It was a pity to have to defile their peace, but the peace of the indifferent dead is held most in the mind of the living, and Lovina was untroubled over the disturbance.

She glanced sideways at me, which I pretended not to notice. When I'd arrived earlier that evening bearing Leo's body, she'd been full of vindictive approval, but that had worn off quickly enough. Leo's face, still frozen in its terrible expression, told part of the tale of his death, but she had demanded more details and I had politely denied them. Her conclusion was that Leo had not suffered as much as she'd expected, and that I was unwilling to admit I'd bungled the job.

"My work is not yet finished, Lady."

"What's left to be done, then?" she asked, unable to hide her disappointment or curb her bitter tone.

"You will see. Now I must ask that he be interred according to my strict instructions."

"Interred? I'd rather hang him from the gates and watch him rot."

"Indeed, Lady, but I have my orders from my lord Strahd. . . ."

With this reminder, she gave in, somewhat grudgingly, and things were carried out. The estate mason was called in along with others to assist, and long before dawn's approach, Leo had been pushed into one of the crypts, a heavy stone was laboriously shoved into the

# P. N. Elrod

opening, and the cement troweled thickly into place.

"Beg pardon, my lord," said the mason, "but shouldn't this gentleman have been put in a coffin first?"

"He was no gentleman," I informed him.

Wisely deciding not to pursue the matter, he bowed, gathered his tools and assistants, and left. Quickly.

Lovina stole another glance my way; this time I met it.

"Why?" she demanded. That single word encompassed a dozen or more questions, none of which I was quite yet ready to answer.

"You will know why tomorrow night."

"Tomorrow!"

"Your patience will be amply rewarded, Lady. In the meantime, I suggest you go on to your bed, spend the day as usual, and meet me here tomorrow after the sun is down. Until then, I cannot tell you more."

It might have been easier had I concluded our association tonight and spared both of us this sort of wait, but the cement needed time to properly set. Better to err on the side of good sense and try her patience a bit, than face a miscalculation and invite disaster.

Lovina was not happy, but gathered her skirts to go back to the house. She paused briefly, expecting me to follow.

I offered a bow. "Forgive me, Lady, but I must stay here for the night and the day as well."

Her eyes narrowed. "For what?"

"Those are my orders."

A silence. Quite a long one. "Is it to do with magic?" she finally asked. She tried to sound collected, but some people find it difficult to be at ease on the subject, and she was one of them.

I spread my hands in a deprecating manner and smiled. She could draw whatever conclusions she chose from that as long as they remained erroneous.

They must not have been too pleasant; she finally left, not so quickly as her men, but with no less determination to get away. I continued to smile after her, partly out of admiration and partly out of relief. She'd grown into a handsome, interesting woman, a credit to her father. Out of memory for him I would not touch her, but it was good for us both that she was gone. Paying honor to a dead comrade was a laudable custom for me, but such civilized manners can be forgotten in the face of deadly hunger.

I resolved to hunt very much elsewhere for my remaining time abroad, and did.

\* \* \* \* \*

Upon awakening the next night, I sensed a human outside my sanctuary and determined it was Lovina waiting for my arrival at the mausoleum. As I'd taken one of its empty chambers to rest in for the day, her early presence made things somewhat awkward, but not impossible. I should have told her to stay at the house until I came for her, but when the thirst is hard upon me, I cannot think of everything. In the end, I chose to leave as I'd entered, as mist, sieving through the many cracks in the unsealed stone of the crypt. It took a goodly time, for I was careful to spread myself very thin so she would be less likely to notice me. I curled to the roof and flowed out into the open air, assuming my own shape only when I was well away from the structure.

My return did not need any stealth, and I walked up boldly, making more noise than usual—in other words, performing a credible imitation of a living man. Lovina was oblivious to my efforts, which was what I desired, after all.

She stood in the doorway, holding a lantern high to guide my steps. It had panels of red glass, throwing out a soft red light that gave illumination but would not destroy one's night vision. Courteous of her, though pretty much wasted on me. My eyes were always well accustomed to the dark. She said nothing as I approached, but gave an odd little start when the light struck me. Perhaps my hair had been disarrayed and the points of my ears were showing. I'd deal with it later, then.

"This way," I murmured, brushing past her.

We went to Leo's crypt. The cement was as solid as any rock by now and I checked it carefully for openings. There were none, thankfully. The mason had done an excellent job. After running a hand admiringly over the smooth joinings, I pressed an ear to the stone.

Yes . . . it was just beginning.

Lovina saw the change in my face. "What is it?"

"Come," I invited. "Listen."

She set down the lantern and also put her ear on the stone. Her hearing was no match for mine, but soon, when the sounds within started to grow, both fear and wonder took her. She straightened and stared at me.

"What have you done?"

"Fulfilled my lord Strahd's wishes and your own, Lady.

Leo Dilisnya has just awakened to his true punishment."

"Is he alive?"

I gave her a hard look. "No. Nor is he really dead."

She made the protective sign of her faith. Its power buffeted against me like a gust of wind, but I'd braced for it and held my place.

"Tell me what—"

I raised my hand. "Just listen."

Reluctantly now, she resumed that activity, as did I. The little stirrings I'd heard but moments ago had developed into louder and more frantic thuds and cries. Before long he began to scream. I could imagine him futilely beating the stone sides, throwing his body against the ceiling and floor, stamping his feet on one end while pushing his hands at the other. No matter that he had the strength of the undead, he would not be able to shift the stone. No matter that he could change himself into mist, he would not find the least crack or pinhole to pour through and escape. No matter that he would soon use up his air, he had no need to breathe.

No matter, no matter . . .

He went suddenly quiet. Thinking, probably. If he'd studied the subject—and by the thorough way in which he'd trapped me earlier, I knew he had—he would be considering all his knowledge now. He would know his strengths and weaknesses, but knowing is not the same as actually experiencing. He would feel the power of his changed body, feel the rage coursing through him as well as the savage joy of his dark rebirth, but most of all, he would feel the overwhelming, gut-tearing, blind madness of *hunger.*

"Strahd?" he called, his voice distant through the stone.

I said nothing.

"You're there. I know you're out there. I know you hear me."

Lovina hissed, "That's *him*. I know his voice."

I nodded, thinking I'd have to make her forget this since she'd heard my name.

"Strahd, you must let me out," Leo calmly pleaded. "You made me, you must free me."

This time I laughed. "Must I?"

"Yes, yes. I am your slave. You know that. I can do nothing but what you command. You are my master."

"You said if you had my abilities, you'd have put them to better use."

"I was wrong. Forgive me, my master. I spoke in ignorance. I was a child, a foolish child. I'm changed now, I know better. Let me serve you. You'll never have a more faithful servant."

"Hoping to play upon my arrogance, Leo?"

"*Noooooo!*" he wailed, losing control. It was a truly terrible sound, worse than any death scream I'd ever heard in battle, enough to move a heart of iron to pity. Lovina shivered from it and looked to me with the whites showing all around her eyes.

"You wanted him to suffer, Lady. When you hear him cry, remember your mother's cries, your sisters', your—"

Her hand jerked up to cut me off. "All right! Say no more. This is what I've wished for, and the gods have granted it through you."

"*Free me!*" Leo shrieked.

Lovina flinched, then forced herself to remain still.

"Please, lord! I will serve you, do whatever you wish."

"Then hear my wish, Leo. Live on for as long as you may and then be damned."

A lull, then more thuds as he beat the walls. His screams were without words again. He was as far beyond human anger as the sky is beyond human touch. No matter. If he could have beaten his way out, he'd have done so by now.

Lovina whispered. "Will he die?"

"Eventually."

"The magic will keep him alive in such a place?"

"Yes."

In a gesture similar to my own, she ran her hands over the cement seal. The lantern threw the twin of her movement on the wall in the form of a harsh shadow. It angled away into darkness.

Leo became quiet again.

"It's utterly black in there," I said, knowing full well that he would hear me. "He can't see anything except the phantoms in his own mind. He has little space around him: a handspan on either side, another above his face, only twice that beyond his head and feet. And he's hungry, Lovina. He's more hungry than you've ever been in all your life. Every moment he's in there it becomes worse. It's as if one great cat is clawing at his belly to get in and a second is inside him clawing to get out. He'll be doubled over by the pain of it, but nothing will help him. He'll gnaw on his own flesh, drink his own blood, but nothing will help him. He'll scream and beg and burn his tongue, calling on the names of the gods, but nothing will help him. He'll beat his head on the stone, hoping to kill himself, but will fail. Only the hunger will kill him. It will consume him like a slow fire consumes the wax of a candle."

Her voice was steady and soft. "How long will it take?"

"A month."

We heard a long, sobbing groan from within.

"When three months have passed, come here in the full light of morning and have your men cut the crypt open again. Take out what you find there and burn it, then scatter the ashes."

She shut her eyes, lifting her chin a bit, and drew in a breath of cold air. A chill had entered this house of the dead . . . and the undead. "A month?"

"Perhaps a little more."

Opening her eyes again, she held them on mine. "Then I shall be here for as long as it takes. I shall be here and listen to him the whole time. I shall listen to him die and pray for peace to come at last to those he murdered that night."

I touched her cheek with one light finger. "And to those he was unable to murder, Lady."

"Yes. To them as well." She did not back away from me, but did stoop to pick up the lantern. Our skin and clothes were washed in red, echoing the color of its glass panes. "I have another memory of that night, of Lord Strahd. I pretended to be asleep—or maybe I *was* asleep and only dreamed it, but I recall my father opening a door and Strahd sweeping into the room. He was a tall man with black hair, and his eyes burned like hellfire. He was drenched from head to toe with blood. It covered him then as it seems to cover us now."

"It must have been very frightening for you."

"I was not frightened. Not then or now."

The silence stretched long between us, and I debated on what I should do next, stifle her memory or. . .

She shook herself and gave out a sigh. "Well, Lord Vasili, you must have great patience to listen to talk about a childhood dream."

"A dream?" I questioned.

"A dream," she said firmly. "A dream out of the troubled past."

"My hope is that the past will not trouble you further."

She glanced at the smooth stone of the crypt. "I think not. Not ever again. Please let Lord Strahd know that I and my family shall ever be grateful to him for his justice."

Lord Vasili smiled . . . and bowed low.

# Chapter Eight

## Tenth Moon, 400

"Lazlo Ulrich, Burgomaster of the Village of Berez of Barovia, understanding that Lord Strahd has a keen interest in any and all tomes relating to magic, wishes to make known to his lordship that he has some volumes, recently discovered, for sale. Lord Strahd is most welcome to come view the books, or, if he desires, they can be brought to Castle Ravenloft for his expert

# P. N. Elrod

inspection. . . ."

If they were spellbooks, I wasn't about to trust them to anyone's care but my own and resolved to travel to Berez myself. Ascertaining its location, I lost no time hitching up the horses, packing a supply of gold and spare clothing, and setting off. It was rather late in the season to be traveling, at least by coach, but there had not yet been a really bad freeze. The mountain roads were soft and treacherous with snow, but still passable if you knew them.

Berez was on the Luna River several miles south of Vallaki, and the only thing to distinguish it from any of a dozen other fishing villages was its huge manor house. It had once been the summer home of some long-forgotten lord and was still a grand-looking structure—from a distance. Drawing closer, the flaws of age and neglect became readily apparent. The cracks in the outer wall, the untended garden, the breaks in the roof, all indicated that its present tenant, the burgomaster, was in sore need of money. If his so-called magical tomes lived up to his expectations, he would have more than enough to restore his home to its former glory. If not . . . then I would make sure he never wasted my time again.

A little after sunset on my second night of travel, I stopped before his sagging, rusted gates, dismounted from the lead horse, and pushed my way into a ravaged courtyard of weeds and mud. Lights shone in one window of a ground floor room; otherwise the place looked quite deserted. I strode up to the once-impressive front doors and briskly pounded.

The servant who answered was a hesitant and pale old

man who peered at the world through faded, lost eyes. He was really too aged and frail for the work, and I wondered why he had not been honorably retired by now. I gave him a card announcing me as Lord Vasili Von Holtz, an emissary of Strahd Von Zarovich. He clutched the note in a none-too-clean hand and vanished into the depths of the house without a word. Having gotten no invitation, but not really requiring one, I stepped inside to wait, politely pushing back the hood of my cloak.

The hall was dark—the servant had not bothered to leave his candle behind when he'd tottered off—but I could see well enough. Muffled by the walls and an undetermined distance, I heard a man's voice throwing questions, and the servant's mumbled answers. Before much time had passed, the master of the house appeared, lamp in hand and a look of fearful hope on his face.

Lazlo Ulrich, for so he introduced himself, bowed and offered a number of apologies of an unspecified nature to me. I gathered that they had to do with his inability to give me a "proper" welcome. He was a huge, tough-looking man, of the sort that would have done well in the company of any of my soldiers, but there was a cringing light in his eyes, which I did not care for.

"I am here to look at the books on behalf of Lord Strahd," I told him, wanting to make my visit as brief as possible. "If you still have them."

He did and was more than willing to show them to me. Raising his lamp, he led the way past dusty rooms filled with damp, musty air and little else. The furnishings were mostly missing, giving me the strong impression that they'd been sold off over the years—that or turned to kindling.

# P. N. Elrod

*Miser,* I thought with a bleak mental sigh. I'd seen Ulrich's type often enough before. Best for me that I not appear too interested in his books. He took me to a cluttered chamber that seemed to serve many different purposes for the house: study, dining, and workroom, poorly lit and with but a small fire on a huge hearth. He opened a decrepit old trunk to reveal a stack of equally decrepit tomes and ancient parchments.

"I was having a bit of cleaning done in the east wing of the house when I found this and looked inside," he said. "Must have belonged to one of the old masters of the manor before me who went in for . . . you know."

"Thaumaturgic studies?" I absently suggested.

He was impressed. "Yes, that's it. Well, I couldn't make head or tail of the writing, so I took them to Brother Grigor, and he said they were magic books. He thought they might not be any good and that I should burn them, but I thought that since someone once went to so much trouble to make them in the first place, they might be valuable . . . to the right person."

"A wise choice, Burgomaster Ulrich."

"Then they're . . . Can Lord Strahd use them?" He watched my every move as I went through them, studying me with the suppressed eagerness of a hungry dog.

"All knowledge is of use," I hedged, while blessing the fates that had made Ulrich favor greed over piety in his decision. The books were quite genuine and incredibly precious. They were also lamentably fragile; time and the damp of the house had eaten into them. I saw myself spending the rest of the winter in careful transcription of their contents to preserve them. Pleasant enough work, though it would delay some of my other projects.

I gave Ulrich a generously fair offer for the lot and in my turn watched the various stages of thought running over his face. First, gratification at the price he was getting, then doubt, as he wondered if he should be entitled to more. Much more. At that point, I made sure to remind him of Lord Strahd's devotion to honesty in all his dealings and his reasonable expectations of honesty in return. The fifty-year-old memory of Berez's headless burgomaster was apparently still strong: Ulrich heartily agreed. Then and there he called for his servant to bring *tuika* to seal the bargain.

Instead of the old man, it was a young woman who answered his summons.

"Marina!" he said, obviously displeased. "I told you to go to bed."

"I'm sorry, Papa Lazlo, but Willy is so very tired. He—"

"So the servant is more important than his master? You've much to learn about the world, girl. No, I don't want to hear about it, just put your tray down and get out."

The girl did so, stealing a quick glance at me as she hurried away. Only then did I get a glimpse of her.

Ulrich poured out a small sip for each of us and offered me a glass. "Here you are, your lordship . . ."

Swaying, I staggered back until my legs encountered a chair, then sat down rather quickly.

"Your lordship? What's wrong? What's—"

I waved him off, pressing a hand over my eyes to hide my face. He continued to hover, fearful and asking questions I could not answer. I was unable to talk, unable to

# P. N. Elrod

think. My mind was quite literally reeling with shock.

Ulrich hastened away, calling for the girl. No doubt he was concerned that I might drop dead in his parlor. The two of them returned, and the girl pressed a cold rag against my forehead.

"There, sir, just be quiet a moment," she said soothingly.

I looked into her eyes, my heart beating so swift and hard that it was like to burst. "Tatyana?" I whispered.

There was no reaction from her. "Would you like some water, sir?"

My hand stole up to touch hers. Not a ghost sent to torment me, she was real. *She was real.* "Tatyana?"

"My name is Marina, sir." But there was some doubt in her tone.

"Call him 'your lordship,' girl," put in Ulrich.

"Your lordship," she said, dutifully correcting herself.

Same voice, same face, same graceful body, she was Tatyana come back to life again. I was absolutely witless from astonishment. Ulrich was so alarmed by my state that he rushed off, muttering about going for help. It never occurred to me to stop him. All I could do was stare at the sweet, beautiful girl before me.

She wore the clothes of the peasantry, poorly fitted, faded and shiny from much use. Her rich auburn hair was braided in the manner of unmarried girls. Other than those differences, and her utter lack of recognition of me, she was the same Tatyana I'd known nearly half a century ago. There could not be another.

A chill that had nothing to do with the cold of the room straightened my spine and ran down through my limbs.

Was this the work of the gods . . . or of dark magics?

*I don't care. She's here again, and that's all that matters.*

"Your lordship?"

"I am all right, Miss . . . Marina. Your name *is* Marina?"

The doubt she'd shown before became sharply apparent. "Oh, sir—your lordship—*do you know me?*"

Her question was so earnest and so intense with troubled longing that it all but cracked my heart, as though I, too, could feel her own terrible pain. All I wanted was to ease it, bring her comfort.

She was trembling. "Please, in the name of all the gods, do you know who I am?"

Her anguish filled me with supreme hope. "You . . ."

"Please tell me. I know nothing of my past."

"Nothing?"

"They found me walking by the river last summer and took me to Brother Grigor. I could not remember anything about myself, not even my name, so he gave me a new one. Then Papa Lazlo adopted me."

"That was very kind of him," I ventured.

She flinched, and a look flashed over her face that told me much more than anything she could say.

"Has he treated you ill?" I managed to keep my voice very smooth and level.

"He treats me well enough, sir—your lordship. But please, you said you knew me—"

"Yes, yes, I do. Your name is Tatyana. Your home is far from here, in a great castle. And you are loved. Loved more than any other woman in all the land."

It was quite a lot for her to take in, and one after

# P. N. Elrod

another, more questions began to pop forth, only to stutter to a halt. She simply couldn't ask them all at once, nor could she decide which to ask first.

"I will tell you everything you want to know," I promised, "but just for this moment, think only on your true name. Tatyana."

She did, and repeated it to herself. "But I don't remember. . . ."

"You will. I shall help you."

If she'd been somehow reborn into the world, then a new beginning was before us—a beginning unmarred by murder and sorcery, free of rivals and old griefs. Very, very few times in my long life had I ever been moved to tears and had never once given in to them. Since my change those many years ago, I thought weeping was beyond me, but now I felt my eyes begin to sting and my vision blur. I dropped my head into my hands, and though their names would have dripped fire upon my tongue, I could have offered up a thousand prayers of thanks to the gods who had sent her soul back to me once more.

I raised my eyes and smiled at her, receiving a faltering smile in return.

It was a start.

But before I could pursue it further, Ulrich returned. Tatyana—for so she would always be named to me—flinched again and rose and backed away, like a child caught raiding the sweets jar. He saw, but let it pass without comment, and stepped aside as a second man followed him in; I was summarily introduced to Brother Grigor.

His sky-blue robe was a familiar sight, but back in the days when Lady Ilona was running things, this specimen would not have been allowed into the orders to scour chamber pots. He was young and vigorous, but dirty, with a long, unkempt beard and tangled, greasy hair. His robe was stained and threadbare; instead of wearing a sensible pair of boots against the cold weather, he was in sandals. This marked him as a member of one of the more fanatic branches of Ilona's faith. They had grown numerous over the decades since the closing of the borders, pushing aside their more moderate spiritual siblings as they played upon the fears of the people. Some few had true faith and thus true power, others had no more power than that which lay in their own minds. Of the two, it was difficult to decide who was the more dangerous. Out of respect for Ilona's memory, I felt a distant pity for those who came to either type of priest for the betterment of their souls.

It was also and only out of respect for her that I rose and bowed to this man now.

"You must sit and rest, Lord Vasili," he pronounced. "You are very pale."

This was something I already knew. There was no advantage in drawing further attention to it. "Thank you, Brother, but I am much better now. I have had such . . . fits before. According to my own healer, they are alarming, but quite harmless. A cup of water was all that I needed, and Miss Marina was kind enough to provide one for me."

I nodded to her, and she had the wit to remain silent about what had really passed between us.

# P. N. Elrod

"You should come to the church hospice, though, just to be sure," he added, perhaps hoping to justify his presence.

Imagining the hospice to be as dirty and flea-bitten as its caretaker, I had no intention of accepting his offer. However, before I could turn him down, he stepped forward and began a cursory examination.

His hand, when it touched the bare flesh of my forehead, was hot.

Burning. Hot.

I winced and backed away from him. "No, don't!"

"What's the matter?" he demanded.

I mouthed the first lie that came to me. "I'm sorry, Brother Grigor, but years ago I suffered a wound to my head. Any sudden movement such as yours . . ." I opened my palms in a humble request for understanding for my "weakness."

Ulrich retreated a bit while Grigor expressed sympathy for my trials in life. An old head wound could account for any number of eccentricities. Better they think me odd than know the truth, and much better if I leave as quickly as possible, lest this holy man touch me again. He was a true believer in his faith, and I wanted to put some distance between us before he began to notice things.

I slipped a gold piece to Grigor (without touching him) as a donation to the church and made it clear I intended to leave. Ulrich made a diffident invitation for me to stay with him for the night, which I graciously declined. He appeared relieved. That made two of us.

"But what about the books, your lordship?" he asked.

I gave him a small bag heavy with gold. "This is the first

payment. I shall return tomorrow evening with the rest. They are Lord Strahd's property now. As you value your life, keep them safe."

My words were not lost on him. He glanced uneasily at the new additions to my collection.

Before turning to go, I looked past Ulrich and Grigor to Tatyana.

*Wait for me,* I silently told her.

\* \* \* \* \*

Ulrich's parsimonious habits dictated an early bedtime for the house, probably as an effort to save on the cost of candles. Not long after my departure, Brother Grigor went back to whatever hole he dwelt in, and the house grew as dark and silent as any tomb. My comparison was not lightly chosen, for the place was certainly dismal and lifeless; the thought of Tatyana wasting away in such wretched surroundings angered me beyond endurance.

It took little effort on my part to enter again and stalk through the halls, looking for her. Ulrich had a large room to himself, the old servant slept in the pantry, and Tatyana had a small chamber nearby. I chose to softly knock on her door: coming in under it as a mist would only frighten her.

She was afraid anyway, or so she sounded when she asked who was there.

"It is I," I whispered. "Let me in, Tatyana."

A bolt instantly slid back, and she stood on the threshold, holding her breath. Her heart was pounding as was mine; I could hear it.

# P. N. Elrod

Locked doors were nothing new to me, but generally they are not for use within one's own house. Once I was in the room and the door shut again, I asked about it.

She looked ashamed. "Willy put it there for me. He thought—"

"That you might need it?"

A nod.

"Against Papa Lazlo?"

She stared at the floor. "Willy doesn't think I should be here without a chaperon."

"Then Willy is a wiser man than Brother Grigor."

"But Papa Lazlo has been kind to me in his way. He said . . . said that if Brother Grigor approves, he will revoke the adoption and . . . and . . ."

"Marry you?"

Another nod as she stared at the floor.

"How generous of him," I said dryly.

She caught onto my contempt and gave me a sorrow-filled look that would melt stone. "I don't belong here, do I?"

"No. No more than a mountain hawk belongs in a cage."

"Tell me about myself. I keep saying my name, but I don't know it. I try to remember the castle you spoke of, but I can't."

"You will."

"How? Please help me."

The furnishings of the room were humble and sparse. She had a narrow bed and a stool and nothing else to sit on. Proprieties be damned, then. "Over here," I said, and took her to the bed. She sat, and I saw in her face that she was suddenly conscious of her surroundings. I pulled the stool up close, but was careful, so very careful not to touch her. Much as I wanted to, now was not the right moment.

"Tatyana, once upon a time you were betrothed to a powerful lord of Barovia. He loved you, cherished you, and desired your happiness beyond all other things in life. But there were traitors in his court who lusted for his power. They came between the lord and you, and their betrayals destroyed and scattered everything that was good. You were caught up in . . . in the dark magic of that night. Many horrible things happened then, and I think that may be why you have no memory of it. I think the gods want you to forget the evil—"

"But must I forget the good as well?"

"That's why I am here, to return that part of your memory to you."

"Who is this lord?"

"Strahd, of Castle Ravenloft," I said, searching her face for the least sign of fear.

"Strahd?" She was still for a long time, thinking hard. She shook her head. "How can it be? He's the lord of Barovia and I am . . . am nothing."

"You are all that is precious to him, more important than life."

"Then why can I not remember him?"

Her voice rose along with her frustration. I raised a gentle hand against it. "That will come, if you can but trust me."

"I think I must already," she said wryly, referring to my presence in her room.

# P. N. Elrod

I smiled, but did not get one in return and so realized that she couldn't see me for the darkness. There was some thin gray light seeping through a single, small window that was useless for fighting the shadows of this house. I myself was hardly more than a talking shadow to her. Spying a candle stub on a rough table by the bed, I pulled out my tinderbox. I soon had a tiny spark going and lighted the thing.

The golden glow of the flame warmed her face and brought back a jumble of heartbreaking memories for me, if not for her. I saw her in the dusk of the overlook garden again, laughing with delight at the roses, or staring in awe at her first view of the valley.

"What is it?" she asked.

I blinked, returning to the sad present, to her cold and musty room with its lowly belongings and unhappy occupant. "Look at me, Tatyana. Look upon me, and you will remember the joys taken from you."

"How—"

"Just look."

Her eyes were on mine, wide with caution, but willing to take a chance.

And then they misted over. A soft word from me and they closed.

"You will remember. . . ." I said. "You will remember the white walls in the sunlight and roses redder than blood and the gray storms of winter pouring down from the mountain and the blazing fire in the hall and the music I made for you there and the silk dresses you danced in and the laughter we shared . . . you will remember. . . ."

Brow wrinkling, she shook her head until I stroked my fingertips lightly on her temples. Her eyes opened, something like recognition coming into them. "I—I see things when you speak. Please, tell more. Please tell me . . . Elder?"

"Strahd," I said.

"Strahd?"

"Yes. Remember the crystal in the chandeliers catching the light, and the lords and ladies swirling about you, dancing in your honor. Remember the prayers in the chapel, and the sweet incense as we asked the gods for happiness and good fortune, and the long days when we walked in the forest, and the time we startled the doe and her fawn, and the night the shooting stars fell like fiery gems over the valley."

"I see them, yes, and you were near us, I was with—"

"Strahd," I said. "You were with *me*."

"With . . . you."

"And I held you close in the garden, and the mists rolled around us like the dancers, and you kissed me."

Somehow we were standing, and my arms were around her, holding her as I'd held her that night. Her rough clothes had been replaced by her silk wedding gown, and her hair flowed wild and rich on her pale shoulders.

"I love you, Tatyana, and you love me. Remember."

"I love . . ."

"Strahd," I murmured into the warm white velvet of her throat.

\* \* \* \* \*

283

# P. N. Elrod

The following sunset once more found me face to face with Burgomaster Ulrich. He'd dressed himself up a bit and had shaved, but having seen him through Tatyana's eyes as well as my own, I was hard-pressed to be civil to the man. We were about the same age—outwardly—so his planned marriage to her was not unthinkable, but it was his casual treatment of her that roused my displeasure and disgust. He was utterly blind to her true worth. Had she been a stranger to me, I'd have felt the same sense of outrage. It was with much relief that I turned over the last payment, gathered the books and papers, and left.

My valuable burdens carefully placed in the long box in my traveling coach, I drove it back to a spot in the forest where I'd spent the day surrounded by lupine guardians. Changing form and taking to the air, I beat my way back to the house, made myself comfortable hanging in a tree just outside Tatyana's window, and waited until all was quiet. Not long after the last hoarded candle had been extinguished, she cracked the window open, and I flew across and entered, resuming my man's shape.

I'd prepared her for this, and because of the understanding established between us with my first taste of her blood, she offered no questions about my nature, nor did she suffer any fear of me. Instead, she opened her arms in welcome and wept from happiness that I had come.

"No more tears for you," I said, carefully brushing them away with my little finger.

"I can't help it. I feel as if I'm waking up after a long sleep. Nothing I did today seemed real; it's only now that

I can touch things and know them for what they are. So much has happened, and so much has changed."

Her words rekindled a joy within me that I thought lost. I pressed her close, content to hold her and think of nothing, to simply drift.

"Will you . . . take me away with you?" she asked.

"Of course I will. Can you think I would ever leave you behind?"

"I don't . . . I . . ."

"When I go, you'll be with me."

"When? Now?"

We needed a few more nights of courtship before I could truly sweep her away as my bride. "No, it's not possible, not yet."

"But please take me soon."

"There's something wrong?" I drew back to look at her.

"Please, Strahd, I am grateful to Papa Lazlo, but I cannot marry him. He said now that he has the money, he'll be able to . . ."

I took her head gently in my hands and kissed her brow. "You need not worry. He will never touch you. I swear it."

No doubt some of the gold from the books had found its way to Brother Grigor, assuring the easy revocation of the adoption and issuance of marriage banns, instead. A pity no one had bothered to ask Tatyana about her views on the matter, but as an orphan in the hands of a zealot who probably thought he was helping her, Tatyana's opinion did not matter.

Again, I was filled with disgust for Ulrich, who had taken this girl under his protection as her father only to violate her trust and feelings in such a cool manner by wanting to be her husband. At least—and for that I was most grateful—he was waiting until things were made legal by the church's blessing before indulging in violations of a more intimate sort.

Pushing his unpleasant presence aside, I gathered Tatyana into my arms and carried her to bed, lying close beside her within its narrow confines. There, I spoke of our life together as it had been and as it would be. And when the time of talk ended and we kissed, she threw her neck back and softly begged me to take her again as I'd done last night.

And I did, resulting in the greatest of pleasures for us both.

\* \* \* \* \*

The next sunset found me outside her window once more, but this time it was closed fast, and though I waited long, it did not open for me. I pressed my ear to the panes and probed with all my senses, but heard nothing. She was on the other side, yet unable to respond to my call. A cold and heavy chill settled on my heart, and I carried that iron weight of panic with me as I hurriedly changed to mist and seeped through the cracks around the window. Inside, I suddenly understood.

The room reeked from prayers and protections. I threw an arm up against the stench, but Brother Grigor had been very thorough. It was not the trap Leo had set for me, but bad enough in its own way. A holy symbol had been hung over her bed, and she wore another on a chain around her neck. The air was so thick with incense and the organic stink of garlic that she was all but suffocated. I saw to this problem by immediately opening the window. The breeze stirring the thin curtains was cold, but fresh.

She opened her eyes and recognized me, but couldn't speak at first. I put my fingers to my lips to let her know it was unnecessary and searched the rest of the chamber for further pitfalls.

Thankfully, there were none. Grigor had confined his blessings and defenses to Tatyana, and though they were fairly strong, they wouldn't last the whole night. I tested them—lightly—and could feel the power wavering already. Tatyana helped by taking off the holy symbol she wore. She was just able to remove the one on the wall before collapsing back onto her pillow. Without that extra pressure to fight, I rushed forward.

"They're trying to kill me," she whispered. Tears filled her eyes and streamed into her temples. Her fingers clutched at mine, cold and lighter than dead leaves. I kissed them and folded them to my breast.

"I'm here now. You're safe."

"But I'm so weak. When Brother Grigor came to look after me, it only got worse. He prayed over me, and I could hardly stand it. Then tonight, he shut up my room and prayed some more. Until you opened the window, I thought I should smother."

"In a little while, you will be yourself again. Brother Grigor is . . . uninformed about certain things and causes you more harm than good with his chants and burnings."

"He was frightened, Strahd."

# P. N. Elrod

"No doubt. Frightened men can be very foolish."

I held her hand and soothed her, easing her own fears as best I could.

So. Grigor had noticed the marks on her neck and correctly interpreted their significance. It couldn't be helped now. I wanted to get her safely away from him, but in her present state, she could not travel. Another concern was over bringing on her conversion too quickly. Her body hadn't had much time to get used to the changes taking place, and there might be danger to her if I pushed things. I had to balance this possibility against the surety of Grigor's ignorant meddling.

Another night and I could lose her.

No. Never again.

"Tatyana?"

Her eyes opened. She could see me quite well, even in dim light now.

"You are weak, and before you can come with me, you must grow weaker—but only for a very short time. Then you will be well again."

She understood, not fully, but on an instinctive level—by means of the special link between us.

"You must do what I say, and then you shall be free. When you waken tomorrow, you'll be able to leave this house and all its problems and pains."

"To be with you?"

"To be with me forever after."

"What must I do?"

"Only gift me with the privilege of kissing you again." I touched her throat with a fingertip.

She gently slipped her hand up to my shoulders. "Yes . . ."

I kissed her deeply, drinking in a portion of her life so that it could merge with mine. She grew white and cold in my arms, but made no move to stop me; her only protest was a soft moan when I finally drew away.

Her eyelids fluttered as she fought to stay conscious. I hurriedly tore open the front of my shirt and, with a diamond-hard talon, dug into the flesh over my heart. Our mingled blood slowly welled from the wound. When I pulled her up and pressed her lips to it, she began to drink.

I know not what pleasure she may have taken; my own was beyond any that I'd ever experienced before. It was more intense than any sharing of love I'd enjoyed while bedding a woman in the usual sense—more intense, and infinitely more desirable. I held her tightly and felt her strength return, even as my own poured out to feed it. Her arms encircled me, entrapped me, but it was right and true. In the past, I'd given everything for her and had lost everything. Here and now, I had nothing left to give but my own life's blood, but it was hers to take, and I murmured to myself, pleading to the dark magics that had made me to grant me this one boon—that she would at last be my bride.

For that, sadly, there had to be an ending to the ecstasy. Reluctantly, so very, very reluctantly, I tried to push her from me. Her strength was equal to my own, though, and she did not want to be moved. My efforts increased the blood flow, and she drank faster, more eagerly. Finally, I had to place the palm of my hand against her forehead and push with all my might, lest we both die. With a groan of misery and bitter disappointment, she fell back upon the bed, gasping for breath like an exhausted runner.

Overcome by the same weariness, I dropped to the floor, shaking from fatigue and sudden hunger. My recovery was slow in coming. When I was able to stand again, Tatyana was already in her last mortal sleep. There hadn't been any chance to say farewell, but no matter. Our next greeting would make up for it. Tomorrow I'd come for her, and there would be no more partings for us ever again.

\* \* \* \* \*

There was nothing more I could do for her except clean away the traces of our blood exchange. I arranged her body more comfortably on the bed and drew up the coverlet. Though the removal of the holy symbols would not go unmarked, I couldn't bring myself to touch them. But an idea had presented itself to me, and as soon as I'd locked the window again and seeped through to the outside, I took steps toward realizing it.

Berez's church had most certainly seen better times. Without the patronage of the town's former lord, or the support of the larger holy organization on the other side of the closed borders, it had inevitably surrendered to the harsh realities of time. Attendance might have been down, either from the indifference of the people or the fact that their spiritual leader was disinclined to believe in the social advantages of soap and water. Whatever the reason, only two people emerged from the midnight devotions, an old woman and Brother Grigor himself.

The woman talked with him at length, received a last blessing, and waddled off to her home.

I waited only long enough for her to fade from sight, then loomed up behind him, a portion of darkness come to purposeful life.

He put up quite a fight and would have raised an alarm if I hadn't slapped a hand over his mouth. Bodily lifting him, I hauled him into the church and kicked the door shut to afford us some privacy. The little entry was poorly lit, making it necessary to go into the chapel where the scented candles still burned. I shuddered, feeling the tepid power of the place, and tried to ignore the ghastly sickness that was beginning to manifest itself in my belly; there was only so much that I could expect from the protective spell I'd summoned, after all.

When I turned him around to face me, his surprise was such as to deprive him of the ability to fight for a few instants. By the time he'd recovered and thought to grab at his holy symbol to wave in my face, I'd secured both his hands with one of mine and had him braced against a wall, high enough for his sandal-shod feet to dangle over the floor.

"Blasphemer!" he gasped, his eyes wild and wide with righteous anger.

"No doubt," I said and wasted no more time. When he saw what was to come, his struggles turned frantic, but he could no more stop me from taking his blood than I could stop the sun from rising. My exchange with Tatyana had left me weak, but I was yet capable of dealing with the likes of Grigor. When I'd finished, I was much revived, and he was in a state of mind considerably more tractable than before. I led him over to a bench and made him sit, then knelt on one knee in order to be at eye level. I must have looked like a penitent sinner asking for help from his priest.

"Grigor, I want you to listen to me very carefully. . . ."

With him dazed from blood loss, it took little effort on my part to bring him under complete control. I spoke, and he listened and accepted everything. My instructions had to be tailored to his own strongest drives, else he might be able to shake off my influence, but it wasn't difficult to think of something appropriate.

"Beginning this very hour, you will start a pilgrimage to the Shrine of the White Sun in Krezk on the western border. Take what supplies you need and go immediately. Do you understand?"

"Yes," he replied faintly.

Excellent.

Again, it was out of respect for Ilona's memory that I did not simply kill the man. He was inconvenient, but no real threat to me. The thought of her inspired one more addition to his quest.

"And Grigor. . ."

"Yes?"

"On your journey, in the name of your god and for the greater glory of all the gods, you will bathe every day. In fact, you will bathe yourself every day for the rest of your life."

It was the least I could do for his congregation.

\*　\*　\*　\*　\*

# I, Strahd

When I awoke, my guardians for the day were restless and whining. The horses, though used to their presence, were naturally upset by this activity and pulled unhappily at their tethers. I dismissed the wolves, freeing them to go about their normal business, and wished them luck. They vanished into the forest and began howling, working themselves up for their next hunt. By the time I had the horses hitched, the night air quivered with many voices, making a savage and sweet wedding song to welcome my bride to her new life.

Mounting the lead animal, I guided them toward the village, stopping the coach on a hill just a few hundred yards above the burgomaster's house. As on all the other nights, no lights showed on this side, but I chose to maintain my usual caution and glided down on silent wings, making a broad circle of the place before landing by Tatyana's window.

I sensed her strongly on the other side. She was only just now stirring. Waking late and languorous . . .

The sudden rush of terror and agony crashed upon me like a physical blow. I thought it must be a blow, for I staggered and fell like a tree into the mud of the yard, helpless. My chest, my heart . . . Fire. . . . Worse than fire . . . my hands scrabbled and encountered nothing, yet the pain was paralyzingly real. I was no stranger to a sword thrust, and that was what it felt like, only a thousand times worse.

Tatyana was screaming.

Shrieking.

And desperately calling on that silent link between us.

Calling on me.

# P. N. Elrod

Then . . .

Nothing.

The last echoes rose in the frost-still air and were lost in the dark.

I groaned and cursed and tried to get up. My limbs wouldn't respond. I blinked and stared at the harsh, bright stars as the iron weight of dread returned to my heart once more. Its chill burden settled on me, heavier than a mountain, crushing, but alas, not killing me.

Oh, to die, to no longer have to *feel* . . .

She was gone. Damnation to the gods, *she was gone.*

All the tears I'd not shed before in my life filled my eyes now. Far, far above me, the stars glittered and danced, mocking my grief. As I lay weeping, drained and in shock, Ulrich quietly approached. I didn't notice him for a long time, not until he spoke.

"Grigor said you were the one," he whispered.

Her blood—our blood—had splashed all down the front of his clothes. His hands were coated with it; one of them still convulsively clutched a great wooden mallet, its red stains smoking in the cold.

"How could you do such a thing?" he asked. "How can you take a young girl and corrupt her with your filth?"

My tears ceased. Thoughts of dying abruptly fled from my brain.

"But no more. She's safe from you. Better that she die this way with her soul purged and ready for the gods than walk the earth under your curse. She's safe and free."

I seemed to see his muscled form outlined in scarlet. He knelt by me.

"And you, may you forever rot for—"

He had another stake . . . and raised it high.

I caught his arm as it came down. He tried to pull away, failed, then brought his mallet around to crush my head, but I grabbed that with my other hand and we rolled in the mud, screeching and bellowing. I was still in near thrall to the pain of Tatyana's death, and weak. He was a strong man in his prime, inspired by vengeance, and in terror for his own life. We were a close match.

But I . . . I had nothing to lose. Nothing. She was gone. And this *bastard* had killed her. Rage gave me the edge.

I wrested the stake from him.

He clawed at my face, my throat, with a grip like a lion.

I rammed the thing into his side. Yanked it out. Stabbed him again. And again.

Writhing, he fell away, screaming as she had screamed. I crawled after him. Pinned his leg with the stake. Pinned it right through to the ground. He squalled and bucked and pleaded and called on his gods as I fell on him like a roaring storm out of hell.

But it was over too quickly.

Much too quickly for his crime.

His blood was spread from one end of the courtyard to the other, but it hadn't taken long at all. He hadn't suffered nearly enough, not as she had suffered, not as I was suffering.

I regarded his mangled corpse with bottomless loathing.

Dead now, he would suffer no more.

And I had . . . eternity before me, an endless march of nights bearing this unbearable loss.

## P. N. Elrod

Nearly half a century had passed, and I'd grown accustomed to the pain of mourning. Then to have her return . . . to have those bleak years wiped from my soul as though they'd never been, to have a glimpse of the paradise that lay before us, and then—

—to *lose* her again . . .

It was too much. Despairing, I wallowed in the mud and gave in to the grief, unable to stop.

\* \* \* \* \*

Slowly finding my feet, I walked toward the house. Too shaken to change form, I pushed in through a door and paced down the hall to her room.

The old servant sprawled on the floor just outside. He was white with death, his frail heart barely beating. I ignored him and braced myself to go in to her.

"Gone," he muttered.

*Yes.*

I stared at the room, at the single lighted candle, at the blood that painted the walls and burst over the bed-clothes . . . at the empty bed.

The impression of her body where she'd writhed in her last agonies was there. She was not. What had that piti-less butcher done with her?

I dragged the old man up. "Where is she?"

His eyes sagged open, wandering. "Poor Marina. Poor child."

"Where?"

He didn't seem to hear or be aware of me. "So pretty. So sweet . . ."

"*Where?*"

Now he winced and looked at me. "The mist took her," he whimpered. "Filled the room and . . . gone. Mist."

His last words. He exhaled once and moved no more.

# Chapter Nine

## *Twelfth Moon, 720*

Winter solstice had arrived, a time of endings and beginnings, a time of renewal and death.

The longest night of the year.

Without sun, moon, or stars, with no means at all of measuring the hours, unless I cared to count the beats of my heart, I still felt the approach of midnight. An important time, for at the precise moment of the turning of the year, darkness was at its deepest, and the dawn at its most remote. The powers were decidedly on the side of the shadows now, not in balance as during the equinoxes, or with the light as during the summer solstice.

In relation to the Art as it applied to me, this was an extremely important time for magical experimentation, but instead of busying myself with the furtherance of my craft, I sat in the study, staring at Tatyana's portrait.

The painting was as radiant now as it had been over three and a half centuries ago when she'd posed for it. The varnish had darkened slightly, but the artist's purpose was yet fresh. Her innocence and lively intelligence shone out, and yet she was strangely distant. No matter where one stood in relation to the portrait, her eyes always seemed to look just past the viewer and on to something else. The artist may have also come under the spell of her beauty and fallen in love with her, for it was agreed at the time that this was his masterpiece. Certainly nothing he painted afterward ever quite matched up to it—not that he'd had much chance to try, since he, along with so many others, had died from Leo's poison on that long-ago summer night.

Much had happened since then, but little had changed. The people still farmed or tended their flocks. They feared me, but were obedient; those who broke my laws rarely got the chance to repeat the offense. Life for most was hard, but they knew things were far more difficult elsewhere.

For Barovia was no longer a land alone in this pocket of existence.

As the centuries passed, the mists at the borders

pulled back, revealing new countries beyond. Other lords like myself ruled them, and like myself, were trapped within their lands. This did not prevent them from warring amongst themselves, but the results were usually indifferent. For instance, Vlad Drakov of Falkovnia had been trying to invade Darkon (among other nations) with tedious monotony for the last three decades. My spies informed me that he was apparently gathering arms and soldiers for yet another attack. In two seasons he'd be ready to march again, content to send his people to certain death or worse in order to salve his pride over past defeats. During my own days of war, I'd have had a commander like him executed for the crime of rampant stupidity.

Not that I hadn't tried. His irresponsible actions had made him rather unpopular, and in exchange for favors from other lords, I'd sent out agents to deal with him. They'd come close, but he'd survived, and the balance of power remained the same, except that, by means of the favors, some of my own goals had been advanced. That was the only reason I'd agreed to the strategy, for without his constant threat, our mutual neighbor, Ivan Dilisnya—since Reinhold's death, the family line had suffered a marked decline—might then turn his full attention on Barovia. My agents had used poison, Ivan's specialty, which kept suspicions high, and kept the two occupied with one another over the years. Perhaps I *should* have provided the agents with a more effective toxin for Drakov . . . but success had not been my true purpose, after all.

And so it went with the other lands enclosed by the

mists. I had spies in each, and they had theirs in Barovia. We could not fight openly in honorable battle, but only by sly and subtle political maneuver. Though I'd have preferred a more straightforward conflict, I played this lesser, if not more demeaning, variation well enough. It was necessary to Barovia's survival—and mine.

But Tatyana looked past me, as if none of this were important at all.

She may well have been right.

I could regard her now with but a twinge of pain. Constant company with the ache had made it bearable; I'd wept away the last of my tears years ago. How many times over the centuries had I met her? How many times had I lost her? I could not say. She ever wore the same face, but under a different name, sometimes a wholly different personality, though somehow I'd always found a way to touch those hidden memories in her heart.

And somehow, I'd always lost her: Marina, murdered by her adopted father . . . Olya, dead from a fever, so they said . . . and all the others, taken from me. Throughout the generations, I'd lost her over and over again, forever trading joy for grief.

If I could just once break the pattern, break whatever curse that kept us apart. In doing that, I might find freedom for us both.

I had tried. Countless times.

I'd made hundreds of forays to the borders, challenging them with my own growing powers, and failing. I'd talked long with the Gypsy tribes that freely traveled the mists, but could not grasp their ways. I'd pored through every book on magic I could lay hands on and found nothing to help me understand the nature of my prison or how to leave it. This night, I should have been working, but there was no desire in me to do so. Perhaps later I might regret the lost time, but for now I did not care.

Midnight was upon me . . . and gone.

Whatever power I might have drawn from its darkness was waning, not to return for another year.

But that was a very short time. The seasons tended to blur past for me. One night I'd be hunting in deep snow, the next be flying in the aftermath of summer heat, the air scented with flowers. Year after year fled by; they piled into decades, massed into centuries.

How many lay before me? And were they all to be as lonely as those I'd already had?

Unable to answer, unwilling to guess, I sat and stared at Tatyana's portrait and felt one more night slipping away into the irretrievable past.

\* \* \* \* \*

The dawn was coming, along with another brief stay in my crypt. Lately, my little increments of death hadn't been enough to provide me with sufficient rest. I first thought that it might have to do with the brevity of the winter days, but instinctively knew that my growing fatigue had another cause.

The fire had burned itself out hours ago. I felt chilled, but not from the cold of the room. This was deeper and more exhausting, the chill of a weary spirit.

I was so tired, as if the weight of all my years had come upon my heart as one vast heaviness that nothing could ever lift. From my heart outward it settled upon me, the very air was too thick to move in, nor did I desire to move. I felt as if I'd been endlessly climbing a mountain and was never quite able to get to the top.

If I could just rest. I wanted to sleep, sleep for more than just a single day, sleep away all my sorrows and lose myself in . . . I wasn't sure.

To drift, dreamless and serene.

To forget.

To . . .

Rest.

# Epilogue

Van Richten turned the page and found the next to be completely blank. He flipped through the remaining pages of the folio. Nothing. Strahd had put down his last lines . . . and simply walked away.

He looked around the study with new eyes, once more examining the girl's portrait—Tatyana, the poor soul. And there, that place on the floor, might that be the spot where

# P. N. Elrod

Strahd had collapsed under the force of the darkness that had come for him?

His muscles sluggish after so much sitting, Van Richten rose, picked up his lantern, and walked through the doors to Strahd's bedroom. There was the window leading to the overlook where Alek Gwilym had died; there was the closet where Strahd had hidden the body. The shadows were very thick here, and a draft from the study caused the open curtains and bed draperies to stir like restless spirits. His lantern hardly made an impression against the . . .

Dark—it was growing *dark*.

He'd forgotten that the looming bulk of the mountain cut the sun off that much sooner. Blessed powers, he had to get *out*.

He swept back to the study, not bothering to blow out the low-burning candles. They could gutter themselves harmlessly enough, and if their condition told Strahd that anyone had invaded his keep, then so be it. The chances were very good that Van Richten would return long before the creature's awakening. He had the knowledge he'd come for, now if the good gods would only bless him with speed and strength to escape this place before . . .

His stiff muscles forgotten, he sped down the stairs, reckless of the uneven footing.

*     *     *     *     *

In the bedroom, a shadow, much blacker than the rest, broke away from one corner and drifted toward the window, which silently opened. The shadow flowed over the

308

sill and paused next to the overlook.

A few long minutes later, the little hunter emerged from the keep into the courtyard, hurrying in the direction of the portcullis.

Strahd Von Zarovich watched his progress with smiling interest. It was amazing that a fellow his age could move so fast, and even more amazing that Strahd could still find such antics amusing. He considered loosing one of his many guardians to deal with the intruder, but held off. If he was like all the others, he'd be coming back soon enough. *Then* Strahd would deal with him.

When the hunter was beyond the drawbridge and lost from sight in the mist, Strahd walked back to the study. His book lay open. He extended a hand and caressed the waiting page, the points of his long nails carving deep grooves into the virgin parchment.

There was so much more to tell . . . and so much more yet to come.

Slipping into the chair so recently vacated by the hunter, Strahd plucked up a quill pen, unstoppered a bottle of ink, and began to write.

# About the Author

P. N. Elrod lives in Texas with her spouse Mark and their dogs Mighty Mite and Big Mac. She made her professional start in writing at TSR with the sale of some gaming modules and an article for *Dragon®* Magazine. A lifelong fan of vampire stories, gangster films, and pulp magazines, she later combined all three into the successful mystery series The Vampire Files. She edits and publishes a Blakes 7 fanzine, has short stories in two anthologies, and is now working on *Death and the Maiden*, the second novel in a new vampire trilogy.